ARTHUR C. CLARKE'S
VENUS™
PRIME
V

Other Avon Books in
ARTHUR C. CLARKE'S
VENUS PRIME *series*

by Paul Preuss
VOLUME 1: BREAKING STRAIN
VOLUME 2: MAELSTROM
VOLUME 3: HIDE AND SEEK
VOLUME 4: THE MEDUSA ENCOUNTER
VOLUME 5: THE DIAMOND MOON

ARTHUR C. CLARKE'S
VENUS PRIME™

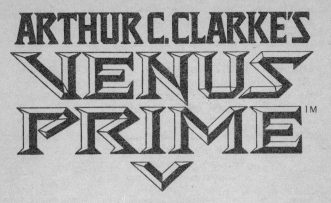

VOLUME 6

THE SHINING ONES

PAUL PREUSS

A BYRON PREISS BOOK

AVON BOOKS ◆ NEW YORK

ARTHUR C. CLARKE'S VENUS PRIME, VOLUME 6: THE SHINING ONES is an original publication of Avon Books. This work has never before appeared in book form. This work is a novel. Any similarity to actual persons or events is purely coincidental.

Special thanks to John Douglas, Russell Galen, Alan Lynch, Megan Miller, and David Keller.

AVON BOOKS
A division of
The Hearst Corporation
1350 Avenue of the Americas
New York, New York 10019

Text and artwork copyright © 1991 by Byron Preiss Visual Publications, Inc.
Arthur C. Clarke's Venus Prime is a trademark of Byron Preiss Visual Publications, Inc.
Published by arrangement with Byron Preiss Visual Publications, Inc.
Cover design, book design, and logo by Alex Jay/Studio J
Front cover painting by Jim Burns
Library of Congress Catalog Card Number: 91-91786
ISBN: 0-380-75350-2

First Avon Books Printing: August 1991

AVON TRADEMARK REG. U.S. PAT. OFF. AND IN OTHER COUNTRIES, MARCA REGISTRADA, HECHO EN U.S.A.

Printed in the U.S.A.

RA 10 9 8 7 6 5 4 3 2

For the Phaeacians have no steersmen, nor steering-oars such as other craft possess. Our ships know by instinct what their crews are thinking and propose to do.

—Homer, The Odyssey, Book VIII
(translated by E. V. Rieu)

PROLOGUE

Klaus Muller stamped his soft boots on the deck of the rented chalet in an attempt to warm his numb toes. The snows of the Jungfrau never melted, and even though it was an early summer evening, a cascade of cold air had spilled down the pass after sunset. Klaus didn't mind a bit; he felt he'd been transported back a century and a half or more to a time when nights like this were ordinary—just as beautiful but not so rare.

In the valley below, the clustered lights of the village, bisected by the black thread of a mountain stream, showed warmly among dark and fragrant meadows. The lingering aroma of new summer grass mingled with the astringent perfume of pine and the subtler mineral scent of ice water spilling over granite. The night sky was crystal clear, a dark blue hemisphere trembling with silver stars, like an old glass Christmas tree ornament seen close.

A small boy's scornful voice broke Klaus's reverie. "You're taking forever. Let me do it."

"No!" came a younger child's frantic reply. "You *made* me miss."

At the corner of the deck Klaus's two sons, red-cheeked and runny-nosed, were jostling each other, contending for the remote control unit of a portable telescope. When Hans, the younger boy, bumped into it the instrument nimbly skittered sideways on its smart-tripod legs.

Papa Klaus hoped he wouldn't have to interfere, but Hans and Richard were laughing, only pretending to fight. They vied for the telescope's controls, both of them eager to find the object that for three nights now had dominated radio and video news throughout the solar system.

That object was an enormous spacecraft, now leaving the orbit of Jupiter on a column of bright flame, diving toward Earth. The ship was thirty kilometers long, the largest artificial construction any human had ever seen, far larger than the mighty space stations that orbited Earth and Venus and Mars, larger than most asteroids, or the moons of Mars. Still, it was invisible to the naked eye, even on such a night of rare good seeing. But its trajectory, readily extrapolated, had been widely broadcast, and with an amateur instrument as fine as the Muller family's a searcher could find it easily.

"There! That's *it!*" cried the younger boy, finally managing the simple program instructions despite his brother's impatient interference. With a whir of tiny motors the telescope had settled itself on its spindly legs and steered its objective to the designated target; it began tracking. And on the monitor . . .

"Oh, oh, *oh,*" cried the boys together, taken with wonder. Then they both fell silent.

Klaus came closer, drawn by the sharp image on the screen. He drew in his breath, then let it out in a wisp of vapor. He'd seen clearer pictures of the thing earlier in the evening, on the video news, but there was something about seeing for oneself, through the agency of a personal instrument, that made the fantastic real.

"They said there were things sticking out before," Hans said.

"It *retracted* them," Richard informed him.

"Why?"

Young Richard paused only an instant before he

said, "They're *aliens.*" A perfectly good explanation—and one identical, if more economically expressed, to that given by most self-proclaimed adult experts on the subject.

Certainly the ship looked like nothing human. There were no bulbous fuel tanks or blunderbuss engine nozzles, no earlike radio dishes or bristling communications masts, no stuck-on cargo holds or miscellaneous knobs of machinery; there were no painted-on flags or symbols or numbers. The object on the screen was a perfect silver egg, featureless as a falling raindrop. Only its deceptively slow, steady movement against the background of fixed stars revealed its awesome velocity.

Just a day earlier the ship could still have been taken for a remnant of Jupiter's shrinking moon Amalthea. A year ago that long quiescent moon had sprouted a network of foaming geysers and had begun shedding its mass. When all the ice was gone, this gleaming object was left.

Early in the extraordinary process an expedition had gone to investigate. Its leader, Professor J. Q. R. Forster, late of King's College, University of London, was renowned for deciphering the ancient language of Culture X, the alien civilization which had left fossilized remains and fragments of writing on Venus and Mars. With him were six other men and women, including Inspector Ellen Troy of the Board of Space Control.

Shortly after arriving, the Forster expedition had been joined under dramatic circumstances—details yet to be revealed—by the most celebrated video personality in the solar system, the distinguished historian Sir Randolph Mays . . . and his young female assistant.

Although Amalthea was the focus of frantic speculation, Professor Forster had done his best to keep his discoveries confidential; only the Board of Space Control knew for sure what he and his team had found in the weeks before the moon's icy husk finally melted away, revealing the hard kernel at its center.

At that moment, according to the Space Board, all contact with Forster and the others was lost—scant minutes before the alien construction erupted in fiery life. No one knew what had become of them.

Now half the inhabitants of the solar system watched the speeding ship with a mixture of awe and apprehension. Soon—a matter of days at its present velocity—it would cross Earth's orbit, approaching closer than any object its size in the memory of humankind.

As Klaus pondered these wonders, the chalet's single phonelink chortled.

Klaus irritably wondered who would be calling at this hour of the evening. His time with his family was short enough; he had left strict instructions with his office against forwarding calls. A moment later Gertrud's voice, quiet but strained, spoke from the doorway. "It is Goncharov. He says he must speak with you urgently." She held the link toward him.

A chill colder than the night lifted the fine hairs on Klaus's neck. Not that he was afraid, or angry at Goncharov, whom he'd known long enough to think of as a friend, but precisely because Goncharov would not have called him in anything less than a real emergency. For his wife's sake he tried to keep his emotions from showing as he took the link.

"Klaus? This is Mikhail. I have a very urgent problem, and I can't talk on the link."

"I know it must be important, Mikhail, but can't it wait a day? I'll be back in the office on Monday."

"Please come to the Embassy tomorrow—I'll send a helicopter for you."

"If it's really that important I can drive down." The North Continental Treaty Alliance's consular offices in the Swiss Free Region were located in

Bern, less than a hundred kilometers by road from the Mullers' rented chalet.

"Yes . . ." Goncharov hesitated. "But then we would have to get your car back to your wife."

Hearing that, Klaus could guess what the nature of the problem was—and that he would not be vacationing with his family the rest of this week.

"Very urgent, Klaus. Only you can help," Goncharov urged.

Klaus sighed. "Pick me up at ten. I'll be packed."

"Perhaps you should also . . ."

"I'll make the necessary calls, Mikhail. And I'll see you in the morning."

"Goodbye, my friend. And I am sorry."

Klaus keyed off the link. He looked at Gertrud's face, saw his wife's pretty features knitted with disappointment and suppressed anger, and he could think of nothing to say.

Something in his expression softened hers. "Next time, *liebchen*, you must not tell the number to *anyone*."

"Agreed, dearest." Klaus glanced toward the telescope's screen, at his two sons engaged in enthusiastic debate over the fantastic capabilities of the alien ship that the little telescope was faithfully tracking.

He turned back to his wife. "Next time."

But there was to be no next time for Klaus in this world. Not by any fault of the alien ship. For when the alien spacecraft finally sped past the Earth, Klaus was underwater in one of his construction firm's deep-sea submersibles, far down in a subterranean canyon that opened from the mouth of Trincomalee harbor in eastern Sri Lanka. He was trying to diagnose the damage to a deep water project his company had spent many years and many hundreds of thousands of new dollars building there, and which on the eve of its official inauguration had spectacularly malfunctioned.

The alien ship had come within a few tens of

thousands of kilometers of Earth but never slowed in its passage of the heavens. Whereupon those "experts" in alien affairs confidently predicted that the ship, once past Earth, would aim itself toward the constellation Crux in the southern skies. For it had long been supposed—and personalities such as Sir Randolph Mays had well publicized—that the home star of Culture X was in Crux.

The ship confounded them. Seen from Earth, it disappeared in bright daylight. It had dived straight at the sun. Within half a day it was licked by solar prominences; a few minutes later it had passed unscathed through the sun's searing outer layers. Using the sun's mighty gravitational field to adjust its course, it accelerated again in a brilliant burst of fire that stretched across the heavens like a thread of molten glass. It shot out of the solar system, heading into the *northern* skies on a hyperbolic trajectory that was aimed—

—at nothing.

Or at least at no target known to the astronomers of Earth. For nine days, the enormous radio antennas at Farside Base on the moon tracked the ship as it continued to accelerate at ten times the force of gravity on Earth, until it achieved over ninety-five percent of the speed of light. What conceivable power source could have propelled the enormous ship to velocities hitherto observed only in subatomic-particle accelerators? Where did it derive the fuel and reaction mass for this incredible feat?

The theorists had no answers to these practical questions. What they could observe agreed with the expectations of relativity: the wavelength of light reflected from the ship shifted markedly toward the red end of the spectrum, and its receding image grew redder and dimmer. Nevertheless, that image was easy to follow with Farside's immense telescopes. This they did for almost four years.

Then, suddenly, the ship seemed to come to a

halt in space. It grew redder still, and darker, never moving. . . .

Years—whole decades—passed on Earth while the barely visible alien ship hung motionless in the sky. Relatives and colleagues of Professor Forster and his companions grew old and died. The skies of Earth grew ever fouler, its land more eroded and barren, its seas more choked with oil, until the whole planet trembled on the verge of a global dying and only the precarious space stations and settlements on the moon and Mars and in the Mainbelt—a few hundreds of thousands of souls—could hope to survive the self-strangulation of the birthplace of their kind.

Long before this unhappy end, even before the alien apparition had departed the daylit skies of Earth, Klaus Muller had disappeared—lost in the depths of the Indian Ocean trying to fix what would have been the Earth's first large-scale hydrothermal plant. From that valiant environmental effort the Swiss engineer never returned. . . .

"Or so it might have been," said Professor J. Q. R. Forster, his bright eyes gleaming with mischief. He watched the firelight glinting in his glass and swirled the smoky Scotch whisky, then took a slow, appreciative sip. "In the likeliest of all outcomes."

"How do we know it won't happen still?" whispered the tall man by the fire, his voice like the rattle of surf on a beach of stones. "Maybe not all the details you've put in for us, Forster, but the broad outlines."

"Kip's right." The woman among the four of them brusquely nodded her head. "Nothing leads me to hope we can prevent the worst of all possible worlds resulting from this debacle."

"But Ari, one might as well say we can do nothing to prevent the best of all possible worlds." Jozsef Nagy was as earnestly optimistic as his wife was dour.

"We'll do what we always have. Our best." Forster

cocked an amused eyebrow and studied the others, not unsympathetically. "One thing we can know. There are at least as many outcomes as there are new stars in the sky outside those windows."

PART
1

ESCAPE
FROM
JUPITER

1

The mansion is made of basalt and granite; it stands on a high tor above the Hudson River. In the past it was a busy place. Now its long corridors and paneled halls are empty, its furniture taken away, its pantries and cupboards and shelves stripped of their contents. The wide lawns that surround the grand old house have grown wild and rank, and weeds have invaded from the neighboring woodlands.

It is evening, early winter; the hazy sky shines with a scattering of familiar stars. Among the known stars are dozens of strange new ones, much brighter, trailing columns of fire like comets. And like comets, the gleaming newcomers seem to quest after the sun, recently set.

Through the tall French doors of the old house, overlooking the lawn, a ruddy light suddenly flares and fades away, then flares again. Inside, in the library, oak logs blaze in the stone fireplace. The man named Kip—whom most people address as Commander—leans his tall frame over the fire, letting its warmth play over his weathered skin; glittering flames are reflected in his cold blue eyes.

There are no chairs in the empty place, but there are enough rolled-up Oriental carpets and pillows of exotic origin—camel bags, embossed leather poufs—to allow the little assembly to sprawl and make themselves comfortable. Ari sits regally on a

Persian rug spread haphazardly on the floor near the fireplace, propped against mounds of pillows. There are enough refreshments on the silver tray in the center of their circle to make the evening congenial.

"More tea, Ari?" Jozsef is the oldest of them; his middle-European accent is heavy.

Ari nods briefly, swiping at her short gray hair—a habitual gesture from an earlier era, when her straight hair was long and glossy black and fell across her eyes. She lets her woolen shawl loosen around her shoulders—the heat from the fireplace is finally reaching into the musty places of the room—and takes the freshly filled cup on its saucer.

"Professor?"

"You have taken good care of me already." Forster seems much younger than the others—until, seen close up, his wrinkled and sunburnt skin reveals itself, stretched tightly over his facial bones. He takes the thick glass with a brisk nod.

"Anything for you, Kip?"

The commander shakes his head. Jozsef pours himself a cup of black tea and cradles it, leaning back against a cylinder of rolled-up carpet, reclining like a Bedouin sheik in his tent. "It will be sad to bid goodbye to this house. It has served us well. But it is joyful to know Salamander's work is complete. I hope that when we are through here this evening, we will have left a record that will serve future generations." He raises his cup a few millimeters, an economical gesture. "To the truth."

The others acknowledge him with stares and silent nods. Ari sips her tea critically, making a face. Forster sips from his whiskey glass and rolls the liquid on his tongue, then swallows. He seems lost in thought.

"You were saying, Professor . . . ?"

Forster looks up as if reminding himself where he is. "Ah. Possibilities . . . But what I'm about to tell you now is not conjecture—or not wholly. It is based upon my personal experiences, upon records, upon my talks with the others.''

''No more fiction about the future, then,'' Ari says tartly.

''Some of what I have to say is, I admit, guesswork. But then I am a xeno-archaeologist, accustomed to operating in the realm of uncertainty.'' Forster sets his glass on the thick-woven carpet. ''Guesswork has proved essential with regard to the actions of the one we call Nemo.''

''We know about Nemo,'' says the commander from the fireplace. ''We've run analyses on all the surviving works of the Knowledge. We've reconstructed what he did.''

Ari gives him a dark look. ''And all still guesswork, Kip. As the professor says.''

''Some things we know,'' the commander says, his words husky, his voice barely audible.

No one contradicts him. The fire crackles and leaps in the fireplace; orange light dances on the coffered ceiling and probes the empty bookshelves.

The young-old man who is Professor J. Q. R. Forster resumes his tale. ''So . . . We found ourselves caught up by the alien vessel, which had come to life and now imposed upon us its own imperatives. There was no argument. There could be none. We must conform—and quickly—or die. . . .''

2

The pressure lock was a blister on the world-ship's perfect diamond skin. Inside, it was a weirdly beautiful place, full of intricate and colorful things that seemed at once alive and machine-like, an alien tide pool at low tide—

—except that its floor was, just now, not so much a floor as an encrusted vertical wall parallel to the axis of the world-ship's crushing acceleration. More than a kilometer across, designed to accomodate spacecraft up to the size of small asteroids, the lock's aching emptiness diminished the only vessel it contained, our rugged little converted Jupiter tug *Michael Ventris*, held fast by a knot of metallic tentacles—a small fish paralyzed by a gigantic anemone.

Without warning, acceleration ceased; suddenly the world-ship and everything it contained was weightless, falling freely toward the sun. Inside the *Ventris*, we began unbuckling ourselves from our couches. But the sudden onset of acceleration at Jupiter had caught some of the crew off guard, crushing them to the padded floors; now they strove to stop themselves from drifting away from the decks.

Josepha Walsh was our pilot—red-haired, slender to the point of skinniness, a youthful fifteen-year veteran of the Board of Space Control. "Let me hear from you, people." She keyed the comm-link and flicked switched on the videoplate monitors. ''What's the situation in the wardroom? Tony? Angus?''

''Well . . . I could heartily recommend lying flat on the floor for ten minutes at ten gees,'' came back our engineer Angus McNeil's drawl, his round face drifting into view on the monitor link from the wardroom, ''for anyone whose spine needs straightening.''

''Right. Would have been a very nice rest, Captain,'' chimed in the cheerful voice of Tony Groves, our navigator, ''had I not been trying to support this damned flowerpot that fell on my midsection.''

''That flowerpot's your helmet,'' said McNeil.

''D'you say so?'' said Groves, pretending astonishment.

''What about our guest?'' the captain asked.

There was a pause before Groves filled the silence. ''Sir Randolph seems to have run out of the necessary hot air to make another speech at the moment. But he is in fact breathing.''

''Pity,'' someone said—McNeil?

''Marianne, are you all right?'' asked Captain Walsh.

''I . . . I'm all right,'' the young woman replied. Along with Sir Randolph, Marianne Mitchell was the other involuntary guest, and, although she was doing her best not to reveal her fear, she was unable to hide her utter weariness.

''We're both all right,'' volunteered my assistant Bill Hawkins, whose acceleration couch was beside Marianne's on the crew deck. He had appointed himself her protector, but clearly he was as weary and frightened as she. ''What happens now?''

''We'll get to that when we have more information, Bill.'' Walsh looked around the flight deck at the glowing console lights, the flatscreens, the surrounding windows that looked out on the huge lock outside. She ran a hand through her brush-cut bronze hair, a gesture of relief, and then gave me an appraising stare. ''You seem to have held up well, Professor.''

''Thank you, Captain,'' I said, no doubt with a

sigh, making no effort to move from my couch. I was, after all, despite my appearance, the oldest of the group. "But I do hope that sort of acceleration isn't going to become routine."

"Same here. I've pulled worse in cutters, but they're built for it," Walsh said. "Apparently our tug's no worse for wear, though. Confirm that, computer?"

"All systems standing by and functioning nominally," said the bland, faintly Chinese-accented voice of the *Ventris*'s master computer.

"Rather warm in here, wouldn't you say?" I complained.

"Can't help that just yet." The hatches were still open to the outside air, saving onboard oxygen. It was hot inside, and humid.

Blake Redfield, whom I'd hired as my other assistant, had gotten free of his harness in the borrowed engineer's couch. "I'll see if there's anything I can do below."

"Check on Mays, will you? I don't want any more trouble with him," said Walsh.

Redfield grunted. "Best bet would be to put him in deep sleep and store him in the hold."

"His compartment will have to do for now. Just make sure he hasn't got a crowbar in there with him."

Redfield nodded and pulled himself down through the open hatch, into the ship's main corridor.

"Hello, *Ventris*. Everyone all right?" It was a woman's voice on the commlink speakers, Inspector Ellen Troy's, strangely distorted with hollow echoes. Though we had previously had time to accustom ourselves to the knowledge that she was talking underwater, we were far from taking the sound of her for granted.

"All still alive, Ellen."

"Good. More news from this end. *Ventris* is to separate from the world-ship before our next acceleration. You'll be put on trajectory to a Mainbelt settlement. Better get started on it right now, Jo."

"What?" That energized me at last. I clawed at my harness. "What was that, Troy?"

"That's . . . good news," said the captain.

"What's to become of the alien vessel?" I demanded.

"What will become of *you*, Ellen?" Walsh demanded.

"I don't know where this thing is headed," said Troy over the commlink. "But wherever it is, I'm riding with it."

"I insist upon accompanying you," I protested.

"I'm not sure that's possible, Professor."

"Why not? The air inside the lock is perfectly breathable. The water is drinkable, the foodstuffs edible. Surely the alien can . . ."

"I'll ask."

"I insist upon speaking directly with the alien. You know as well as I that . . ."

Again she interrupted me. "I'll convey that request and get back to you as soon as I can, sir. Jo, prepare to launch. You only get one chance."

Forster looks up from his nest of cushions on the rug opposite Ari and Jozsef, addressing his remark to the commander. "Later, we learned what Nemo was thinking and doing in the minutes that followed. It was hardly the first time we'd disastrously underrated the man. . . ."

Moments after we'd come out of acceleration, McNeil had carried Randolph Mays—still bundled in his spacesuit, limp as a sack of laundry—to his sleeping compartment and locked him in. Redfield told me he tested the door a minute later; otherwise, Mays was alone and forgotten. He struggled out of his suit and pushed it into a corner of what had been designed as a two-person cabin; his spacesuit was bulky enough to make up the difference.

Ducking his head under the negative-pressure hood of the personal hygiene unit, he rubbed water on his face; I picture him letting himself smile with the pleasure of it, then prolonging the luxury by running a chemosonic shaver over the wiry gray whiskers which had sprouted on his chin since our precipitate departure from Jupiter orbit. Not half an hour earlier, he'd been a dead man. He'd been sure of it.

Surely he must have spent a long time studying his face in the mirror. It was a big, square, deeply seamed face, thick-browed, with a wide mouth and bunched muscles at the hinges of the powerful jaws. A predatory face. But a distinguished face. He'd worn this face long enough—well, almost long enough—to get used to it.

When he got tired of staring at himself he lay down on his bunk and stared at the gray metal bulkhead. For Sir Randolph Mays—the name he bore in his current manifestation—had nowhere to go and no reason to go anywhere.

"Randolph Mays," "Jacques Lequeu," "William Laird," just plain "Bill"—he was a plastic man who had appeared repeatedly over the years, revealing himself as a leader in the affairs of the now-defunct Free Spirit, the milleniums-old secret society that had long predicted the reappearance of the aliens. Who was he in reality? No one knew.

He'd plotted to kill us all, every member of our expedition, and he'd come uncomfortably close to succeeding. But he knew that none of us could seriously entertain the notion of doing to him what he'd tried to do to us. That none of us would want to waste time being his jailer. That after some discussion we'd come to the conclusion that since he had no conceivable further motive for killing us and nowhere to run to if he did, we would simply try to maintain reasonable caution in is presence—probably by telling the computer to keep track of his whereabouts, and by never allowing him outside the crew area alone, and of course by keeping the medicine cabinet with its therapeutic poisons locked up, and so forth and so on—and otherwise we would ignore him.

Coventry has no physical dimensions, but it is

a tangible place nonetheless. No one would talk to Mays. When we sat down to eat, there would be no place in our circle for him. If he came into a room, everyone else would leave it—or if that was inconvenient, we would talk and look through him as if he didn't exist.

Nemo, Troy had called him. A man without a name is no man at all. Before long even that label would seem superfluous, as I'm sure he knew. Persuaded by our self-altered perceptions, the crew of the *Ventris* would forget about him. We would pretend he didn't exist, and soon we would believe it.

Advantage his. He'd spent more years of his life in solitary meditation than any of us could imagine.

He meditated now upon the immediate future. Nothing in the Knowledge—which the Free Spirit had worked (and often murdered) to preserve—had prepared him for what was happening, much less what was yet to come. Except for an insignificant difference in numbers, he and his enemies were evenly matched.

Only possession of the *Michael Ventris* gave us an edge. So . . . how does one disable a spaceship?

Really, the possibilities were endless, although pragmatism imposed a few restraints. Most vulnerable were the engines and fuel tanks—but it was not likely he'd be able to get outside the crew module without alerting his captors. We would ignore him, see through him, only while he was somewhere in sight. Like a rattlesnake on a rock, he'd be camouflaged only so long as he didn't move. For the same reason the hardware of the ship's maneuvering systems, life support systems, and radiation shield were protected; getting at them required going outside.

From inside he could blow a hole through the wall of the pressure vessel which was the crew module. He'd have to get his hands on explosives, which were in the equipment bays with the other tools—which still meant going outside. In a pinch he could attack the control consoles barehanded.

No doubt we'd be able to stop him before he did much damage.

Which left software. Appropriately named. As it was for all complex systems, software was the soft underbelly of the *Michael Ventris*.

I see Nemo grinning to himself then, stretching thin lips over voracious square teeth. In the solitude of his sleeping compartment he spoke aloud. "Computer, I'd like to read. Please display the catalogue."

"Do you have a preferred category?" the computer asked in its politely neutral voice.

"Poetry, I think," said Nemo. "Epic poetry."

Then the light on the videoplate monitor in the bulkhead blinked redly, and the freckled face of our pilot gazed in at him coolly. "Mays, we're preparing for an immediate launch. Put your suit on and strap yourself down."

"I hear you, Captain Walsh."

"Do it."

He put on his suit—all but the gloves. He had work to do on the computer, quietly, without talking, using the keyboard.

The rest of us were at our regular launch stations, Groves in the navigator's couch on the flight deck beside Walsh, McNeil at his station behind them. Those not needed to direct the ship's operations were in their couches below, except for me. I stayed where I was, on one side of the deck, nervously eyeing the chronometers. I pulled my portable synthesizing translator from the flap of my suit and began speaking rapidly, filling its memory. I was frantic to get off the *Ventris* before it left the alien ship, and I had a single chance, at best, to plead my case.

The pre-count began. We were visible to one another on the tiny commlink videoplates. The men's faces were shadowed with whiskers; all of us were tired and sweat-stained.

Groves stared at his readouts thoughtfully, his

dark brows knitting at the bridge of his fine straight nose. "Not to step on any toes, but at first glance it doesn't seem we've got the delta-vees to make it to any of the Mainbelt settlements. My charts show we're moving at forty kps retrograde."

"You're not steppin' on *my* toes, if that's who you're referrin' to," said McNeil, whose brogue tended to thicken when he was in a contrary mood. He tapped the visual display in front of him. "Consumables are just about consistent with regainin' Ganymede from Amalthea orbit. We've drawn down heavily in past days. H-two, LOX—not to mention food, that sort of thing."

The commlink speaker sounded with the weird ringing of Troy's underwater voice. "All right, a little better data to give you. Your launch window comes up in just under ten minutes."

Walsh said, "Some concern here, Ellen. Consensus is that we don't have the consumables."

At that moment the *Ventris* was rocked gently in the cradle of the world-ship's mechanical tentacles. We could hear the grappling of automatic couplings and the venting of gases.

Troy's voice continued, "Thowintha assures me that *Ventris* will be fully supplied before departure with liquid hydrogen and oxygen, food, fresh water . . . all necessary consumables."

"That appears to be happening now," said Walsh, watching the gauges. "We're taking on fuel."

"And ver' nice of him, Ellen," said McNeil, ". . . or of it, or whatever . . . but I'm wonderin' whether the alien's notion of food is similar to our own."

A series of shrieks, whistles, clicks, and booms threatened to overload the speakers. When it subsided, Troy said, "Thowintha says that what is needed will be provided." She added, amused, "Hope you like sea food."

"What of my demand, Inspector Troy?" I shouted, addressing my question to the blank videoplate where Troy's face would have been on a normal transmission. "I *must* be allowed to speak to Thowintha. *Immediately.*"

"I'm sorry, sir, but I can get no acknowledgment from Thowintha yet," the invisible woman replied.

I had done my best to control my temper, but I was losing the battle. I could feel my features reddening. Furiously, I tapped at the keys of my translator. Troy was not the only one who could speak the language of Culture X.

The pilot and navigator and engineer watched the changing graphics on their consoles.

Outside, automatic hoses bulged and writhed.

Walsh said, "Before we launch, I think the professor would agree that what we signed on for, we accomplished. . . ."

"I didn't sign on for anything," said Marianne Mitchell, whose green eyes were bright and unblinking in the pale monitor that showed her face. "I just want to go home."

"That's where we're headed, Marianne," Walsh said gently.

Hawkins felt the need to come to her defense. "Some people may think there's a reason to . . ." The talkative young postdoc stopped himself in midsentence, I think because whatever question he'd been about to answer, nobody had asked. He swiped at the lock of fine blond hair that had floated into his eyes. "Well, I'm coming with Marianne, that's all."

Obviously he was; his non sequitur got no reply. Outside the hull, the hoses uncoupled and retracted in unison—we could see them on the videoplate, like an octopus ballet.

"Ellen, do you read me?" Walsh asked, but got no reply.

"Inspector Troy!" I cried out desperately, but the commlink remained silent. "I want Thowintha to hear this." I held up the translator, which began to emit clicks and spats and booms, a good simulation of the alien speech, I thought, but for the puny resonance of the synthesizer's tiny speakers.

"Seal all exterior hatches and locks," Walsh ordered, over the din I was making.

Her magnificent coolness failed to impress me as it should have. "But Captain Walsh . . . !" I protested—shouting at her, I fear.

"Sorry, Professor. Looks like you're coming with us. Why don't you help us out and turn that thing off?"

Troy came back on the commlink. "Your message has been received, Professor."

I clicked off the synthesizer. "Yes? And?"

"Thowintha says the world-ship is about to undergo accelerations that . . . mm . . . make the one we just went through look puny. You couldn't survive. No unmodified human could. You must go with the others, sir."

The *Ventris*'s computer said, "All exterior hatches and locks are secured. *Michael Ventris* is sealed and pressurized."

"Our tanks are full, we're powered up and ready to launch on a one minute count," said Walsh. "Copy that, Ellen?"

"Copy you're ready to go," Troy said.

Then McNeil jerked in his chair as if stung. "Captain, look at that. We've a significant mass anomaly!"

"Go ahead," she said.

"Showing deficit after resupply of . . . of sixty-seven kilograms. In the crew module."

"Somebody's missing," said Walsh. She searched the monitor screens one by one. Groves, McNeil, and I were on the deck with her; Mitchell and Hawkins were in their couches on the utility deck; Mays was in plain view, having strapped himself to the couch in what had become his private sleeping compartment. "Where's Blake?"

To our surprise, it was Inspector Troy who answered. "Blake's with me."

The blood raced to my scalp so fast that I could

feel my skin blazing under my restored hair. "You deceived me, Troy," I said, sure that she had conspired to keep me from the crowning achievement of my life. "All of this is intended . . ."

"Sir, I said no *unmodified* human could survive the coming course change. It was Thowintha's assessment that you personally could not have survived the necessary modification—however much you might wish to believe otherwise. I am sincerely sorry, sir."

I went a little crazy then, and slapped at my harness release. "It's not too late for me yet, to see . . ."

Troy said, "Please start your count, Captain Walsh. The pressure lock is opening."

Displayed on the flight deck flatscreen, the diffuse blue glow which filled the enormous empty space beneath the dome had dimmed; a black well had opened in the center of the dome and was spiraling outward; the pattern of starry lights which decorated the concave ceiling was fading out, to be replaced by other, dimmer lights—the real stars, shining through the vanishing gossamer stuff of the lock.

"Thirty seconds and counting," said the computer.

There was another light in the sky, its source invisible from the *Ventris*. But through the flight-deck windows we could see a blazing oval moving like a theatrical spotlight across the filigreed wall of the vault, as the sun sent a slanting bar of what seemed to our dark-adapted eyes like fierce illumination through the lock's widening aperture.

"The whole world-ship is rolling like crazy," Walsh said.

Half out of my couch, I struggled to get back into it, knowing I was too late. The others were too busy to notice me or see my hot tears.

"Ten seconds," said the computer. "Nine. Eight. Seven . . ."

The *Ventris* began to move at an angle to the ship,

borne aloft on the same unfurling tentacles that previously had locked it firmly in place. Stretching—seemingly without limit—the delicate metallic tendrils lifted the tug lightly through the hole in the roof, into the blazing light of the sun above.

"Now we're accelerating *away* from it," said Groves.

The tendrils had curved back upon themselves, coiling themselves like a spring. To some cosmic observer watching this scene from afar, it would seem that the huge shining ellipsoid had budded, emitting an almost invisibly tiny polyp from a cyst on its side.

McNeil said, "The world-ship . . . it's *throwing* us!"

With a snap like a slingshot, we were hurled into space.

". . . Three. Two. One."

A solid boom, massive and comforting to those of us on the flight deck, thundered through the *Ventris* as our main rocket engines fired—

—followed almost instantly by a sharp, crackling cough. To me it felt and sounded as if somebody had just dropped a piano on the roof.

Stars were suddenly streaking across the real sky outside the windows and jiggling crazily across the image of the sky on the flight deck's flatscreen; the *Ventris* was out of control, tumbling in a violent, spiraling spin. I had gotten my harness fastened barely in time.

"Number two main engine misfire," McNeil said. Most of his bulk, like mine, was thrown upside down against his harness, and all trace of Scottish accent gone from his expressionless voice.

Alarm sirens were howling, red lights were flashing on all consoles.

"Auto-shutdown one and three," Walsh said quietly and without hurry, as if this sort of thing happened every other day or so. "MS to auto-stabilize."

"One and three to auto-shutdown. MS to auto-stabilize," McNeil confirmed.

"Computer, status please—first approximation, in order of criticality."

"Life support systems nominal. Auxiliary power systems nominal. Maneuvering systems nominal. Fuel stores nominal. Other consumables nominal. Main propulsion system condition red. Number two engine out of commission. Number two engine H-two pumps out of commission. No fire . . . No danger of fire."

"Computer, carry on."

"Present position and velocity not computable from available data. Internal accelerational forces misaligned by . . ."

"That's enough, computer." Walsh shot a crooked glance at Groves. "Any guesses on a heading?"

"We should be in a lot of trouble," Groves replied.

"Well, are we?"

"I think not, Jo." He indicated a threadlike pattern of light unraveling on the navigation flatscreen. "Looks like the world-ship is about to . . ."

There was a bruising jerk—

". . . grab us back."

—the first of several jerks that repeatedly hurled us against our harnesses. I groaned woefully, suddenly concerned with keeping my dinner down. Outside the windows, stars stopped spiraling and started bouncing. Then, abruptly, they settled into a smooth wheeling pattern.

"Look!" Groves pointed excitedly out the flight-deck window. A hard-edged plain of diamond-bright metal had appeared, cleaving the heavens, to spread itself solidly beneath us. The sun and stars were doubled in its polished depths.

"What's happening?" I asked, sounding pitiful.

The *Ventris* was so close to it that the world-ship filled our sky; in its perfect diamond-like surface we could see the reflection of our own tiny vessel against the panoply of the wheeling universe.

"Later," Forster tells his listeners, "I learned of the words—remarkably few words—that passed between Troy and the alien just then. . . ."

Do you wish the human beings to survive? Thowintha asked her without preamble. Whether she did or didn't—whether the other humans lived or died—seemed a matter of indifference to the alien. *If they are to survive, they must be made to conform to the living world.*

Water transmits sound much better than air; although Thowintha was far off and invisible, Troy heard the alien's words as if they came from beside her. *How shall they be made to conform?* she called into the dark waters.

They must conform as you do now. As your companion will. They must live within the waters.

How are we to make water-breathers of them? she demanded. *You said the professor could not be modified. And now there is no time.*

We have other means to save them, besides modification. You must persuade your fellow human beings of the necessity. From what you have told us, this will be a great obstacle.

Why do you say so?

Because you are—what do you call yourselves?—'individuals'.

That will not be an obstacle, Troy said firmly.

What the alien did not understand is that individuals have an instinct for survival far more intense than that of beings who regard themselves as merely the organs and limbs of a collective body.

For when Troy came to us and said, to live you must let us drown you, we quickly replied, let us drown.

3

> "Like the egg it resembled, the huge spheroid of the alien world-ship was filled with warm fluid," Forster continues, "a broth of saltwater, thick with life. . . ."

Water is virtually incompressible. Creatures who live in water, having their tissues and hollow spaces filled with water, are unbothered by accelerations that would crush an air-breathing human. Wholly submerged in dark water, our lungs and other hollow places flooded with water, our tissues and organs infiltrated by microtubules that bathed us in water-borne oxygen and cleansed us of impurities and bubbled all corrupting influences away, our seven naked bodies swayed in a kelp-like forest. We seemed to swell like pods from the pulsing transparent tubes and veined leafy ribbons that bore us.

We slept for half a year. We might have slept that way for eternity, dreaming. . . .

As for myself, a professor of xeno-archaeology, late of King's College, University of London, I dreamed what I believed—that I had brought myself and the others with me to the culmination of my life's work, pursuing the traces of vanished Culture X. Scenes of my lifelong chase replayed themselves vividly, from my first amazed boyhood encounter with reproductions of the dusty and enigmatic fossils of Venus, to my discovery, on the hellish surface of that very world, of the extraordinary Venusian tablets, twice the cause of my near-death—from which, the first time, Ellen Troy had saved me at great risk to her own life—and finally to what I was sure would be my triumph in orbit around Jupiter. And although the future hid itself, even in dreams, a warm confidence now suffused my expectations. I had gotten what I wanted after all, and surely the end of our journey would be the alien homeworld in Crux, a planet never touched by humanity revealing itself in all its majesty and unimaginable strangeness. I dreamed, and at the edges of my musing consciousness, alien masses flocked like choirs of angels. . . .

Ari interrupts Forster's musings. "What of the others?"

The professor eyes her. "Later—much later, we were to have longer than we could have then imagined to come to know one another, to learn one another's deepest thoughts. My friends never forget what they dreamed then, or thereafter. This is a little of what they told me. . . ."

In her sleep, Josepha Walsh told me, she inhabited an underworld more congenial by far than the darkness in which her body was actually submerged, a world of sky-blue waters and glowing reefs and squadrons of fishes as bright and energetic as fireworks—a glorious underworld like that which lay beneath the Caribbean reefs of her girlhood. Shining brown gods came striding across the sandy seafloor, wreathed in smiles and flowers. One of them became her lover, before she lost him. But she was sure, in her dreams, that someday, somewhere, she would find him again. . . .

Awake, Tony Groves was a lively elf; drowned and dreaming, melancholy overcame him. His pale mother flitted at the outskirts of a dark urban dreamscape; his tradesman father, mostly absent when Tony was growing up and in reality now long dead, was ever-present, taking more of an interest in the boy than he'd ever shown in life, but expressing himself, even here, only by nagging: was young Tony prepared for his maths test? Would he pass the swimming examinations that so terrorized him? And just what ideas had Tony been putting into his younger brother's head, to make the lad decide against seminary? Precisely why was Tony so . . . perverse . . . so inadequate . . . ?

Angus McNeil wasted little of his dreamtime on his childhood, his damp and brown-hued Scottish boyhood. He lived in fiery fantasies of planetfall. Awake, McNeil was a private man, like most of the men and women who spent the bulk of their lives aboard the working ships of the solar system. Only a few professional spacefarers have families in the regular way; the others make do instead with a shifting network of seldom-seen friends and occasional lovers. Ascetic of necessity, accruing hefty credits but with no place to spend them in space, McNeil indulged his considerable appetites between cruises. He was a voracious reader of books, old and new. He wanted knowledge, of whatever kind, whatever its source. But in his dreams he was not a reader. In his dreams tom-toms pattered, ouds moaned, houris whirled, and sweet wine flowed. . . .

Marianne Mitchell had read much in her peripatetic college career but never since childhood anything in the way of fantasy. Her wildest nightmares before this fell far short of the true situation. Now she dreamed desperately of normalcy. She was back in a college classroom, or she was back in her dormitory room, or in her mother's Park Avenue apartment in Manhattan, or wandering the corridors of the Metropolitan Museum—which in her dreams, curiously, was hung only with representations of alien life forms—or she was perched high on the rail of a close-hauled ketch, tossing her luxuriant hair in the breezes of Long Island Sound.

Young men crowded these halls of memory; it was with irritation that she recognized Bill Hawkins's sincere English good looks among the anonymous suitors who approached her almost everywhere she turned. But another face confronted her whenever she turned away from Bill, and Nemo's leer set her to screaming inside. . . .

On Amalthea, young Bill Hawkins had dreamed of oak-paneled lecture halls gleaming waxy gleams, of scholarly philological triumphs; then he had been caught up in the real-life excitement of our first explorations of the alien vessel. Now he dreamed of dark-haired, green-eyed Marianne, of the wooing and winning and losing of her, in endless variations upon his own recent past. Bill had learned that nothing binds a wanting but indecisive man's longing like the realization that the woman once within his grasp has lost her patience, has decided to get on without him. . . .

Who can say what Nemo dreamed? Surely the man so recently known to us as Sir Randolph Mays was more accustomed than we knew to the nature of the drifting consciousness which trapped us all. I think his "dreams" would have startled us, anchored as they were in specific memories and pointing to hard-edged (if then only potential) alternative futures.

We do know that more than once in the eternal night that threatened to dissolve their very flesh, Nemo's eyelids rolled back and his pale eyes, hard as pearls, gazed implacably upon our drifting bodies. . . .

We know it because every day another human came to visit us, although we were oblivious to her. She swam freely and consciously in the rippling half-light among the swaying bodies of the drowned. Her slender body was as hard-muscled and lithe as a dancer's; her short blond hair swayed gracefully as she swam, as if each strand of it were alive. She was more at home in the water than anyone else of her species could have been. The slits beneath her collar bone gaped to accept the inrush of water, and the petal-like gills between her ribs fluttered as water flowed through her. Her bare limbs undulated rhythmically as she swam.

At first only she experienced the days that passed—experienced them in the present tense; at first she was alone, free (and condemned) to explore the vast watery realm of the alien ship by herself. Occasionally, at unscheduled moments, at times that seemed without rhythm, she found herself in the company of the only other waking sentient creature who inhabited that endless volume of water—as she did on the very first day.

"They talked that first day, and Ellen Troy—your daughter, Linda—recounted their conversation to me much later," Forster explains. "And so it was that I learned her secret name. . . ."

Seen at a distance, the enormous animal swimming ahead of her might have been a giant squid from the oceans of Earth, although a closer look revealed many differences; the resemblance was accidental but not random, for organisms adapted to speed in the water tend to assume the same torpedo-like shape no matter what their evolutionary history. She pursued the silvery-gray, many-tentacled creature as swiftly as she could, tracking the alien by its odor in the water, taking the water through her mouth and nostrils, analyzing its rich and intricate chemical nature at a level that verged on consciousness and that she could call to consciousness whenever she willed it.

For years my parents conducted what came to be known as the SPecified Aptitude Resource Training and Assessment project—SPARTA for short. Later the Free Spirit tried to destroy my memory. I forgot my name for a while, but I remembered something of my upbringing. So I called myself Sparta.

The alien adjusted itself to her speed in the water. *What purpose had they, these . . . your parents? The* creature's question streamed out behind it as if in a string of ringing bubbles as it moved easily through the life-encrusted corridors, hardly rippling its propulsive fins. The waters through which they swam, she following in its wake, teemed with glowing, multicolored life.

Whatever "Thowintha"—a corrupt and approximate rendering of a name whose sounds consisted of bubbling hisses and resonant thuds—was doing could apparently be done in a leisurely fashion. At least for the moment, the alien (Sparta—as she always thought of herself—had as yet received no hint of the creature's reproductive systems, or its place or orientation within those systems, and considered him'er neither a he nor a she) had no tasks more important than the one sh'he and Sparta were engaged in now, the exchange of stories.

Sparta blew bubbles and spat clicks. *There is a prejudice in our culture that ranks individuals according to a single measure of intelligence. My parents wished to disprove that prejudice.*

Such an idea is beyond our comprehension.

There is much about us you do not comprehend. She smiled inwardly at the thought. *We have trouble comprehending ourselves.*

They spoke in the language that humans (chiefly myself) had reconstructed from a few ancient artifacts, which I had labeled that of Culture X. Granted, my reconstruction was far from perfect. But Sparta was learning Thowintha's true language rapidly, limited in her attempts to reproduce it only by her physique: her body was a fourth the volume of the alien's and her clicks and booms and squeaks were feeble by comparison.

Nevertheless, the creature seemed to comprehend her watery words. Whether sh'he and Sparta fully understood each other's meaning was another question, one that might take both their lifetimes to answer.

To begin with, Sparta suspected that Thowintha did not have a firm grasp of the notion of individuality. For her part, Sparta certainly did not fully understand what Thowintha meant when sh'he said, *We are the living world.* To Sparta's eye, Thowintha was a single body, but sh'he referred to his'erself only in the plural and, moreover, seemed to regard his'erself as somehow actually a part of the world-ship. But by ''we'' Thowintha apparently meant more than the ship itself. Thowintha assumed unity with those who had built it, now absent and long dead—or perhaps asleep somewhere in its depths, as Thowintha had slept for unknown ages. There were no others of his'er kind in evidence in the vast ship, whose volume exceeded thirty-five trillion cubic meters.

While Thowintha answered Sparta's questions on these subjects without reservation, the answers often made little sense.

The alien quivered and emitted an intermittent stream of bubbles. *Your . . . parents. They succeeded in healing this aberrant mode of thought?*

The aberrance persists among all but a few of us, as it has for centuries. An amused stream of bubbles flowed from Sparta's nose. *Perhaps you think us mad.*

Thowintha suddenly darted ahead with strong beats of his'er fins, vanishing into a green-glowing corridor.

Sparta swam doggedly after, wondering what urgent business had suddenly arisen—or if the conversation had made the alien uncomfortable.

They were swimming inside the enormous structure-within-a-structure that we had called, because of its many murals and sculptural representations of familiar but unknown life forms (actually Mays had called it this, and his name stuck), ''The Temple of Art.'' One such work of art had turned out not to be a piece of sculpture at all; it had been Thowintha his'erself, who had rested in perfect stasis for who knew how many milleniums. As yet none of the other pieces in the so-called Temple of Art had come to life, but Sparta regarded everything around her with wary respect.

As for the Temple, it was no temple at all, and its relationship to art was obscure; it was, as nearly as Sparta could determine, the bridge, the area from which Thowintha in some way that was unclear to her participated in the operation of the world-ship.

The maze of narrow intersecting corridors opened into a cavernous hall whose filigreed walls radiated shades of dark purple and blue. Sparta knew the place; she knew that the innumerable bright glowing patches on the shadow-clotted walls—walls that reached higher than any Earthly cathedral—represented the stars as seen from the ship's orientation in space, which moved as if projected on a planetarium's dome. These stars were not projections, however; each glowing patch was alive, a colony of some phosphorescent planktonic organism, and the physical movement of the whole ensemble of living light was somehow coordinated to the precise motion of the ship.

Thowintha hung suspended in the middle of this bowl of heaven, in water that swarmed with glittering galaxies of other life, ctenophores and transparent shrimp and swarms of tiny jellyfish that pulsed with neon colors, pink and purple and green. A shimmering sound as of underwater bells issued from the alien's siphons; the living stars on the walls dimmed and rearranged themselves. When they reappeared, moments later, the relationships among them were similar, but the orientation seemed skewed.

Look at the heavens, said Thowintha.

Above her, in the highest reaches of the shadowy planetarium, the star map had assumed a peculiarly contracted quality, as if the whole sphere of constellations had been squeezed into a narrow circle. *I see it. What is it?*

This is the next stage of our journey.

Where is our destination? Sparta asked.

There where you see it, above you, replied Thowintha unhelpfully.

Sparta saw only the crowded constellations of

Earth's northern sky. If the center of the planetarium dome were to be taken as the aim-point of the world-ship—a not unlikely assumption—then the ship's destination was somewhere in the constellation Gemini, near the plane of the Galaxy.

What is the name of that place?

It is a non-place. There followed a staccato series Sparta could not decipher.

Sparta lapsed into trance. In the milliseconds that passed, she evaluated the implications of the peculiarly contracted star pattern on the ceiling far overhead. It was instantly clear: this was the forward view of a spacecraft traveling at nearly the speed of light. In the next few hours the world-ship was to undergo far greater accelerations than those it had needed to leave Jupiter's orbit.

Sparta came out of the trance that had passed so quickly no one would have noticed. *So that is why we drowned them.*

That is why.

Thus the ark that carried us all continued its headlong dive into the sun. Inside the photosphere, stealing some of the sun's gravitational energy, the world-ship whipped itself up and away from the solar system and, minutes later, engaged its own awesome engines. For nine days the world-ship accelerated at forty times the gravitational acceleration normal to Earth. Then acceleration stopped. We fled through empty space, weightless.

Now our abandoned tug was secure again in its nest of half-living machines, a small and awkwardly shaped human artifact intruding upon the ethereal blue hemisphere of the enormous lock. Sparta guided herself along one of its landing struts, pulling herself easily toward the equipment bay airlock, which stood open.

Inside the ship she moved deliberately, working her way up from the life support deck, past the sleeping compartments, through the common areas, toward the flight deck. With every extraordinary sense at her command she probed the *Ventris*'s space-worthiness, seeking the malfunction that had prevented its escape. Earlier, there had been no time to search, but it should not take long to find the cause. She knew at least as many ways to sabotage a spaceship as the man called Nemo.

Reason and intuition suggested she waste little time on hardware. On the flight deck she kicked in full system power from the ship's capacitors. From beneath her fingernails, conducting polymer PIN spines slid like cat's claws; she slipped them into the handiest set of IO ports and lapsed into trance.

For a second or two her consciousness was wholly inside the computer; she swam in the datastream as easily as she swam in the world-ship's waters, although (being only a tug's memory) this was a much smaller pool. A rank odor rose instantly in the code, and she followed the sour current to its source.

In the last minutes before the *Ventris* had been abandoned, someone had accessed the computer's central nets through the library program. Unlike Sparta, Nemo had no PIN spines under his fingernails to slide out and allow direct computer interface. What he had was an ancient and sly sophistication. He knew how to infect a system through its outlying terminals, introducing a worm through quotidian traffic—in the course of ordering a meal, or summoning a bookfile from the library, or adjusting the temperature and humidity of his solitary sleeping compartment.

A bookfile had given him access. In minutes he had been able to fashion a worm from borrowed chunks of other programs, a worm that would assemble itself when the main engine countdown sequence was initiated, a worm designed to eat up sensor feedback from the engines.

Seconds after launch, the number two motor had started to overheat. Its fuel and coolant pumps had shut down. The launch had aborted.

Sparta examined the clever worm, rolling it over, dissecting it from end to end. She left it in place. Less than two seconds after she had dropped into trance, she resurfaced into real-time consciousness and pulled her spines out of the ports.

Among all life forms disease is unavoidable. Best to excise the diseased organs.

Most of us do not think that way. Most of us are reluctant to kill those who disagree with us.

We have noticed. Still, it is better to cut off the diseased feeler. Another will grow in its place.

We are not made like you. Besides, another would not be the same.

Thowintha was silent a moment, before emitting an emphatic series of sharp clicks and hollow booms. *Denial of sameness is a heavy burden.*

For whom?

For us and you. For the living world.

4

The second day of our weightlessness passed.

Sparta gazed upon the body of the man she loved. He floated entangled in gossamer veins of pulsing fluid . . . entwined by suckered tentacles . . . sliced open by glass-edged knives. Dark blood drifted from him in veils, to be absorbed in the luminous mucous that throbbed in the waters around them both.

Then, with exquisite care, the thousand instruments of Blake Redfield's transformation detached themselves from his body and retracted, while Sparta watched in fascination. The world-ship's machines, half alive, possessed of their own intelligence, had performed his surgery with less trauma and much less fuss than the Earthly surgeons who'd done the same job on her.

Sparta watched him fondly. She'd been away from him for most of the past year, had seen him only intermittently before that; now, when she was with him—and especially when he didn't know she was watching—she had a tendency to become fascinated by his freckled (and after ten days without a shave, auburn-bewhiskered) half-Chinese, half-Irish face. Handsome, in her eyes. Wonderfully so.

Already a strong swimmer, bigger than she was and with heavier muscles, he had been modified by experts. Now he was like her. For although she'd designed her own reconstructive surgery, it had been done uncannily well; with her lithe quickness they would be underwater equals.

As she watched, the crimson intakes beneath his collarbones opened, taking water into the passages beside his lungs, where the muscles of his thorax forced it out again through the slits between his ribs.

At the same moment his eyes opened. He closed them again immediately, then blinked stupidly, as if trying to clear his vision. She knew what he was experiencing: the darkness around him was filled with colored lights that formed no coherent picture for human eyes.

"Aigan'dz*ee*you."

"But I can see you."

"Aizong*fun*nee." Bubbles streamed from his mouth; his vocal chords hummed with air from lungs that borrowed it by oxygen exchange with his new gills. He could not understand his own words, much less hers; his effort to speak produced nothing but gong-like ringing in his ears.

"Not funny. You sound wonderful."

For a moment he said nothing, only peering goggle-eyed into the gloom.

"*Zell*. . . ." He paused to listen to the sound of his words. "*Hhelll* . . . not earring."

"You'll get used to it. The brain is a plastic organ."

"Yah?" He assayed a ghastly grin. " 'Peshly mine." He strained to focus on her: she was a blurry shape in the darkness. "I wonderrr . . . owww . . . mean, *hhhh*ow thaiver . . ."

"How they ever what?"

" 'Skovered *star*z. Figuroww*grav*tee.'Vended *spais*shhhips."

"They have eyes, but vision is not their primary way of understanding the world." Sparta paused. "Did you understand me?"

He nodded. "Libbit."

"Information space is big, a lot bigger than the

little slice of the spectrum that registers on *our* retinas.''

''Sohh you tole me.''

She smiled. ''So don't be a perceptual chauvinist.''

''Easy for *you* to say,'' Blake mumbled. It came out as a string of low-pitched echoing rumbles, accented by a tingling fizz. Already he was hearing better, and forming words that were easier for both of them to understand.

He drew in a deep draught and, with conscious effort, expelled it forcefully through his gills. The skin flaps covering his gills were rosy at the edges with healing flesh; they stung in the salt water. He felt tender and vulnerable. He held his arms awkwardly away from his sides, shy of brushing against the new organs, moving them only when he started to sink in the water.

Sparta sympathized with his discomfort but said nothing. In a day or two he would love his freedom to move in the water, as she did. Air would come to seem a thin and unsupportive medium.

They had a world to play in, and months to play in it. She taught him all her tricks—how to use the oxygen in his lungs, borrowed from his bloodstream where his gills had captured it, to control his buoyancy; how to consciously control the CO_2 level in his bloodstream; how to use a mix of gases to produce the full range of clicks and resonances needed to speak the language of so-called Culture X in its original, underwater form. And she taught him what he considered her best trick: how to excrete from his modified salivary glands a mucous that could form a tough membrane over his entire body—mirror-bright mucous, like mother of pearl or the reflector eyes of clams, and vanishingly thin, tough enough to function as a pressure suit in vacuum, reflective enough to protect against wild swings in temperature. He amused himself by

blowing silver mucous bubbles as big as basket-
balls, so strong they could hold compressed air.

Together, they explored the deep.

Thowintha had told her the route to the very
center of the ship, taking an hour or more simply
to describe it, never repeating him'erself, somehow
confident that Sparta would remember it. Aided by
her "soul's eye," the dense knot of artificial tissue
implanted beneath her forehead, she did remember it. Perfectly.

They descended slowly through the shells of the
ship, following winding pathways that might have
seemed accidents of nature, their arrangement no
more rational than the tunnels of an ants' nest. All
around them the translucent walls glowed prettily
blue, giving the water the color of a clear tropical
sea on Earth some eight or ten meters below the
surface. Larger chambers opened beside and above
them, their interiors barely glimpsed; stalactites of
gleaming filigreed metal hung from the ceilings of
the long galleries, or stood straight out from the
walls. Streams of tiny glittering bubbles rose everywhere and looped about almost aimlessly, seeking
the most minute pressure and temperature differences. The bubble-streams were reminiscent of an
aquarium's aerators; quite possibly they had the
same function.

The dive was long, but they were in no hurry.
The first ten vertical kilometers took them almost
six hours of ceaseless swimming. Occasionally they
refreshed themselves by pursuing the darting fish;
what they could catch, they could eat. That was
the way this world was.

Light and pressure did not change with depth;
the scenery changed so constantly, however, that
it could have run together into a featureless smear
in minds less focused than theirs.

Once they swam out into a seemingly bottomless
chasm whose walls glittered with living jewels,
where wreathed cables of half-living stuff hung like
garlands or twisted ceaselessly above the watery

void. Everywhere they were surrounded by life, shoals of silvery fish and fingerling squid darting about, veils of plankton hanging almost motionless, silently tearing and then reknitting themselves in the clear water. They caught sight of larger creatures below, moving slowly through shadowy crevasses, not of Thowintha's kind. They swam smoothly across the chasm and entered another winding cave.

From time to time they came to a wall or a smooth floor which grew transparent and dissolved before them—until a brief surge of current would carry them effortlessly through what moments before had been a solid barrier. These were pressure locks, and it was soon evident (as Sparta had suspected from the expedition's previous explorations) that the water pressure inside the worldship varied little from level to level. It was a huge ship but a small world, and its self-gravity was miniscule; pressure was regulated much as the cells of the human body regulate pressure, by constantly adjusting the molecular structure of their containing walls.

Only the sounds changed, and those gradually. In the upper levels of the ship the water had been filled with the insect-like chitter and skirl of countless organisms, punctuated by the occasional bark of a fish or the click of closing shells or claws. Barely audible beneath this mostly soprano chorus there beat a dark, low tone, like that of a giant heart.

As they went deeper, the frantic natterings of life grew less insistent. The dark heartbeat increased.

Below twelve kilometers, the nature of the view changed, subtly at first and then—with their passage through a final domed pressure lock—abruptly: all lifelike forms, whether sculptural or real, had vanished, left behind in the upper regions, to be replaced on every side by mirror-bright columns, narrow and cylindrical, and wire-fine catenary arches of diamond stuff like that which formed the world-ship's flawless outer hull.

The water in this innermost chamber was perfectly clear, undiffused by organic matter and unstirred by swaying towers of bubbles. Perhaps a kilometer below where Blake and Sparta hovered, breathing in slow pulsations, the shining radial shafts of the columns converged steeply upon something bright and spherical, throbbing with light in the depths.

They forced bubble-rushes of oxygen from their lungs where, having borrowed it from their gills, they had stored it. Slowly they began to sink.

Sparta *listened*.

The water boomed with the throbbing of the thing at the heart of the ship. They saw it plainly now. It looked like a sea urchin, tiny, but with very long spines.

The taste of the water that flowed through Sparta's throat and gills brought nothing unusual, beyond the astringency of a higher concentration of dissolved oxygen. She detected no gamma radiation, no neutrons.

After several minutes of passive sinking she and Blake floated a few meters away from the apparent outline of the pulsing light, which seemed wholly without inner substance or structure. No physical object was visible at the origin of the luminous sphere. Even the light itself seemed to recede as they drew closer to it—surely that was a function of their pupils' adjustment to its brightness.

The diamond "columns" that radiated in every direction were not columns at all, but slender cones which sprouted from one another in tapering branches until a mere score of hair-fine filaments slimmed virtually to invisibility upon entering the globe of light. The pattern was reminiscent of arborized neurons.

They swam as close as they could, until the diamond reticule barred them from approaching any closer.

"It's taking energy from the vacuum," she said.

"It's a captured singularity," Blake said in wonder.

"A singularity," she agreed. "But captured? Or created?"

They found Thowintha inside the Temple bridge. The living stars on the high vault had assumed a tight, highly resolved pattern, concentric rings of red and blue light. *We are near*, sh'he said.

Near our destination?

Another burst of indecipherable sounds from the alien.

We do not understand you, Sparta said.

Do you understand the concept of small ice-bodies?

Sparta looked at Blake. He formed a silent word: "Comets."

We think perhaps you mean what we call "comets," she said.

An old word: originally it meant 'hairies,' Blake added.

Thowintha emitted a plosive noise they thought might indicate amusement—if indeed Thowintha was capable of being amused. *'Hair' is not a common characteristic among us*, said the alien. *What we call small ice-bodies, you call comets. This place we name Ahsenveriacha—Whirlpool in the classical speech.*

Whirlpool? Sparta repeated.

"Nemesis," Blake said to her.

It was a name not heard recently. In the late 20th century physicists and astronomers had hypothesized that the sun was one member of a binary star system—that like many stars in the universe it had a companion star. Supposedly this small companion had an eccentric orbit and periodically perturbed the cloud of comets surrounding the solar system, causing some of them to fall inward toward the terrestrial planets and a few even to collide with those planets. But the supposed companion star, dubbed Nemesis, had never been found, and the hypothesis had been abandoned.

What sort of thing is Whirlpool? Sparta asked.

No thing. A singular region of time and space.

A singularity! Blake said.

A black hole? Sparta asked Blake.

"If the sun's companion had collapsed into a black hole before anyone started looking"—Blake paused, excited—"that would certainly explain why they never found it."

Black hole. Thowintha's percussive sounds expressed appreciation. *A fine description.*

But why is this place our destination? Sparta asked.

This . . . black hole . . . is of the kind that rotates rapidly, giving access to other regions of time and space. We must return to it to reorient ourselves in the universe.

Reorient ourselves? Blake asked. *Then our final destination is not predetermined?*

We have choices, Thowintha said simply.

Apparently they were limited choices, however. Thowintha's explanation was far from explicit, but Sparta and Blake gathered that decisions coded milleniums ago in the genome of the living worldship were now expressed in its nervous system. When the ship, temporarily inhabiting the orbit of the false moon Amalthea, had emerged from its protective mantle of ice, it had searched the skies for a pre-programmed target and, having found it lying sunward, had set off straightaway. Even Thowintha, the voice of the ship, was seemingly helpless to alter its path until the final stages of their outward journey.

A few years earlier or later in Jupiter's orbital progression, Whirlpool—Nemesis—would have lain in a different direction from the world-ship's starting point; crushing accelerations would have been needed instantaneously, to free the ship from the grip of the solar system. Instead the sun's pull was an asset, and thus the humans were given a few short days in which to prepare themselves. Only the accidental particulars of time and place had saved their lives.

Thus spoke Thowintha, and they believed everything sh'he said.

"A singularity in the heart of the ship, a singularity in space . . . controlling us like a rock on a string," Blake said later, when they were alone. "In a universe like this, I'm not sure I know what it means to have a choice."

One moment the world-ship was falling toward an invisible place in the sky. The next moment the sky was ablaze with rainbows.

And a moment after that, a sun burst in the heavens. . . .

What sun is that? Sparta asked, watching in awe. The living constellations on the ceiling of the Temple bridge had almost instantaneously rearranged themselves, representing the new view of the heavens; the glowing patch of organisms that represented the new sun made a disk so sharp-edged, so yellow-hot, that it seemed to Sparta almost as if she were seeing it in reality.

We call it Enwiyess, which in the classical language means, approximately, Plain Yellow. And we give it a number to distinguish it from the many millions of others of its kind. Thowintha emitted the watery burble that might have been a laugh. *You call it the sun.*

The sun?

Our sun? Blake gushed bubbles of amazement.

Yes.

We left our sun at least two light-years behind us, Blake protested. *Those constellations aren't the same as our sky.*

Whirlpool warps space and time. We have emerged in a region of space-time three billion years earlier than we left. The star patterns were different then.

Three billion years . . . earlier? Sparta waved her arms in a graceful if unconscious imitation of Thowintha's tentacles, a gesture which to all of them indicated puzzlement.

You have a clock which tells you this? Blake asked.

Thowintha waved feelers at the vault of the Temple. *There is our clock. We know—we remember—where and when we are.* The huge creature turned toward them, its tentacles rising like a ballerina's skirt. *You may waken the humans from their sleep.*

PART
2

VENUS,
VENUS
PRIME

5

Jo Walsh blinked water from her eye-lashes and sneezed again.

"Are you cold?" Troy asked.

Dough, I'b olig, Walsh said nasally. *Ed's fuddawadda.*

I watched this exchange, half conscious, from my own corner of the *Ventris's* smelly wardroom. It wasn't just warm in here, it was downright hot; the water beaded on our bare skins, and we felt as if we were in a steam bath.

Walsh snagged a restraint on the padded wall, pushed her hair out of her eyes, and vigorously shook her head, banging the palm of her free hand against her ear. *Hade wadda id by ees,* she said. *Bakes be dizzy.* She pulled her palm away from her ear with an audible pop. "That's better." She looked around, saw me, and gave me a sickly smile. "Where are the others?"

"Getting into their clothes," Troy said. "Claim they need the pockets."

On the far side of the room, Tony Groves was coming awake. He was pale as a fish, and looked half dead; six months' growth of beard curled on his chest. "Guess I'll be off to find some pockets for myself," he said, intending it lightly, but he seemed desperate to escape our attention. Troy's touch on his shoulder seemed to restore his calm. "I'm okay now, thank you very much," he said as Troy tried to help him steer toward the corridor.

To go about naked is not an occasion for offense in this century, of course, although to furless, tool-obsessed humans, clothes are more than a convention, they are a necessary convenience. No doubt the longer Troy lived in the water, the less she missed them. She crouched in front of Walsh again, comfortable in her skin.

"Nemo?" Walsh asked.

"He's safe where he is."

"How long were we underwater? It seems like about ten minutes since you put us to sleep."

"Nine days of acceleration at forty gees. Six months coasting. Nine days of *de*celeration, at forty gees again."

Walsh stopped sponging. "Mary, Mother of God."

Troy raised an amused eyebrow. Jo Walsh, religious?

"Where did the power come from?" Walsh asked. "Where did the reaction mass come from?"

"The motive force is invisible."

"How does it work? What does the alien say?"

"Sh'he can't explain. Sh'he claims sh'he's not what sh'he calls a tool-grower. Sh'he's a, uh, a map-reader."

By then I was far enough out of my muzzy confusion to exclaim, "Let's have a look." Troy looked at me warily, but I plunged on. "We could take the Manta down. Even if we can't see this phenomenon, we might very well pick up some clues. We hardly scratched the surface of this world-ship, in the time we had. We never got really deep inside it. Does Thowintha object to our having a closer look?"

Troy held up a hand, halting my rushing speech. "Blake and I have already looked, Professor. There was nothing."

"You already . . . ?" I stopped myself, realizing I was still too weak for anger.

"Nothing there except a bright light."

"Nothing!"

The captain took up my cause. "What is the protocol here?" she demanded of Troy. "I mean, I can't figure out if we're guests or prisoners. Or just barnacles on the back of a whale."

"We are Designates," Troy said.

Walsh didn't hesitate. "*You* are a Designate, maybe. You can live down there, go anywhere you want. Which doesn't answer my question."

"Sorry, Jo, I can't do better at the moment."

"Six months! We must have hit ninety-nine percent of lightspeed. Which implies . . ." She thought a few seconds. "Four years from Earth, at least. Including redshift."

"The Lorentz equations seem to be on the tip of your tongue."

"I'm a pilot."

"It's a bit more than four years," Troy said. "You see, we've passed through a black hole."

Walsh and I exchanged incredulous looks. "I suppose I should have asked before," she began—

—but I was quicker. "Where *are* we?"

Troy's breath caught and the word came out almost as a sigh. "We're at Venus."

Within the hour the expedition had gathered in the tug's wardroom to hear what Troy had to tell us. Heat and sonic massage had resurrected us from the pasty wrinkles into which we'd slumped. We men had shaved our cheeks and chins of our Rip Van Winkle beards; the women had spent some minutes brightening their eyes and lips. Troy, her skin stretched taut over long muscles, so white it was almost translucent, seemed content as she was.

"Where's what's-his-name?" Hawkins muttered, to no one in particular.

"Blake's in the world-ship, if that's who you mean."

"Not him . . ."

"So's Nemo. But not free to move around. I didn't wake him up," said Troy. "You people have to decide what's to be done. He sabotaged the ship's launch sequence—very skillfully, very quickly, in just the few minutes he was left without direct supervision."

"Quite a feat," said Groves.

"I left his handiwork in place in the computer, if anyone wants a look," Troy said.

"I don't need convincing," said Marianne Mitchell. "If I've got a vote, we should leave him down there for good." From the silence, it was plain no one disagreed with her.

"Damage reparable?" asked Angus McNeil quietly. The engineer was more concerned about the integrity of his ship than about the fate of their unwanted guest.

"Again—*you'll* have to judge," said Troy. "I can erase the worm. It's up to you people to put the ship back into commission. The world-ship's machines may be able to help, if you can communicate your needs."

"Tony and I'll have a look."

I spoke up then. "This assumes the *Ventris* is still of some use to us. But is that a reasonable assumption, Inspector Troy?"

"Just now I can't see very far into the future, Professor," she said, giving me a look that implied more than her words. "Since we last talked, the world-ship has traveled two light years from the sun in the direction of the constellation Gemini. It reached almost ninety-nine percent of light speed before it entered a spinning black hole, apparently the remains of a binary companion to our sun. We came out of it—Thowintha calls it the Whirlpool—practically right back where we started, a couple of light months from our own sun. A few more hours and we'll be in a parking orbit around Venus."

"Then perhaps there's no need to repair the *Ventris*. Surely the world-ship can simply transfer us to Port Hesperus."

Troy took a deep breath of the air that must have seemed very thin to her; her gills flared involuntarily. ''The catch is that the time—or date, or however you wish to express it—is a few billion years earlier than when we left.''

Marianne gasped; Hawkins said ''Lord, *now* what do we do?''

''Thowintha hasn't told us what to expect,'' Troy said firmly. ''Maybe sh'he doesn't know. But from some hints sh'he's dropped, I don't think we're alone here.''

''Could it be . . . Culture X?'' For I had suddenly seen the possibilities, and leapt so far to a conclusion that I startled even myself. ''Surely it's possible! We may have been brought into the past to see Culture X at work. Perhaps we are to be permitted to observe the, uh, terraforming of Venus. If terraforming is the word for it.''

''If Culture X is the word for *them*,'' said Hawkins, speaking with unusual unpleasantness. He gave me a withering look, as if to suggest that I was the one who'd gotten us all into this fix—which I suppose I had.

His unpleasantness was echoed by Ms. Mitchell's heat. ''I don't think *permitted* is the word I'd use for any of this.''

I took their criticism, forcing myself to bear it in silence. I was no longer in charge of their fates.

''What *do* they call themselves?'' McNeil asked mildly.

''They call themselves *we*,'' said Troy. ''Just *we*.''

''We can't go on calling them Culture X,'' Hawkins retorted, thinking to needle me for having proposed the term many years earlier. ''We're not dealing with artifacts, we're dealing with live creatures. One live creature, anyway.''

At that, Groves spoke up brightly. ''Ever since the Ambassador came to life, I've thought of him as an Amalthean.''

''That's the way I think of her, too,'' said Walsh.

''It, I mean,'' said Groves.

''Very good,'' I said. ''Amaltheans they are.''

We talked a while longer, until everyone had

asked their questions—What was the alien like? What was inside the world-ship? How did we *know* we were three billion years in the past?—but only confirmed that the most pressing questions were unanswerable.

It seemed to me that, remarkably fresh as they were after their ordeal, my friends had lost the edgy, prideful carriage natural to them at Jupiter. The ego quirks, the small competitions that had arisen on the expedition to Amalthea were rapidly giving way to private concerns. For one thing, the alien clearly had no need of our professional skills. Thowintha was keeping us alive for purposes of its own. Or simply from indifference.

No goal or objective, no matter how difficult or far in the future, would by its achievement put an end to our adventure. Only death would do that. We had already taken on the stolid look of wagon-train pioneers heading into unexplored country, hoping we would find a place for ourselves, but knowing we would recognize it only when we came to it, if we ever did.

Finally, after one interminable pause, McNeil had the last word: "Now that that's out of the way, what's for dinner?"

We laughed, more from relief than amusement. And dinner wasn't long in coming. Shrimp and squid and seaweed tasted fine to a crew that had been fed intravenously for months.

I only regretted that we were still inside our cramped spacecraft, with no way to see what lay beyond the gleaming hull that enclosed us.

6

"Long afterward, I learned what was outside the ship," Forster tells his listeners. "I had described to me what none of us could see. . . ."

The diamond moon, our mirrored world-ship, was falling smoothly toward the sun's own mirror, bright Venus. But as it fell, it left behind it other lights in the sky, startlingly near, glowing streamers that hung in the star-mottled night like battle flags aimed at the sun.

The night was full of comets.

The mighty exhaust flared briefly, and the world-ship lost orbital speed, steeply descending toward the planet's cloud tops. Those of us aboard *Ventris* would have been startled at the sight of these clouds. Although they were as high and dense as the clouds of our later epoch, these clouds were not the sulfur-yellow color of industrial smoke, but the bright, steel-edged blue of water vapor.

The thirty-kilometer-long world-ship sank into them, diminishing slowly in relative size and brightness against the disk of the planet, until at last it was swallowed in the mist.

Green, a thousand shades of green—the green of hard shiny leaves and of feathery fern fronds bejewelled with moisture, and textured green that dully glistened, hanging like bolts of green brocade down the faces of red-black cliffs . . .

A millions years and more of hard, steady winds and unceasing rains had carved these basaltic crags into knife-edged scallops of rock, standing a thousand meters out of the implacable surf of a seething gray-green sea.

The misty sky was black with swirling bird-things, like a sprinkle of ink drops on thick white paper; the cliff tops were smeared chalky white where the creatures nested. Reefs encircled the shore, and in coves at the base of the cliffs, edging beaches of red-gold sand, pliant trees like coconut palms bent smoothly under the burden of the hot wind. The cliffs stretched away to the east and west for hundreds of kilometers. White waterfalls fell from them into the shallow green sea, falling with the rain into water that was ceaselessly bubbling, whipped with foam. The oceans of Venus, almost a hundred degrees Centigrade at the surface, were on the very edge of boiling.

Although there were the things like birds to look upon what happened then, there were no sentient creatures to see through the kilometers of steaming, rain-swept air. The million eyes of the circling bird-like creatures, unthinking scraps of life, only registered a shape, coming out of the cloud-roof—

—a huge diamond shield, a perfect convex mirror reflecting a green world of wavetops and clifftops, of wet vegetation and curving reefs—and of tens of thousands of inky marks darting about the white sky, screaming, circling the cliffs and skimming the steaming waves . . .

The immense apparition thundered out of the cloud-bellies and settled seething into the sea on columns of bright flame. Matching columns of roaring steam rose to hide it, before they were dissipated in the wind. Frothing green surf crashed against the mirror wall; a sucking maelstrom swirled around its flanks as it slumped to a grinding halt. It had sunk as far as it would go.

Thirty kilometers long on its n
much less even when lying on its
now, the world-ship had settled in
deepest chasms in the oceans of Ve
were nowhere more than two kilom
The bright skin of the great ship soared
cantilever-like, curving upward into the clouds
of the lower atmosphere, far exceeding the
height of the nearest cliffs. Rain ran down its
sides and fell in veils to the shadowed waters
beneath. Hot primeval seas rolled in unchecked
ranks of spume around it, flowing toward the
breaking shore.

Forster pauses in his recitation. "Meanwhile,
deep in the interior of the world-ship," he presently resumes, "other momentous events were un-
folding, hidden from us. . . ."

"Something seems to be happening up there,"
said Blake, his words ringing through the waters of
the Temple vault.

Sparta, swimming into the deserted bridge behind him, followed his gaze. On the intricate surface of the vault, the star map had vanished.
Clusters of light were coalescing; unlike the livid
celestial displays she'd seen before, these clusters
were multicolored, the colors almost hot, throbbing in neon hues like the living creatures that inhabited the internal waters.

As if stimulated by her thought, the water within
the bridge suddenly trembled and swirled with colors in three dimensions. Creatures that for six
months had drifted casually through all the watery
spaces of the ship, even allowing themselves to be
caught and eaten, were now galvanized into frantic
but coordinated activity; squadrons of squids and
schools of fish flashed blue and orange and whirled
away in tight formations, dispersing like single organisms to the right and left, up and down. Clouds

owing plankton and blushing jellyfish pulsed
intricate watery abstractions.

Suddenly Thowintha appeared in the cathedral-
like heights and swam downward toward where
Blake and Sparta hovered. Sparta had never seen
the alien move so fast—Thowintha was an underwater rocket, and his'er mantle, which had not
changed its shade of pearly gray since we humans
had first encountered him'er, now radiated a kind
of mottled blood-orange.

As the huge creature darted past them, sh'he
emitted a burst of sound: *We are coming to question
ourselves as to the right course.*

Seconds later sh'he exited through one of the
narrow passages at the base of the vault, leaving
them rocking in his'er turbulent wake.

Blake looked goggle-eyed at Sparta. "We?"

"In this case, maybe 'we' means 'they'," she replied. Overhead, on the surface of the vault, the
multicolored clusters had brightened to aggressive
hues, forming an unbroken circle below the ring
that represented the exterior water line. "We'd
better find out what's happening."

They swam a winding path down through the
world-ship's labyrinth of corridors, reaching the
outside sea level, going deeper still. Sparta led
the pursuit; they were already far behind the racing
alien, but Thowintha's aroma lingered in the water, a trail she followed easily.

It was a long swim to the nearest lock. When
they reached it, its great dome was already opening
to the sea outside. Coming upon the scene, the two
humans paused, keeping to the shadows, floating
motionless a hundred meters behind Thowintha.
What they saw amazed them.

Centered in the aperture, the alien was a silhou-
ette framed against green water. Clouds of lesser
animals swirled like flashing fireflies around
him'er, darting to and fro in nervous formation.
Outside the ship, from far above where the surface
of the Venusian sea seethed and bubbled, a mot-

tled green light sifted through the clear, cool waters beneath the waves to fall upon a horde of tentacled sea creatures, some smaller than Thowintha, some enormously larger—bigger than the giant squids of Earth, as big as small whales—but all made to the same basic plan: hooded and gilled, bright-eyed, many-armed, streamlined.

Colors ceaselessly swirled across the flesh of their mantles, rich hues of pink and purple, bright with bioluminescence. Patterns formed and dissolved there, teasing the eye to imagine coherent images which were gone too quickly to identify, if in fact they were images at all. Their clumps of tentacles coiled and uncoiled in some enigmatic ballet.

All of them seemed to be sounding off at once. A choir of pipe-organ thunders and sleigh-bell glissandos made the waters ring—so loudly that Sparta could visualize the standing waveforms of the harmonious symphony projected as rippling shadows on the sandy ocean floor below.

"I thought I knew the lingo," Blake said, expelling bubbles from his chest, "but I'm missing most of this."

At the sound of his words the alien symphony abruptly ceased. Every slotted yellow eye in the crowd suddenly swiveled in its hooded flesh to peer at Blake and Sparta. Blake's outburst had revealed their presence to the alien horde.

Mantles darkened from red to deep purple; in one voice they demanded, *Who are these?*

Thowintha replied. *Guests, come to share our counsel.*

Instantly the chorus began again, louder, once more incoherent to the "guests." Sparta, who'd had more practice with the language than Blake, caught a few words in addition to common nouns and standard verb forms *(we come, we do, we make, we are)*, words such as *coordinates, alternates, interference, waveform, collapse, frustration, violation, probability*. . . .

Blake's mouth formed a bubble: "Ellen . . ."

She held a finger to her lips to shush him.

Thowintha again added his'er voice to the chorus; this time sh'he was as incomprehensible as the rest, and as loud as any of them. As harmonious as the racket sounded, a powerful undercurrent of conflict was unmistakable. There was a movement in the horde of swimming creatures, and the flanks of the formation closed in, thickening to form a living pocket in front of the lock. All view of the waters beyond the writhing crowd was cut off.

Blake shot a worried glance at Sparta. They had only a few seconds to wait. Thowintha suddenly turned a startling shade of blue. With a heave of his'er mantle and a spasm of his'er tentacles, sh'he move aside; the tiny squid and shrimp that had been darting frantically about behind him'er in the amphitheatral space swirled away in delicate spirals, like sparks from a burnt-out Catherine wheel.

Outside the lock, the center of the close-packed school of aliens swelled gracefully open, like the diaphragm of a camera lens, into a circle framing the ocean beyond.

Come with us, sang the choir.

Blake glanced questioningly toward Thowintha, uncertain if *their* alien had joined in the thunderous command. Sensing their concern, Thowintha delicately lifted his'er tentacles. *We are in agreement*, sh'he said, and like a bass line, a harmonious chord simultaneously sounded from the choir outside.

When shall we return to you? Blake wondered if he sounded as forlorn as he felt.

You are not leaving us, said Thowintha. Again his'er words were reinforced by the chorus outside, in mysterious, instantaneous communication.

The two pale humans, each possessed of only four rather stiffly jointed "tentacles" not ideally suited to swimming, struggled through the water into the midst of the alien host.

Blake allowed himself a nervous inward smile. The scene had suddenly put him in mind of one of

those baroque ceiling paintings filled with cheru-
bim and seraphim and ascending saints swaddled
in pink and blue satin.

''Blake had no way of knowing that I had
dreamed of just such clouds of angelic aliens,'' Forster says with a smile. ''Neptune's apotheosis. But
of course I had imagined them in quite a different
sort of heaven.''

She and he floated together, their hands just
touching, as the encircling school of aliens guided
them lightly through the clear currents with a thousand strokes of their tentacles—like tiny tongues
licking their bare skin. Although they were surrounded by the wriggling creatures, the aliens had
thoughtfully left the view ahead unobstructed;
Sparta and Blake could see an approaching settlement, which was big enough, perhaps, to be an
entire city.

It was a city of coral caves, dark arches in the
white carbonate cliffs—deep old coral reefs pep-
pered with caves and garlanded with living stuff.
Only here and there did a bit of silvery metal ex-
trude to sway in the currents—a wide parabolic net,
perhaps, with the shape of a radio antenna but the
apparent mass of a spider's web, or a set of ribbon-
thin spires like corroded stalagmites, reaching for
the surface high above. To Blake it resembled nothing so much as a ruined city he'd once seen in an
isolated canyon in Greece, a monkish Byzantine
city eroded to rows of collapsed vaults in the limestone hillsides, one stratum upon another.

But this was a living settlement, teeming with
glowing busy creatures who moved in six directions at once and filled all the space between the
coral canyon walls; like Arabs, these seemed not
to mind rubbing up against each other, perhaps
even found reassurance in doing so. Occasionally a
vessel of odd design floated through the living
mass—some were small bright spheres like bub-

bles; others were larger, and could have been mistaken for organisms themselves.

"Is this what you expected from Neptune's palace?" Sparta's words were bells in the water.

"Nope. No mermaids about." Blaked eyed her mischievously. "Present company excepted."

Her laugh was a strand of purling bubbles.

Sparta and Blake came as ambassadors from a foreign land, grandly escorted. Or so they imagined. Except for their escorts, however, none in the crowd of sea creatures took notice of them.

"They don't seem very surprised to see us," Blake said.

"It's almost as if we'd been expected all along."

"They may think we understand more than we do." She filled her lungs with borrowed air. *Tell us what we are seeing*, she bellowed, addressing no one in particular. *Describe the purposes of these structures, these machines*.

There was momentary silence, as if the aliens were again surprised to hear the humans speak. Then in one voice they said, *What you sense is real*.

Blake and Sparta waited, but that was all the aliens had to say before again taking up their worldless chant. Clearly they had not understood Sparta's question, or not as she had intended.

Or perhaps they did not want to be bothered answering. For instead of leading the humans to some grand hall or chamber, they swam right through and over the alien "city" and on into the empty waters beyond. What Sparta and Blake had taken for a center of civilization was merely an outpost en route to their destination.

The sea bottom dropped away; what had been a rippling sandy floor changed to a featureless slope of rocks and black mud that fell off steeply into opaque depths. The waters grew cool and dark and empty, but for strange winged fish that now and again slipped by on solitary errands of their own. Sparta and Blake, despite continual boosts from helping tentacles, had to make increasing efforts to keep up with the alien convoy; their chests heaved with the strain.

The group around them had grown silent except for a sort of low-toned, wordless chant, but there was a sound in the water that gradually resolved into a rich symphonic chorus, prodigious in its range of frequencies, from throbbing bass to shimmering treble. The sound ebbed and flowed, trailing long strands of melody; whether the dynamic was internal or due merely to the shift of the currents, it was impossible to tell. Not knowing its source, the humans had no way of knowing if it came from just beyond their vision or from far on the other side of the planet, a distant sound carried like the songs of Earth's great whales through thousands of leagues of ocean.

Sparta looked at Blake, who was rapidly growing too tired to speak. There were words in the chorus, most of them incomprehensible, but recognizable as sentences nevertheless. More than one song was being sung; there seemed to be several melodic lines antiphonally intertwined.

Blake was exhausted and on the point of calling for rest when she touched his shoulder and pointed. There was movement in the waters ahead—a writhing, coruscating mass, a sphere of struggling life as dense and bright as sardines in a net. Each "sardine" was a colorful, tentacled alien.

The strange apparition was vast in size—a lifesphere like a human egg cell coated with a million glittering sperm. And their convoy was like a spaceship of flesh—about to land on a planet of flesh.

Just before they struck it, the "planet" split open beneath them. They were inside an immense sphere of water, its shell a mass of pulsing life, ringing with song as loudly as the inside of a bronze bell.

7

For so many hours that Blake and Sparta had lost track of time, they had been captives inside the sphere of choiring aliens. In all likelihood the aliens were themselves unaware of their guests' discomfort; it was certain that their sense of time was very different from that of the humans.

Very little seemed to have happened, despite the constant writhing of bodies and the ceaseless, ever modulating song. There had, for a time, been a display of imagery in the center of the watery sphere: veils of color and moving strings of colored lights racing hither and yon and formations of tiny colorful polyps dancing in precise but, to the human observers, wholly meaningless geometric arrangements. All this could have been the alien equivalent of a water ballet or a viddie comedy or visual aids for a sales pitch. As much as they tried to pay attention, Blake and Sparta could understand no more than scattered words and phrases of the conference that went on all around them. This was not the vocabulary of Culture X as they had learned it, and even the words and phrases they recognized sounded strange in their ears.

Finally Sparta stopped struggling to understand; she lapsed into a dreaming trance. . . .

In trance, the few words she had understood were added to every other environmental clue that had impinged upon her consciousness. She did not hurry this trance; this was not a computation—not merely a computation—but a search for a deeper understanding. . . .

She awoke.

She waited for a moment's pause in the ebb and flow of sound that vibrated the waters all around them. Then, pushing the sounds out of herself with all the energy she could muster, she said, *Forgive us and hear us.*

Blake watched her, mystified.

The aliens fell silent. Then, in a single voice together they sang, *We hear the guests.*

Honored hosts, we are your future, against which you must test all that you do and decide here, Sparta said. *We do not, we cannot, threaten you. But you must help us to understand. Only in that way can we help you to understand.*

As if something like this had been expected, her words—to them, they must have been very quiet words, although she was exerting herself to the limit of her strength—were quickly taken up by the swimming creatures and repeated and amplified.

There followed another momentary hesitation, while her paraphrased remarks echoed and faded away.

Blake watched her curiously, wondering what she had thought would happen. He did not interrupt; she would explain when she was ready. Long ago he had resigned himself to trust her actions, even when he found them incomprehensible.

Chords crashed around them: *How shall we help you understand?*

Show us your great work, Sparta said immediately. *Tell us your story.*

Wait, came the ponderous reply, and a great echoing call went up, like the moan of a conch-shell trumpet.

Sparta turned to face Blake. "What we're listening to may sound like the Hallelujah Chorus, but it's a fight. And it's been going on for a long time."

"What's it all about?" Blake asked.

"I'm not sure. Whatever it is, it has something to do with us."

A section of the living sphere bulged inward and opened in an eruption of squidlike bodies. Into the opening a shining shape intruded, as big as a zeppelin. The thing had an enormous hemispherical canopy, subtly multicolored by thin-film interference of light waves in the quivering soap-bubble colors of mother-of-pearl; below it dangled a long skirt of slender tentacles and veil-like pink membranes. Above, the vessel was nobbed with spiral windows and barnacle-like projections. Below, its tentacles and fleshy draperies ponderously, rhythmically, stirred the water.

Blake peered at it. "What's that, an animal or a submarine?"

"It's a medusa," Sparta said.

"Like the ones on Jupiter?" he said, disbelieving.

"Related, anyway," she replied. "And I think we're about to find out what this species does."

Acting on some unspoken signal, dozens of aliens moved in close around the humans, tumbling and sliding past each other like minnows thrashing in a tank, although they were so quick and agile there was no sense of struggle or crowding. The humans were deftly herded below the medusa, toward its center, where in a living jellyfish the mouth and stomach parts would be.

They were not eaten, however. The aliens guided their guests into the interior of the vessel, urging them on with a thousand feathery nudges of tentacles; they might have been in the gentle grip of one enormous, amorphous, softly glowing organism.

"I wish they'd give us time to see," Blake protested.

"It looks familiar," Sparta said. "Like the worldship."

They were in a maze of transparent bulkheads

and passageways writhing with organic shapes that may or may not have been alive. Then, abruptly, they found themselves inside a transparent blister on the very top of the huge dome, looking straight into the teeming ocean.

"What are we looking at, a hologram?"

"Reality," she replied. "Through an invisible window, only a few molecules thick."

Somehow the diaphanous window withstood the extreme water pressure without apparent strain. Inside the transparent chamber with them were two or three dozen of the squid-like creatures— some, tiny graceful shapes, sparkling with bright blue and orange, others much bigger, green and copper hulks—who filled the watery space with multiphonic sound, all speaking together.

All that you see—all but the balanced salt ocean itself— we carried here. Now regard how skillfully we have worked to fulfill the Mandate.

Blake and Sparta exchanged a puzzled glance. The medusa began to move. Peering to the side and backward, they could see the great trailing veils rising and falling, oaring the craft in a smooth forward glide. The huge sphere of living creatures that surrounded them opened, then closed again behind them as if expelling them, and their supple vessel was soon moving swiftly through featureless benthic waters.

Out of the darkness below, a wide barrier reef rose before them; soundlessly, their vessel moved into what seemed a crowded freeway for fish, a passage between walls of chalky coral skeletons covered with living coral and a hundred species of urchins and sea stars in scarlet and pink; shrimps danced nimbly among the anemones; crabs stumbled frantically after floating crumbs; the water between the walls was thick with schools of striped and glittering fish. Effortlessly, the vessel twisted and turned among them, following the random turnings of the corridor.

Observe, sang the creatures who surrounded them.

The harmony of the myriad creatures is gloriously perfect. Carbon life arises from the sea floor and floats in the waters. Above us, carbon life covers the surface of the land and takes wing in the skies. The delicate web is complete; the elements are in dynamic balance.

They came into an open lagoon. Flotillas of real jellyfish pulsated above them; the bottom was lost in inky blue depths.

The light-eating creatures of the shallow waters die and sink to the ocean floor, carrying their carbon with them. The light-eating creatures of the land surface die and decay, adding their carbon to the soil. All the myriad creatures feed on the light-eating creatures and on each other. Thus all exist in complex harmony, a model of the place of origin. The song was a hymn, with a quality of having been often rehearsed, completely lacking in spontaneity.

These seas are beautiful, filled with life, Sparta said, pushing the appropriate booms and clicks out of her chest, meanwhile attempting an engaging smile—and wondering what impression a smile made upon them.

At her glance Blake took the hint, and he hummed sonorously along with her when she added, *You have done well indeed.*

But as Sparta gazed into the green-blue waters, as clear as the tropical seas of Earth, she knew they were less enriched with nutrients than a colder, hazier, plankton-laden ocean would be. Yet these were the higher latitudes of the planet. Perhaps the seas of Venus were not as full of life as their hosts would wish.

As if changing the subject of her unvoiced thoughts, the vessel suddenly heaved itself upward. Bubbles and jellyfish flowed away over the invisible curving dome and the mother-of-pearl hemisphere around it, and they broke surface.

''*Whoaaa . . .*'' Blake couldn't hide his surprise.

Water poured from the dome; the churning waves receded below them; they were moving through thick clouds, clingy as wet gray cotton.

Even submerged in the vessel's interior waters they could sense the acceleration. Sparta stared up into the clouds and pondered what might be at issue here.

Not all the local contingent had seemed pleased by the arrival of the world-ship, she thought, or by the appearance of Blake and herself. Yet none of the aliens had seemed to show the least surprise. At the great convocation, when she had made her brief speech (*Honored hosts, we are your future . . .*), it was as if she were playing a part that had been written for her long, long ago.

She knew then, beyond doubt, that she and Blake had been expected. Designates, were they?

But maybe a Designate was the equivalent of a plumbing inspector. Blake had had the same thought. "Get the feeling they think we're here to check up on this Mandate of theirs?"

"They referred to 'a model of the place of origin.' As if that were the standard."

"Their home world, I'll bet—and they're trying to reproduce it here."

"What we're trying to do to Mars. In our time."

"But what we're trying—*will* be trying, three billion years from now—strikes me as a little looser, a little more . . . adaptable," said Blake. "Or am I being chauvinistic again?"

"It's early to judge. We haven't seen much."

"We already know they like to do things by the book."

"By consensus, anyway."

We are eager to answer your questions, said their guides, filling the water around them with insistent nervousness—reminding them that it was not, after all, very polite to speak a foreign language in front of one's hosts.

We have many questions to ask, Blake said, taking the initiative. *We wish you to explain the construction of your vessel. . . .*

* * *

Again Forster pauses in his recitation, leaving his listeners in anticipation while he sips from his lukewarm glass. For a moment his thoughts seem far away from the bare library in the house on the Hudson; in the fitful shadows cast by the fading firelight, his expression is obscure.

Resuming his tale, he said, ''Redfield got a fuller response than he'd anticipated. Everything he and Troy asked was answered; it would form the basis for what knowledge I have been able to gather and preserve concerning the beings we had chosen to call Amaltheans. . . .''

8

The world-ship stood above the waves, higher than the highest mountain on Venus, rising a fourth of the way into the planet's thick clouds. On Earth, it would have reached above the stratosphere. Well up the side of the towering, cloud-hidden mass, the great pressure lock that housed the *Michael Ventris* stood open to the driving rain.

On our flight deck, McNeil was busy with an artificial-reality helmet and gloves, looking for damage to the number-two engine's fuel and coolant plumbing. The AR system let him crawl through the pipes and valves like an ant, immersing him in convincing visual, aural, aromatic and tactile sensations as he pushed his way through pistons and past pump rotors, squeezed through injector nozzles, and scrambled over the pitted surface of the combustion chamber without ever leaving the engineer's couch. Yet if his senses told him he was no bigger than an ant, he was required to be much more discriminating; the concentration required for the job was exhausting. After two hours going over the ground at millimeter scale he'd found no serious damage—still, he'd explored less than half the area affected by the malfunction, and he had a long way to go.

I watched him work while I filled file after file of

my journal, occasionally wishing I had the requisite skills to take some of McNeil's burden.

Walsh climbed onto the deck as McNeil was pulling off the helmet and gloves. "Want me to take over?" she offered.

"Need to rest my eyes, that's all." He bent forward to peer out of the flight deck's wide windows, blinking at the kilometer-wide circle of sky outside. The direction of the planet's gravity put the big dome at a sideways angle to our tug; our floor, however, was still a level floor.

The hatches of the *Ventris* stood open. The atmosphere of *this* Venus, three billion years younger than the one we had known so well, was actually breathable—a little rich in oxygen, perhaps, but that nicely compensated for our present high altitude—and the thick warm wind was rank with the odor of organics, the smell of the jungles and seas far below us and of the microbial life that inhabited the clouds themselves.

"Thoughtful of the alien to open the door for us," McNeil mused, watching the blowing clouds. "I wonder why."

"It's nice to know we're not forgotten," said Walsh. "How's the diagnostic coming along?"

"I've a ways to go yet, but the hardware seems all right—seems we shut down in time to keep from burnin' anything up. And Tony tells me he's got the software all cleaned up." McNeil passed his hand wearily over his head, then leaned back in his couch. He looked up at Walsh. "The *Ventris* is functional again, or will be soon. We've a sturdy little Jupiter tug at our disposal."

She read his unspoken thought as easily as I did. What good does it do us? Where do we go from here?

Even as we pondered these questions, the events that would determine our future were happening without our participation, or even our knowledge. . . .

* * *

Sparta and Blake were carried swiftly aloft by the huge medusa. After many minutes of streaming grayness the sunlit cloud-tops of Venus flashed into view, a shining plain below them, and the last wisps of vapor vanished from the window. Above them spread the deep velvet of starry space.

The aliens paused, only their wordless music continuing, taking on a melancholy air. When the voice of the choir again filled the vessel's waters it was feebler, with many of the creatures abstaining. *This is what frustrates our efforts*, the remaining ones sang, and there was no mistaking what they meant.

Unfiltered through electronics, unmagnified by optics, unrepresented by pixels on a viewscreen, living or otherwise, Blake and Sparta were confronted with the spectacle of a night sky full of misty comets. Still the alien ship continued to rise, until it was hanging high above the cloud tops.

You have been struck by objects like these? Blake asked, blowing the phrases into the close-packed waters. He peered out through writhing bodies at the comets that crowded the night sky, which seemed magnified by the bubble dome.

Repeatedly, within the past million circuits of the sun, the aliens replied. *Innumerable objects smaller than those which are nearest to us now. And many larger*.

As they spoke, the medusa appeared to reach the apex of its trajectory and began to fall smoothly back toward the clouds.

But apparently these impacts have not destroyed your work, said Sparta, *nor killed the life you have sown and nurtured*.

For a moment there was no answer. Blake and Sparta listened with interest while high-frequency bursts of sound passed back and forth from one side of the water-filled chamber to the other, in some kind of dialogue.

Outside, the clouds rushed up toward them, faster and faster. Blake took a last look at the thousands of pale cometary banners set among the stars. ''Seems likely two or three of those billiard balls are going to make direct hits," he said to Sparta. "Assuming they're incoming at typical delta vees—thirty or forty kps—the first of them could be here in a day or two."

"What then?" Few people had a more encyclopedic knowledge of explosions—how to make them, their effects—than Blake; blowing things up was his hobby, perhaps his addiction.

"Depends on the mass. If they're typical . . . say ten to twenty kilometers in diameter, with the density of water"—he briefly pondered—"a bang on the order of a thousand million megatons."

Her eyes widened.

"Big, all right." He nodded enthusiastic agreement with her unspoken comment. "A crater maybe two hundred kilometers in diameter. A thousand million tons of molten rock and steam shot into the atmosphere. Tidal waves right around the planet, again and again, until the perturbation finally damps out."

"Life?" Her drowned words were almost inaudible.

He shrugged—it had the effect of flaring his gills. "Hard to know. This isn't Earth. It's a lot hotter here, the cloud layer's a lot thicker. Firestorms? What they used to call nuclear winter? I doubt it. It's awfully wet out there."

Sparta said, "The world-ship could roll over like an egg."

"Well, but it's no ordinary ship."

The high squeaks and whistles of the furious conversation around them ceased; when the aliens resumed speaking in the lower, slower phrases that humans could understand, it was apparent that only about half the creatures in the room were joining in the chorus.

In the past there has been destruction, but the great web of life remains whole, they sang. *The threat is not from impacts.*

Accompanying this song was a sustained dissonant bass note.

The threat is from what, then? Blake asked.

From water.

Water!

Just then the medusa was swallowed by clouds. Sunlight failed and the watery observation room seemed to contract and darken; crowds of raindrops inched across the outside of the window.

The great thickness of clouds that now shroud this planet did not exist when we arrived. Instead we found a salt world like that which had been mandated. A world with clear skies and sparkling salt seas.

The voices of those who apparently had come out second best in the recent difference of opinion now piped in, in strident antiphony. *For many millions of cycles we had traveled in search of such a place. Our work went forward joyfully.*

Until the first comets appeared in the skies, the other choir chimed in. *More and more of them accumulated.*

Out of the Whirlpool, said their opponents. *We had not known of its existence until we sought the source of the comets.*

In their curiously harmonious version of disagreement, the groups took turns playing chorus. *They were soon appearing in the skies at a frightening rate—*

—When we located the Whirlpool and determined its orbit, we knew that collisions were inevitable and would continue for a million revolutions of the planet or more. Each comet brings a thousand million tons of water vapor to the atmosphere of this planet—

—Already the water-vapor concentration near the surface exceeds twenty parts in a hundred. Condensation is warming the atmosphere rapidly—

—Water now rises so high that when it evaporates it dissociates into oxygen and hydrogen, and the hydrogen escapes into space.

Blake blew words at Sparta. "How do you say 'moist greenhouse effect' in the language of Culture X?"

We calculate that within another one hundred million circuits of the sun, all water will disappear, the aliens continued. *The oceans will be dry and all that we have done will vanish, baked to dust.*

Why not steer the comets away? Blake asked.

How is that possible?

Go out there and push them into new orbits, Blake replied. *You have the technology to move far greater masses than a comet, at far greater velocities.*

More high-pitched shrieks and whistles ensued.

"It must be hard to keep a secret in a totally communal society," Blake said to Sparta.

"Not from us—until we can understand them better."

When things calmed down the prevailing group sang again, in tones that struck Sparta and Blake as tinged with astringency. *What you suggest has been advocated. Is this then what the Designates have been sent to tell us?*

Well, it seems obvious. If it has already been suggested, why do you delay? Blake asked cheerfully.

Vessels of this kind are unable to travel far from the planet, came the quick reply. *Only the vessel in which you were brought here is capable of distant journeys.*

In that case, couldn't you . . . ? Blake began.

But Sparta softly forestalled him. *What is the fundamental objection?*

This time it was the minority faction who answered her, their voices booming as one. *Such action is contrary to the Mandate. So it is claimed.*

The din that followed (as Blake Redfield later described it to me) "was like a bunch of kindergarteners with kazoos pretending to be a twentieth-century rock band."

Meanwhile, all of us aboard the *Michael Ventris* were assembled in the wardroom to hear the captain's address. "The effects of Nemo's sabotage have been repaired. Our simulations indicate the ship is in A-OK condition. It's time we gave some thought to our next move."

They tell me my eyebrows quiver when I'm being temperamental. "I hope we are not expected to arrive at a final decision about *that* within the hour.''

"Just openin' the dialogue, Professor.'' McNeil had the grace to grant me a weary smile.

"Estimate of the situation and all that,'' Groves put in.

My nod was rather impatient. They were condescending to me. All but Marianne Mitchell. Her green eyes looked dull, and sweat stood out on her pale face. Hawkins hovered over her, full of solicitation.

Like me, Walsh had noticed the sudden sickly pallor that had come over the girl. "Are you all right, Marianne?'' she asked.

Marianne looked wildly about at the faces now studying her. Though she knew us all well, she might have been staring at strangers. "I just want to go home,'' she cried, and burst into wrenching sobs.

Hawkins tried to put his arm around her then, and for a moment it seemed that she might allow it. But she stood up abruptly, thrusting out her hands as if to fight her way through an enclosing web. As she made for the corridor she stumbled in the unaccustomed near-Earth-normal gravity; Groves leaped up to steady her, but she pushed at him resentfully and hurried down the ladder to the deck below.

"Bill!'' Walsh said sharply, as Hawkins jumped up in pursuit. "Leave her alone. Give her a few minutes to herself. It's best.''

Hawkins turned angrily on the captain, on all of us. "The poor thing is desperate! That monstrous man dragged her into this hell without giving her half the chance we had.'' He meant Mays, but his next salvo was aimed at me. "Not that *any* of us were given any reasonable foreknowledge—any truly *informed* consent.'' I said nothing. Young Hawkins was not himself just now. Walsh tried again to calm him, but he wouldn't be interrupted. "What sort of people has she found herself stuck with—possibly for the rest of her life! Us! Look at us! No wonder she longs to be home!''

''Don't we all,'' muttered McNeil, who called no place home.

It seemed to me that Hawkins was borrowing Marianne's grief to reinforce his personal pique. ''There's no theoretical reason why we *shouldn't* be able to go home again,'' he burst out. ''If this huge thing we're riding in could drag us three billion years into the past—if that's what it really has done, and what evidence do we have of *that?*— why then, it ought to be able to go the other way just as easily. We ought to be able to *make* it do that.''

One could allow something for Hawkins's youth and passion, but really . . . ''We know very little about the capacities of the Amalthean ship,'' I said tartly. ''We have no influence whatever over those who control it.''

''Troy and Redfield seem cozy enough with the powers that be,'' Hawkins retorted. His big hands went to his sides, perhaps unconsciously stroking his rib cage where we had seen the red gashes of her gills. ''She changed herself to be like one of them. And Redfield must have allowed himself to be changed to be like *her*. They care very little about us, if at all.''

''Look, Bill, nobody blames you for the way you feel,'' said Groves. ''Right from the start, Blake didn't make himself accessible in the way . . .''

Hawkins laughed in that unpleasant way, which was becoming habitual. ''They *chose* to be down there. They made it plain they'd rather be living in the water. Apparently they don't even care to be humans anymore.''

''Do us all a favor, Hawkins, and stop interrupting everyone who speaks to you,'' McNeil said sharply, shifting his muscular bulk. ''As it happens, I'm deeply in debt to Inspector Troy. It's no secret—I'll tell you the story, if you insist—that if not for her, I'd likely be in prison at this moment.

Happened right here at Venus. But speaking for myself, I certainly do not feel *abandoned* by her.''

My agreement came out as a growl. ''Troy saved my life, as you all know. In my mind there is no question whatever about her humanity, or Redfield's. There are, however . . .''

''Spare me, please.'' Hawkins stood up melodramatically, rebelling like an adolescent at our attempt to impose discipline upon him. ''I'm going to see Marianne.''

McNeil was on his feet in a wink, blocking the corridor hatch. ''Cease pestering the poor girl for two minutes.''

''I certainly . . .''

''Sit *down*.''

Hawkins's jaw worked silently a moment before he sat down, and McNeil studied him impassively before resuming his own seat. He nodded to me. ''You were saying, Professor?''

''Mmmhhmmmaaa.'' My eyebrows must have done calisthenics, but at last I recovered my composure. ''Well then. First, let it be clear that I make no further claim to leadership; certainly our mission has fulfilled whatever goals I set for it, long ago. But I will say this. Despite all our work, we know very little about . . . about these *Amaltheans*. Yet we still have some means to continue our exploration. There is, for example, the submarine.''

''The Manta?'' McNeil asked. ''What good is that to us?''

I drew myself up until I was as erect as I could be. ''For most of the past six months, assuming what we've heard is true, we've been living in a sort of suspended animation. And by necessity, during our few days of consciousness we've been in an essentially reactive frame of mind. We reacted to the events at Jupiter, we reacted to the opportunity to leave the world-ship, we reacted to the failure of that effort, and we've reacted most recently by repairing our fragile and possibly useless planetary craft. What we haven't done is plan or take the initiative. We haven't even taken time to think.''

"Let's think, then." Groves again—but his eagerness and good cheer sounded oddly forlorn. "Let's do more than that. Let's explore. Who knows, we may even figure out how to run this world-ship for ourselves.''

"Or at least learn how to persuade those who *do* run it to take us back where we came from,'' said McNeil with a rueful smile.

"What if Troy and Redfield try to stop us?'' That was Hawkins, of course.

"Why would they want to stop us?'' said McNeil, astonished.

Before Hawkins could launch himself into a new diatribe, I spoke up. ''I vote with Mr. Groves. We should inaugurate a new exploration of the world-ship. And a look outside, should that prove practical. And an investigation into the nature of the Amaltheans themselves.''

9

Forster pauses to watch the commander tend the fire; he does so obsessively, poking at the coals, staring into them as if seeking in them the answers to questions too elusive to express, too portentous to suppress. There is a brief flare of orange light, which momentarily overwhelms the faint vision of multiple misty comets seen through the tall library windows.

The commander catches Forster's eye, suddenly aware of his attention. "Go on," he says, his voice rasping, his shadowed face more menacing, perhaps, than he intends.

"Certainly." Forster nods agreeably and turns back to Ari and Jozsef. "In our earlier explorations of Amalthea, Redfield had been the chief pilot of the Manta. He had absented himself, and since the status of the *Ventris* seemed to be one of indefinite standby, Captain Walsh undertook to prepare the submarine for our new explorations." He clears his throat, more loudly than necessary. "In the course of doing so, she departed from her mandate—and thereby made a disturbing discovery. . . . "

Walsh had done the checklist in the equipment bay and everything checked out fine, so she'd lowered the sub through the inner lock, into the worldship's waters. She lay there looking at the control console, waiting for a warning she didn't really expect to hear. With the interior lights on, the hemisphere of the *Manta's* bubble was a distorting mirror that showed her an inverted image of herself.

Looking into that diminished self-portrait, she reflected that this whole trip was an example of the way things were *not* supposed to turn out. This was more like what they warned you about when you showed up at the Academy; this was why all the squats went through a couple of days of stone-black solitary at the start—to see who would freak right away, to see who would never survive a wide-awake to the moon, much less a wide-awake to Mars or the Mainbelt.

Some learned right then they'd never make it in space. Couldn't stand the screaming boredom. Some found it out a few weeks or a few years later. Most who'd gotten as far as the Academy's gates made it, though—because they'd figured out how to beat the system. Their secret was that they *couldn't* be bored. Their imaginations were too lively, their anticipation too keen. They were the sort who would put up with two or three months of machine tending (most Space Board ships were about as glamorous as the *Ventris,* or even less so; the Space Board had only a dozen of the sleek white fusion-torch cutters), if in exchange they got a week of action on some far-flung outpost of the solar system.

It didn't matter that the action was never as adventurous, the venue never as exotic, as in their dreams. As long as they lasted as Board pilots— until age thirty-five, say, or forty at most—their fantasy lives kept them fooled. When reality finally caught up, there were pilots in line behind them and desk jobs begging for their experience. Seems the Board had known about their kind all along; the test protocols were specially made to find candidates with those secret dreams.

From the start, Jo Walsh had much more than a pilot's dream.

In a service dominated by North Continentals, therefore by pale skins, even her looks were special. She was one of the Board's rare women of color; her forebears were black African and Arab, with a dusting of Portuguese by way of the Caribbean sugar planters who'd owned her slave ancestors three hundred years before. Walsh herself had the bold geometric features and rich deep color of a Benin bronze.

She had the reflexes of a shark fisher, a skill she'd acquired summertimes while still a little girl, to the delight of her widower fisherman father and the horror of her teachers. And she had extraordinary mathematical aptitude—of the sort that cascades randomly through the human gene pool to concentrate, seemingly by magic, in the offspring of Hindu clerks and Greek peasants and Hungarian Jewish refugees and Eskimo pipeline workers and other such folk—in other words, striking anywhere, anytime. Thus she had the makings of a fusion-torch captain.

Even that was far from the sum of her. She was certainly the daughter of her parents, a child of her green island and the clear seas surrounding it, and of the sunny superstitious people who inhabited it. In the late 21st century the concept of "nation," as a geopolitical reality, had been obsolete for half a century. But every minority-language group on Earth that had been trapped inside boundaries not of its ancestors' making still craved nationhood. Cultural imperatives may become diluted; they do not dissolve, but persist for countless generations. People are not immune to ancestral magic.

Josepha Walsh was not a prisoner of magic, but neither was she proof against the interference of the gods. In retrospect, then, none of us should have been surprised to learn that she'd been recruited by the Free Spirit before she became a cadet. Throughout the worlds they trolled for promising children, and they'd spotted her when she was fifteen, when she'd already been frightening the nuns for two years with her precocity and talent.

Having been forced to choose Jesus over Ogun or Chango by the sisters, it now seemed that a third and higher way was opened to her, that the Pancreator was Jesus and Ogun and Chango rolled into one—the Pancreator, who had made all things and was the fount of Knowledge and would be bringer of Paradise on Earth. Looking back, it was clear that agents of the Free Spirit—one, anyway, in the persona of a certain Jesuit padre—had steered her into mathematics and physics at parochial school, and then into the Space Academy itself. They'd been eager to plant another of their own inside the most active arm of the Board.

After the first year, the Academy let cadets have weekends free; the campus, such as it was, was in New Jersey (a Space Academy on Earth needed nothing more than classrooms and access to a shuttleport), and it was an easy trip from there to Manhattan, where she attended the secret meetings of the *prophetae*. But with closer inspection of that collection of half-remembered mix of history and myth they called the Knowledge, her belief began to waver.

By the time she graduated from the Academy, she'd come to believe in nothing beyond practical matters except quantum theory and curved spacetime. The Knowledge was incomplete, she was persuaded, and its preachers were con artists; if there were aliens about—and this much she did believe—they were not here to bring salvation to the *prophetae* of the Free Spirit. She had also pieced together enough of the program of the Free Spirit to know that as long as she remained a member she was a traitor to the Board and the Council of Worlds. But it was too late for her; anyone who tried to leave the Free Spirit was marked for death.

Then, on her first assignment, she encountered a

gravel-voiced, sun-blackened Investigations Branch commander. He'd been watching her, he said; he knew her for one of the *prophetae*. But to her surprise, he didn't arrest her. Instead he recruited her into his own secret service. . . .

He and his colleagues called themselves Salamander. Like her, they'd been members of the Free Spirit; like her, they believed in the essential truth of the Knowledge but knew it was being used to distorted ends. They'd survived their apostasy, most of them, by arming themselves and disguising themselves or going into hiding. A few, like the commander, operated openly from positions of power, daring the Free Spirit to strike. And a few pretended to be Free Spirit yet. This was the role the commander asked Josepha Walsh to play.

She continued her Space Board career and rose rapidly in the ranks. A cutter captain sits in the left seat by the age of twenty-six or seven or not at all; Josepha Walsh made it at twenty-four. Simultaneously she continued her ''secret'' membership in the Free Spirit.

She was never more than a soldier for the *prophetae*, who left her in the dark and gave unexplained orders—orders she was expected to carry out without question. Sometimes she did so; at other times, risking her life, she only pretended. Thus she ''killed'' her first, ritual victim, a member of Salamander who upon her warning changed identities and vanished, leaving only a convincing death report.

Although Walsh was not privy to the councils of the knights and elders of the *prophetae*, she discerned their broad objectives and observed their maneuvers. She managed to convey what she knew to the commander. Sometimes the commander was able to arrange her missions to bring her into contact with Inspector Ellen Troy, even before Troy herself had appreciated her place in the scheme of these events. It was Josepha Walsh who carried Blake Redfield to the moon, with his news that the alien home star was in Crux; it was Josepha Walsh who planted the suggestion that the mystery of the Martian plaque could be solved on Phobos.

It was natural that Josepha Walsh would volunteer for detached duty with the Forster expedition to Amalthea, an assignment that suited both Salamander and the Free Spirit. But before it could begin, the Free Spirit had been suddenly beheaded, deprived of half its ruling council, by Ellen Troy operating as a free agent—out of control and out of her mind.

Walsh did not recognize Sir Randolph Mays when he (quite literally) crashed the Amalthea expedition, bringing Marianne Mitchell with him. For Mays's part, although he must have recognized *her*, he evidently thought it more efficient to kill her along with the rest rather than try to make use of her. No one except the commander knew that Josepha Walsh was Salamander, not even Redfield, who was Salamander himself.

And no one at all knew—when Mays was finally forced to admit who he was, when Walsh realized what he'd done and tried to do—that she had made a private resolution. For at that moment the chief and principal among the *prophetae* of the Free Spirit, the eldest elder, the most honored knight, the one who had fouled the Knowledge, twisted Walsh's aspirations, dishonored her, and tried to murder her and her crew—*that* one had come within her grasp. Even now he drifted below her in the warm waters of the world-ship, unconscious and vulnerable. It would take only this supple Europan submarine to search him out and put an end to him.

Which is why Josepha Walsh, in the midst of the grandest adventure of her life, an adventure such as she had dreamed about since she was in her teens, was nevertheless mad with impatience and the boredom of enforced inactivity, and why she did what she did. No revenge is sweeter than revenge extracted for ruined dreams.

The submarine we had nicknamed the Manta

had originated as a research vessel on Jupiter's moon Europa; below that moon's thick rind of ice was an ocean, devoid of life but rich in dissolved minerals. The Manta was intended to be wholly independent of the surface: its "gills" were suffused with artificial enzymes with which it absorbed the oxygen in the water; other artificial proteins carried the oxygen to all the sub's internal systems that needed it, including its human passengers. Underwater, the submarine propelled itself by the rhythmic beat of its ray-like wings, which were powered by the molecular complexification and decomplexification of engineered molecules. Since the Manta's internal peristaltic pumps could equalize pressure equivalent to depths far greater than any that occured naturally in the deepest trenches of Earth's oceans, the shallower oceans of Venus posed it no challenge.

Without saying a word to the rest of us, Josepha Walsh now steered it downward, into the depths of the world-ship.

Her search was swift and precise. We'd gleaned enough from Troy to know where we'd spent those months of suspended animation, and it was a chamber not far from the lock where the *Ventris* was parked. The Manta's wings carried it downward like an angel of death.

In a few minutes she was there. Nemo, however, wasn't.

Forster cast a shrewd eye about him: once more he had his small, select audience hanging upon his words. He paused a moment to watch reflected firelight flaring from the bare paneled walls of the library before quietly resuming his narrative. "What happened in the minutes before Walsh came upon the deserted drowning chamber? We will never know for sure. From Troy I have a version of events, but she did not witness them. Perhaps Thowintha is the source. . . ."

* * *

Deep in the dark waters of the world-ship, a drowned man's eyes open to pearly slits; his slug-like, wrinkled fingers clutch at the tubes that feed him and bathe his organs in oxygen.

Nemo has slept when it suited him to sleep and dreamed when it suited him to dream. It has ceased to suit him, so he has come awake. Over the decades he has learned more about seizing and shaping his own consciousness than even yogis know. Now he would seize the rest of himself.

The life-sustaining nutrient tubes and oxygen-exchange membranes in which he is entangled are not connected to primitive pumps or ponderous tanks of air; these are miniaturized enzymic systems, far more sophisticated if similar in principle to those humans use in submarines or to breathe the thin carbon dioxide atmosphere of Mars. It hardly matters that these gossamer systems have not been intended for mobility.

Nemo leaves the kelp-like strands and tubes undisturbed in their symbiotic attachment to himself but uproots them from their anchors in the encrusted wall of the chamber in which he has been a floating captive. Wreathed in polymer seaweed, he swims slowly into the watery labyrinth, aspiring to the fate of the *Wasteland*'s drowned Phoenician sailor:

> . . . *As he rose and fell*
> *He passed the stages of his age and youth*
> *Entering the whirlpool.*

Now Thowintha floats alone in the waters of the Temple bridge, studying the parabolic paths that are depicted in glowing streamers on the vault of living lights. The alien's tentacles barely waver in response to the tasted sign, borne to him'er on the eddies, that a human has entered the Temple.

I find you alone, Nemo says. *Like me.*

We are never alone.

Nemo's pale, bony figure hangs in the luminous

water, garlanded with trailing polymer membranes. Awkwardly, he paddles closer. *That is your manner of speaking, honored one. It does not express fact.*

Nemo's manner of speaking is peculiar indeed—barely comprehensible—since the human has to make the sounds of Thowintha's language without benefit of lungs or the resonating gas bladder the alien possesses. Instead, Nemo speaks feebly with his tongue and lips and presses hand-claps and finger-snaps into service when necessary.

Nevertheless, he is understood. *You have isolated yourself,* Nemo says. *You have set yourself against the others of your kind. You have brought Troy and the rest of us humans here for purposes of your own—for the sake of a scheme you hatched in your own mind, who knows how many hundreds of thousands of years ago in your personal history. When I first laid eyes upon you, I mistook you for a mere animal. Now I know. You are the Pancreator.*

These sounds are without meaning to us, the alien replies.

You do not fool me.

A shimmering sourceless sound fills the Temple, then fades away. Nemo waits.

But Thowintha forms no words.

What will you do if I demand to leave? Nemo asks.

That does not concern us.

Even if I explain to the others of your kind why you are really here?

Nothing is hidden.

So you say. You can kill me easily, says Nemo.

Thowintha's mantle brightens and, without warning, sh'he swims swiftly away.

I imagine Nemo allowing himself a cold smile, full of teeth that are ghastly in the pale blue light. His big hands and feet flail the water and he sinks slowly toward the depths of the world-ship, trailing life-sustaining weeds behind him as he seeks the way out.

* * *

"The alien let him escape?" Jozsef is amazed.

Ari gives her husband an impatient glance. "The creature was hardly human. It could not be expected to understand."

"If you will excuse me, Doctor, I suspect it understood very well indeed," says Forster. "And that all that happened subsequently was considered in the alien's calculations."

"Do you mean to say, *that* is why I will never see my daughter again?" Ari angrily demands of him.

But Forster's reply is mild. "She contributed equally to her fate. She and Redfield. . . ."

10

The commander places another billet of split oak on the fire and pushes it firmly into place, ignoring the flames and sparks that shoot up around his wrists. Outside the bare library's windows the last skylight has faded; the descending celestial lights are bright enough to intrude even into the warm interior.

"I've asked them to bring us a hamper of sandwiches," says Jozsef, "whenever anyone is hungry."

"Not yet," says the commander. "A few things . . ."

"Yes, Kip?"

"Professor Forster has done an impressive job of reconstructing events which he did not witness—he has even included some that *no* one witnessed. . . ."

"Kip, please," says Jozsef, disturbed by the commander's ill-disguised irritation.

"I have no intention of deceiving you," Forster interjects, his gingery eyebrows rising in indignation. "My intention is to be explicit about my sources."

"You have been. I want to know what you think all this means."

"There is a very interesting conversation which Inspector Troy reported to me some years later. . . ."

"No, I want to know what *you* think," says the commander. In the firelight he is as fearsome as Baal; the fierce glow renders his gaunt face in black shadows, in rough-hewn slabs of dark flesh.

The others exchange glances. With visible effort, Forster lets the unpleasantness pass. "Very well then. It's clear Venus was doomed. Our voyage into the past was partly a rescue mission. Thowintha went back to get his'er compatriots out of a tight spot—before the rest of the Amaltheans could 'amputate' them. Which is what they do to those who don't fit in."

"An elaborate rescue," the commander remarks.

"It was more than that," says Forster. "The settlers had traveled a million years from their home star, searching for a place to exercise their Mandate. The mission to recreate their home world was programmed into their genes. They found our sun and with it Venus, a planet covered with oceans and blessed with clear skies—a stable planet, not wracked by an active geology or a swerving climate, without Earth's wandering continents and ice ages. What they planted there would persist forever, so they thought. . . .

"For millions of years everything went as planned; they succeeded in virtually reproducing the ecology of their home. Then Nemesis appeared—what they call the Whirlpool. Repeated bombardment by comets created a moist greenhouse, which raised the temperature of the oceans and saturated the atmosphere. When we arrived, water was evaporating, and atmospheric hydrogen was being lost to space. Venus was already on its way to becoming the carbon-dioxide furnace of our era."

"A tragedy, certainly," says Jozsef. "But why the . . . well, 'political conflict' is probably not the right phrase. . . ."

"The split was precipitated by evolution. The Amalthean settlers had observed phylogenetic saltations, new adaptive lifeforms unlike anything catalogued in the Mandate. This horrified them. They believed they had only two alternatives—to let nature take its course, and thereby lose everything they had achieved. Or to accept change as inevitable, bend with it, adapt themselves to it—even take charge of it."

"Take matters into their own tentacles, as it were," Ari remarks lightly.

Forster allows her a dry grin.

"What if they did take charge?" Jozsef demands. "Why *not* take charge?"

"For one thing, they would have had to deflect the comets," replies Forster. "Only the world-ship was capable of that."

"Yet the medusa-ship you described seemed to defy gravity," the commander objects. "If it could fly without wings, surely it could travel in space."

"After years of study I am still fundamentally ignorant of Amalthean technology," Forster replies, "but I gather that their vessels borrow energy from the vacuum. They are dependent upon a sort of macroscopic analogue of the quantum effect; their range is governed by solutions of the amplitude of possible vector states. The world-ship calculations yield a wide amplitude; thus the world-ship is capable of interstellar journeys at near light-speed. The much smaller medusas, however, have a severely constrained amplitude."

"Clear as mud." The commander's words are hardly a growl.

"Anyway, the little ones couldn't do the job, and the big one wouldn't."

"Why not? From your description, Thowintha seems a flexible sort." Jozsef still presses for an understanding of policy issues, as if the motives of aliens are no more obscure than the motives of delegates to the Council of Worlds.

"Thowintha's involvement in this is deep," says Forster. "Sh'he does not regard his'erself as an individual—none of them do—but it's clear to me that sh'he is *primum inter pares* where what we call the Adaptationist faction is concerned. However grudgingly, sh'he, or the group sh'he speaks for, came to accept the evolution of local populations away from the ideal of the Mandate. It must have been hard for them; we may well have witnessed the final break between the parties. Indeed, we may have helped precipitate it.''

"You may even have been *recruited* to precipitate it,'' says the commander.

"That occurred to some of us.''

"Then Nemo was part of this plan, too?'' asks Ari.

"I don't pretend to understand how. For example, how did Thowintha know he would be on Amalthea? How did Thowintha know he would escape? Somehow Nemo understood that Thowintha did not represent the majority of the aliens, that they had left themselves no room to maneuver.''

"I'm confused,'' Jozsef interjects. "As long as Thowintha controlled the world-ship, sh'he could go anywhere in space and time sh'he wanted.''

"It wasn't the only world-ship,'' says the commander, gazing through the window at the light-streaked sky. "We know that now.''

"On the contrary, in reality there is only one world-ship,'' Forster says sharply.

"I'm even more confused,'' Jozsef admits. "Thowintha's ship—the ship you found at Amalthea—is also the ship they came in on?''

"Yes, but it represents only one possible state of the total system.'' Forster nods toward the framed patch of night sky. "Other possible states co-exist with it.''

"But surely the superposition of states described by quantum theory occurs only at the microscopic level,'' Ari remarks coolly, "and then only until some observer interferes.''

"According to those who claim to know . . .''

"Who would that be?''

"McNeil, and I trust his judgment,'' Forster replies sharply. "Theories of quantum gravity suggest that linear superpositions of alternative states spontaneously reduce themselves to one . . . *reality* . . . upon encountering significant space-time curvature. Travel into the past introduces a second order of alternative states.'' Forster allows himself a smile. ''Although I'm not certain we ever convinced poor Bill Hawkins that time travel was actually possible.''

''I'm certain you haven't convinced me,'' the commander growls. ''What's to prove this isn't some elaborate dream, some programmed hypnotism, begun while you were in—what did you call it?—the drowning chamber?''

Forster fingers his empty glass, and Jozsef quickly takes the hint, filling it with ice and whisky. The professor nods his thanks.

''True,'' he says then, ''time travel was always considered impossible. But solely on the grounds that messages sent to the past might generate paradoxes. In this case the superposition of alternatives insures that that won't happen.''

''Nothing you've said rules out paradox,'' objects the commander.

''I'm told that the collapse of the wave-function prevents it,'' Forster answers. ''We are not faced with multiple realities, only multiple possibilities. There is one reality. If a message sent to the past were to interfere with another message—a contradictory message—one vanishes. It never existed. The wave-function collapses. If one of us interferes with himself or herself, one of us vanishes. If a world-ship interferes with another version of itself, one of them vanishes.''

Ari smiles ruefully. ''Were you really in danger of meeting yourselves?''

''It seems that in this century, yes, we might have been, as a matter of fact,'' says Forster, his eyes widening at the thought. ''And at Venus, Thowintha had that immediate concern. Precisely because, at that moment, not everything approaching Venus was a comet. . . .''

* * *

So many hours had passed while the flying medusa explored the seas and jungles and cloudscapes of Venus that Sparta and Blake had almost lost track of the time. Finally the vessel brought them to the great ridge of cliffs where they had first left the ocean; there it once again sank beneath the boiling waves.

The wriggling alien lifeforms poured out of the vessel, pulling the humans along at first but, to their surprise, soon leaving them to swim for themselves. Sparta said, "They may desire consensus, but they're about to split. If they haven't already."

Blake tucked his chin in agreement. "At least two parties. The hail-to-the-Mandate types. And the ones who want to be creative. How the hell we tell them apart—short of a quick course in counterpoint and antiphony—is beyond me."

Approaching the convocation, they knew something was wrong.

They had left behind a perfect sphere of life, wriggling with energy; what they saw in front of them was like a cell infected with a virus, a misshapen thing seized with waves of distortion, convulsions that rhythmically flattened and puckered it and threatened to split it wide open. Upheavals momentarily dislodged black particles—individual aliens—who struggled desperately to regain contact with their fellows.

The total mass of the conglomeration seemed much larger. And the song that came from the massed singers was louder than before, weirdly strident and dissonant.

Threat of dissolution became reality when the huge sphere tore open, spewing out creatures into the dark waters. What had been empty interior space, defined by a disciplined throng of intelligent creatures, was now an inchoate suspension of mindless, struggling animals.

The human eye will make patterns of almost anything it sees, and Blake later reported that he recognized structure in the chaos—that what seemed like a bundle of dark rods, a spindle consisting of hundreds, perhaps thousands, of bodies, some streaming one way, some the other, had formed between two wobbling amorphous shapes in the light-streaked water.

Sparta saw it too. "Like a cell dividing," she said.

They hung motionless in the depths, abandoned by their escort, which had dispersed and fled to join the writhing chaos ahead. "I don't like the looks of that mess," Blake said. "I don't think I want to choose sides."

She shook her head. "We've already chosen sides. Humans can't be anything but Adapters." She sounded less than enthusiastic.

"Is that bad?"

"Good or bad, it's our nature. We get nervous whenever we try to think five years into the future. For us, any institution that keeps the same name a thousand years is unimaginably ancient. Conservation means trying to save the last scrap of something that disappeared before we noticed it." She was silent a moment, after her angry outburst. Then she said, "Now I'm sure that you and I being here is not accidental."

"What do you mean?"

"Because we are what we are, Thowintha chose *us*." She started to swim toward the boiling remnants of the convocation as if drawn to it by duty.

Blake reluctantly swam after her, thinking that there were lots of unexplored options short of taking sides in an alien free-for-all—in a pinch, one could always blow something up—but he had no intention of leaving her side. Following her, he dived into the chaos.

The crowded aliens were using their siphons to jet through the waters in phenomenal bursts of speed, but even in the midst of upheaval the racing bodies never struck each other or did worse than graze Sparta and Blake. Nevertheless they were buffeted by churning currents. Blake felt he'd been plunged into a cauldron of molten metals—a little more colorful and, he imagined, only a little less warm—as immense mantled-and-tentacled bodies hurtled past them, glowing with ruddy hues that reminded him of quenched iron and burning sodium. The water smelled of acid and copper.

The confusion seemed to abate as the humans drew near the center of the spectacle. The spindle-like bundle of rods of swimming bodies was retreating now, withdrawing from both ends, and the division of what had been a great sphere into two still-wobbly spheroids, one larger than the other, was almost complete.

If Blake hadn't been breathing with gills he would have choked on what he saw. At the coagulating nucleus of the larger of the "daughter cells" swam a pale apparition, a rag-bundle imitation of a human being shrouded in trailing seaweed. *Nemo.*

A moment later, they heard the message of the cacophonous chorus: *The false Designates are diseased limbs. They must be cut away. Then all will be well.*

With these words the living structure of which Nemo was the focus contracted and became better defined. It was like looking into a medusa's mouth-parts, a devouring hole surrounded by a million writhing tentacles; to Blake—hyper-alert, seeing everything as if time had slowed down—it seemed that the attention of that black eye was focused upon him and Sparta, that every real slit-yellow eye that ringed it and defined it beamed malice, that the whole creature made of creatures was about to convulse around them and swallow them up.

From nowhere, immense fiery wings spread themselves over them, dropping a veil before their sight of the evil heart of the ravening lotus. A single alien only—his'er mantle ablaze with opalescent fire.

Like an earthly squid's, two of the alien's tentacles were equipped with prehensile suckered pads;

much longer than the others, these elongated still more and wrapped the two humans around their waists. Of the menacing alien song, only a grinding wordless moan was left to vibrate through the waters.

Thowintha had never touched Sparta or Blake before; as sh'he did so now sh'he sang in tones that conveyed immense tenderness and protection—*All will be well*—and they surrendered their bodies and wills to his'er care.

Water gushed from Thowintha's siphon. Sh'he jetted away, trailing the human pair—unlike an earthly squid, which swims "backwards"—like streamers from a kite. Their faces distorted into theater masks as they tried to avoid swallowing water. They flattened their arms against their sides and pointed their feet, streamlining themselves.

With the humans in tow and a myriad of fiery miniature squidlings streaking after them like sparks from a bottle rocket, Thowintha soared away from the disintegrating convocation. In moments sh'he was over the reef settlement Blake and Sparta had seen on their journey from the worldship, its wide canyons and coral caves with their strange artificial structures now wholly abandoned. Blake would have asked why, but his velocity through the water made speech impossible. He rolled slightly in Thowintha's grip to look backward along their trail. The ocean was thick with bodies, jetting after them in pursuit.

Do not be concerned. It is not too late to avert collapse, Thowintha boomed.

Collapse! Blake wanted to shout questions, but could only ponder the word instead.

During all this, my companions and I were exploring the world-ship. As Walsh had reported to us, Nemo was gone. We could see for ourselves that the drowning chamber was empty. Only the kelp-like trailing membranes that had so recently sustained us all remained.

We hadn't closely questioned our captain on her motives for coming here before us—that could wait until later, when she was less reticent of the truth—and for the time being we accepted at face value her statement that she'd been giving the Manta a test run. But her news had disturbed us enough to make us nervous about separating. Did Nemo intend another attack on the tug? We had learned not to attribute ordinary motives to the man. We'd left McNeil and Hawkins and Marianne Mitchell very much on their guard inside the *Ventris*.

But meanwhile Nemo's escape lent new urgency to our explorations. Walsh and I peered through the forward bubble of the craft's polyglas pressure chamber; poor Tony rode blind, squeezed into the crawlspace behind us. The Manta left the drowning chamber and beat its way through kilometers-long winding corridors.

Before we'd left Jupiter we'd grown familiar with the path to the Temple of Art, and soon the Manta reached the Temple's central vault. We saw there what we had never seen before: the lofty vault was alive with living stars.

"Tony, can you get your head up here and look at this?"

"Give me a minute, Jo." One reason we'd picked him to go with us was because—after myself—he was the smallest of us; even so, it took strenuous slow-motion acrobatics for Groves to get himself forward, his head upside down between our knees, where he could peer upward through the bubble in a position to study the ceiling. "Hmm," he murmured.

"Yes? Well?" Perhaps I sounded more irritable than I felt—I was more nervous than irritable, really, not because of Nemo but because I'd put myself on the spot. The closer we came to the world-ship's control center, the less certain I was that anything useful would come of it. How did one be-

gin to decipher the alien mind, even if, after thirty
years of hard work, one could claim to comprehend a few thousand words of the alien language?

Groves spoke up. "That pattern's pretty much
identical to the one the *Ventris* calculated for us with
Troy's input. It's the way the sky would look three
billion years ago—from when we left Jupiter, I
mean. Good deal of uncertainty, of course. Couldn't
pay me to trust any computer's notion of planet
positions over that span. . . ." He trailed off incon-
clusively.

"You were about to say something else," Walsh
prompted. Groves was a private man and modest,
which made his reputation as a navigator easy to
overlook. But he'd managed to land Springer on
Pluto when all that famous explorer's assumptions
proved mistaken, and his colleagues had known
who deserved the credit.

"Well, Jo, it's simply that there are a great many
lights in this particular sky that don't show up in
Ventris's reconstruction. If you watch them for a
minute or two—which is about how much time
I've had here, lying on my back—they seem to be
following cometary orbits."

"You can tell, that quickly?"

"Oh yes. They're moving *fast*, and they're very
close—which is why their motion shows at all."

"What does that portend?" I asked.

Groves hummed some more while framing his
answer. "Rough guess, you understand." Upside
down he gazed at us. "I'd say one or two of those
comets are just about to hit us," he said. "Maybe
next week. Maybe tomorrow."

"The Amalthean must know about this," Walsh
said.

"That's what makes . . ."

"There's something else," Tony said, breaking
in.

"What?"

"I don't know what," the navigator replied.
"I'm lying here on my back, looking at it. I don't

even know how this imaging system is made, or where it gets its data. Assuming for the moment that I'm looking at something like a realtime planetarium . . . well, there's one object up there which is three times brighter than a typical comet, and it's incoming at twice a comet's velocity. Right on top of us."

"Good Lord," I said.

Walsh said nothing. Her attention had been attracted by movement in the Temple, well below the glowing ceiling, where bright moving stars, gold and turquoise and ruby, were gathering in the darkness, and among them shadowy shapes, infiltrating the waters around them.

"Professor . . . We're not alone in here."

Moments later the Manta was surrounded by creatures as large as Thowintha, blazing like electrical signboards and bombarding our hull with frightening sonic reverberations.

"Are we being attacked?" Walsh asked.

"Maybe we're under arrest," Groves said at almost the same moment.

But from the muffled noises I was hearing, I didn't think so. "Turn on the hydrophones," I said to Walsh.

She did. The suddenly clear, urgent voices of our "captors" sang in unison over the Manta's interior speakers.

"What are they saying, Professor?"

"Roughly, *We want to help you. Do not interfere.*"

"Yeah? Where but where did they come from? Who *are* they?"

"Help me rig up the translator to the phones. Perhaps I can respond."

Walsh pulled circuits as I keyed words into the translator, but before we could finish, a new flurry of sounds filled the water. *Do not worry.*

"We're moving!" Groves shouted.

All will be well. The aliens were doing something to the outside of the hull. A swarm of tentacles descended over the bubble viewport. There was a pause, then an ominous sound.

Poor Groves screamed when he realized what the aliens were doing, a wailing cry of terror that filled the cramped interior and did not cease.

"My God, they've found the emergency hatch release," Walsh shouted. Her hand had reached for the switches that would fire the Manta's auxiliary rocket motors, but before she could open the safety covers the hatch split and water shot in through the opening as if from a fire hose.

The force of it propelled me into the polyglas window, and I remembered nothing more.

Thowintha kept his'er grip on Sparta and Blake but made no attempt to evade the brilliant horde of aliens that crowded into the submerged lock with them. The impermeable molecular layers of the giant lock immediately began reassembling themselves, spiraling rapidly inward. Thowintha swam powerfully upward through the glowing caverns and corridors of the immense ship.

The once lonely ship was transformed. All around them swarmed busy aliens on errands of their own, creatures moving so effortlessly through the water that Sparta and Blake were embarrassed by their human helplessness. No matter how adaptable, naked humans, stripped of their tools, are among the most ineffectual of beasts.

It was doubtful that the Amaltheans could have understood their emotions. Thowintha certainly seemed indifferent to their feelings. Sh'he acknowledged only their curiosity, lecturing them as sh'he swam; his'er voice had acquired an eerie resonance, for his'er thoughts were formed simultaneously among the mass of creatures scattered throughout the ship—perhaps with the ship itself—and voiced with all their voices, which filled the surrounding waters.

What sh'he, *they*, had to say was part theoretic,

part fantastic, part inconceivable. Sparta and Blake absorbed what they could of it.

After many minutes of strenuous effort, Thowintha released them. *You must explain to them what we have explained to you. There is very little time.* Then sh'he was gone.

Blake and Sparta emerged from the water; the world-ship sealed itself behind them. Beside them, the tilted dome was filled with air, still warm, still rich with the rank perfume of Venus. The lock's metallic tendrils wound themselves gently around the humans and lifted them swiftly into the open cargo bay of the *Michael Ventris*. They felt their feet on hard metal decking; the tendrils whispered away, leaving them to stand shakily, unsupported by the buoyancy upon which they had come to depend.

The crew module hatch was locked. "Who goes there?" Hawkins's voice boomed at them over the comm speaker.

"Troy and Redfield," Sparta said.

"Open up, it's urgent," Blake added.

The hatch opened slowly. Hawkins peered at them suspiciously, holding a titanium spanner in plain view. "Where are the others?"

"We'd hoped to find them here," Sparta said, pushing past him with effort. If he had chosen to resist, she and Blake would have been helpless. They found McNeil and Marianne Mitchell in the wardroom, looking as strained and nervous as Hawkins.

"Walsh and Groves and the Professor went exploring in the Manta, Inspector," McNeil explained. "They're overdue."

"Nemo's missing," said Marianne. "The captain says he escaped."

"We don't really know," Hawkins said, "maybe he . . ."

"Never mind that now," Sparta cut in. "The world-ship is about to undergo another massive acceleration. It's imperative we get you into the water.''

Their breath stopped, and the blood drained from their faces. Sparta might have pronounced their death sentences.

Marianne was the first to speak. ''This time are we going home?''

''It's out of our hands,'' Sparta said.

The aliens and their gentle machines received the bodies; in the drowning chamber, Walsh and Groves and I were already floating on the artificial tides, seeing nothing, awash in dreams.

Sparta and Blake watched us until all were safe. She turned to him with a flick of her hands, relieved to be in the water again. ''You have sucker marks on your tummy,'' she said. Her underwater voice had become her accustomed voice, filled with nuance. She looked down at herself. ''Me too.''

He didn't reply. The two humans swam hard through the ship's warm and swarming waters. ''They're going to fail,'' Blake said angrily. ''They know it and it's making them crazy. We're seeing the disintegration of their society.''

''They have no experience of failure.''

''Not even experience of the unexpected.'' He feigned amazement. ''Send out an ark, a starship full of pioneers, carrying every species two by two—or whatever the magic number is where they come from—with orders to reproduce the home-world right down to the last virus. But forget to tell them they might bump into something a little *different.*''

''They know secrets of nature we humans may never learn for ourselves . . . that most of us are two impatient to learn.''

''Different histories, different stupidities. You're the one who said we can't help being Adapters.''

''Because we've short-circuited evolution, replaced slow physical modification and hard-wired behavioral change with fluid culture. We grew up with volcanoes and earthquakes, glaciers that came and went, sea levels that rose and fell. Disaster keeps us on our toes.''

''Whereas their species is hundreds of millions of years old, maybe billions of years old. Certainly they came from some ancient and never-changing place.''

''Even on Earth, some designs change very little over time. Dragonflies. Scorpions. Sharks.''

''Squid,'' Blake suggested.

''We can help them,'' she said.

''Why? What difference does it make to us if they fail?''

She turned her cool-eyed gaze upon him. ''More than their success is at stake here. Thowintha brought us here because sh'he thought we could help them. And for something else.''

''Which would be?''

''I believe it was in order to create our own destiny.''

He blew a stream of bubbles. ''What can we do for these characters? I can't even keep up with them in the water.''

''You already helped. You suggested steering the comets.''

''An idea that got shot down pretty quick—besides, now that I think about it, it's too late. Even if they could bring themselves to disobey the Mandate.''

''You mean because there's too much water vapor in the atmosphere of Venus already.''

He nodded. ''The greenhouse is irreversible.''

''I agree,'' she said. ''I wasn't thinking about Venus.''

He looked at her, surprised. ''Earth?''

She shook her head sharply. ''Mars.''

''That's impossible,'' he said without hesitation. ''Mars has a tenth the mass of Earth, a fourth the diameter—a much greater surface-to-volume ratio. It's the opposite problem from Venus. You couldn't keep an atmosphere, and if you could, you couldn't keep it warm.''

"Nevertheless, they did it. As we know from the Martian plaque.''

He looked exasperated. "First of all, if they did it, they did it without *our* help . . .''

"Are you sure?''

"And second, they failed.''

"Maybe not this time. It seems to me we've been living a different history ever since we flew into that black hole.''

"Mars is the same size no matter what history we're in,'' he retorted. "If you want to help them recreate Crux, Earth is the next logical choice.''

"I would like to persuade them otherwise.'' She reached out a supplicant hand and rested it lightly on his shoulder. "I need your help.''

He could not, after all, hold out for long. The prospect of bombing Mars, an entire planet—with *comets*—was wildly irresistible.

Thowintha hung in the glowing waters of the Temple bridge, surrounded by others of his'er kind. To Sparta and Blake the strong beating of his'er mantle, its steady tempo, suggested deep contemplation. After several minutes of silence, his'er mantle glowed bright red and vibrations erupted around him'er. *You command us to do this?*

Who are we to command? We suggest this course of action.

We will do as the Designates suggest. We will make the vessels you need. We will even teach you to pilot them. The waters rumbled with his'er amusement.

How will you do that? Blake's eyes widened in surprise.

We will teach you how to think, said Thowintha.

We know how to think, he said angrily.

But Sparta said, *We are eager to learn your methods of control.*

Thowintha's mantle subtly shifted from crimson to purple. *Our vessels take their power from the vacuum.*

We relay that power from our core. As distances increase, losses increase.

Losses?

That is to say, the probability of nonexistence increases. Ratios are easily calculated. For us, these matters are of little consequence. For such as yourselves, individuals, there may be a different weighting.

Sparta looked glumly at Blake, before addressing the alien. *We will wish to contemplate the ratios of which you speak*, she said, more reasonably than she felt.

No sentient eye had observed the landing of the world-ship; no sentient eye observed its departure. The ocean around its landing place was deserted for many kilometers around. Superheated, that patch of ocean boiled in frenzy, evaporated; a vortex of cloud swirled around the fiery column that the ship left in its wake.

Soon it was high above the clouds; the sphere of the planet became a disk. Venus was left behind, and the gleaming diamond moon fell smoothly toward the sun.

Comets pursued it. Comets—and one other giant diamond moon, exactly like itself. . . .

11

"The fastest incoming object was in fact a world-ship."

"A world-ship!" Jozsef is astonished.

". . . Coming to carry the Amaltheans on Venus to safety—a world-ship piloted by Thowintha his'erself, as sh'he had existed three billion years previously. *Our* Thowintha intended to be elsewhere when his'er alternative self arrived."

"You mean that right then, the alien introduced the first fork, the first branching path in space-time," says the commander.

"That's a fair assessment," Forster agrees. "The first of many." His aquiescence gives him a moment to sip thoughtfully from his glass.

The commander, like a cat worrying a mouse, will not let go. "What will be the effect of all this? That's what we *must* know."

"I'm afraid we'll have to wait to find out, Commander. Right now all I can do is continue my narrative . . ."

"You said you learned something from what my daughter told you," says Ari.

"I learned much, although I learned slowly." Forster sets his glass aside and resumes his tale. "Diving into the Whirlpool, our path could have branched in many ways. Already

111

drowned, most of us had no say in our fate. Only one other could claim to be in control— but how much did Thowintha control his'er *own* fate . . . ?''

PART
3

THE GARDENS
OF MARS

12

"On Amalthea, at Jupiter, I had had the luxury of limitless time stretching before me," Forster continues. "My journal entries were sporadic, mere notes. Now, not knowing if each moment would be my last opportunity to record what I had seen, I began to keep careful records, beginning with this account. . . ."

Again we found ourselves dripping wet and choking for air in the overheated interior of the *Ventris*, floating weightless in the crowded wardroom. This time Troy was not there to ease the transition.

"Nothing to show for our resurrection except a bit of pucker," McNeil said morosely, grabbing a roll of his belly fat and scrutinizing it. "In my case, quite a bit of pucker. If they're going to drown a man, they might have had the courtesy to let him lose a few grams in the process."

"We've bloody well escaped from the jaws of death," Groves said through clenched teeth. The little navigator was shivering uncontrollably.

Walsh eyed him sharply. "Tony, I think you'd better come with me to the clinic." He protested feebly, but she said, "That's an order, not a suggestion." She hooked an arm around his shoulders and pulled him into the corridor.

Hawkins and Marianne Mitchell left for their

quarters without a word to McNeil or me. I found McNeil eyeing me speculatively, stroking his chin. "I don't believe we've been under for more than a few days, Professor." I felt my own chin, and understood what he was driving at; our beards were short. That suggested that, wherever the world-ship had emerged from the Whirlpool, the black hole was still close to the sun. Which further implied . . .

"There be comets out there. A hornet's nest of them, with us in the middle."

We felt the *Ventris* move. I followed McNeil to the flight deck. Outside, the world-ship's great lock was opening in front of us, and the tentacles that held us in place now moved us forward. The aliens were thoughtfully positioning the *Ventris* outside the lock, in space.

There we hovered, tethered to the world-ship by invisibly fine tentacles. To anyone looking on, tiny *Ventris* would have seemed a hummingbird escorting a Zeppelin.

Captain Walsh joined us on the deck and named what we saw but could not quite acknowledge: "Mars!"

The planet below us was recognizable, barely— a golden shield hanging in the starry sky. But its gleaming north polar cap extended halfway to the equator; its plains and mountains of red and yellow and black were veined with riverine seas of dark blue, reflecting ranks of cloud which sailed across what must have been a crystalline sky; even from space, we could see dark thunderheads crawling over the desert, sending spears of lightning to the ground.

"How's Tony?"

"His biostats are okay," she said. But she did not mention his psychostats.

McNeil pointed to the streaked heavens. "Comets again." Walsh only nodded, but I could hardly contain my excitement, for I thought I knew what we were about to witness.

We didn't have long to wait; the aliens had timed our resurrections closely. A bubble of intense light flared on the plain below, then another and another. The soundless violence threw shock waves radiating outward through the atmosphere, stunning clouds into existence and almost as quickly blowing them to tatters, throwing concentric rings of shadow onto the desert floor to interfere with each other like ripples in a still pond. In less than a minute, a hundred incandescent holes had opened in the disk of the planet, seemingly breaking through to a universe of unbearable brightness beyond.

And from the driest wastes of Mars, steam began to rise.

The spectacle went on for hours. I stayed glued to the windows while Walsh found other things to do. McNeil went below and, as he told me later, broke out a bottle of medicinal brandy—"Private stock, I assure you"—and persuaded Groves to join him.

"Tony seemed in despair that we'd found him out. He confessed he has an absolute horror of drowning. It's why he never went back to Pluto, he says; in the old days it meant going into the tank for four years. He claims what we've been through is worse."

"Then he's an even braver man than I knew," I said.

McNeil shook his head. "Not the way he tells it. He claims he was taken by surprise both times—first by Troy's orders, then when the aliens cracked open the Manta. Says he can't face it again."

I found nothing to say in reply.

When Groves appeared on deck we all pretended nothing had happened. The poor man looked pale as a fish; he watched what was happening on the surface of Mars a long while in silence, then turned to me and grinned weakly. "Beyond anything in the wildest imaginings of xeno-archaeology, eh, Professor? Culture X arrives on Mars."

But I'm afraid I was too absorbed to acknowledge his pleasantry. To see a planet struck by cometary fragments simply awed me.

When at last the bombardment subsided, I broached an idea to Walsh. I pointed out that Mars was less than half again as massive as Jupiter's moon Ganymede, for which the *Michael Ventris* had been over-designed. "What's to prevent us from taking the *Ventris* down to the surface under its own power? With cooperation from the Amaltheans, we could document the transformation of the planet on the site!"

"What's to prevent us?" Her reply was tart. "How about the equivalent of nuclear holocaust?" She nodded to the scene below.

I conceded we should have to wait to be sure the bombardment, or at least the worst of it, was really ended, that the atmospheric storms had subsided and the flash floods had run their course. But I persisted, and at last persuaded her.

"All right. Provided the lower atmosphere quiets down and we stay in touch with the world-ship, I've no personal objection. But I won't take a chance on getting stranded. I don't itch to live out my life on a lifeless planet."

I replied that I did not think Mars would remain lifeless for long.

She scheduled a meeting of the crew for later that night.

Eventually we reached consensus, although not without a certain amount of emotional bullying on my part. As I had hoped, McNeil and Groves were all for the adventure: McNeil is a thoroughgoing, cheerful Stoic; as for Groves, I'm afraid he would as soon die alone on a primitive planet as face another move in the drowning chamber of the world-ship.

Hawkins and Mitchell posed a problem, however. I had already suspected the difficulty, for Ms. Mitchell's cabin was next to my own, and in the confines of a small ship like ours it was impossible to avoid overhearing conversations one would normally prefer to avoid. Thus, while we were still at Venus, I had found myself involuntarily eavesdropping—keeping quiet not so much from prurient interest as from an intense desire not to interrupt.

"Marry me." It was Hawkins, his voice heavy with urgency.

"What if I did?" she replied rather sadly. "What would that change?"

"Would you marry me if we were back on Earth?"

"Living on the mud flats with the blue-green algae?" Her laugh was short and sharp. "Playing Adam and Eve?"

"I mean Earth the way it was."

"Get me there and I'll give you an answer."

"Maybe we're not three billion years in the past."

"What do you mean?"

"Maybe this is all a show. The professor claimed he knew what to look for on Amalthea, but he never told the rest of us until we got there. So maybe this situation too isn't . . . real."

When she spoke, she sounded years older—or at least more mature—than he. "It's real, Bill. And no way out."

"How do you know that?" He spoke in an intense whisper, broaching a conspiracy. "I'm not saying there's not an incredible technology at work here. Maybe it's alien technology. Maybe not. Maybe it's something a lot less mysterious."

She was so surprised that her laughter, this time, seemed almost happy. "Welcome to Disney-Cosmos. This way to Alien World."

"Why not?" His voice was hoarse, the charge of his emotion almost frightening. "They're in some big fight, some power struggle—Forster, working for the Space Board, Mays . . ."

"Nemo."

''He's not *nobody*, no matter what we call him.''

''We *should* have killed him after what he did.'' She was serious. ''He deserves to be dead.''

''Should I have done it?''

''No. You're saying that for my sake. What I did with him was my own doing, Bill. You can't fix it.'' There was silence then, and I honestly tried not to listen, but I heard her tell him, ''I don't expect you to take me home. But if you can, I'll love you the better.''

At that moment Jo Walsh called me to the flight deck, and this convenient interruption spared me further intimacies between them. . . .

Hawkins's conspiracy theories were not confined to chats with Marianne; he'd hinted at his suspicions to others as well. Now that we had met to discuss our future, the time had come to confront his extreme form of denial.

''Mr. Hawkins, you have suggested that we're the victims of a charade, mounted by me, perhaps, or mounted by the Amaltheans for unknown reasons.''

''How . . . why do you say that?'' Is it only the young who manage such exquisite mixtures of anger and guilt?

''This is a chance to satisfy yourself of the truth. On the surface of this planet, acting without supervision, we'll be able to conduct any researches of which we're capable. I guarantee you freedom of movement.''

He wavered visibly, pushing a hand through his limp blond hair, but came back strongly: ''Since we will, after all, require the aliens' cooperation, how can we pretend that we are independent?''

And so we went back and forth for a few minutes more; in the end Hawkins brought himself around. He was not wholly bereft of a scientist's natural curiosity—he was mightily intrigued to see for himself a transformation which, as I proposed, would culminate in the inscription of the Martian plaque, that glimmering shard whose meaning he had learned, if I may say so, at my knee.

Marianne Mitchell, throughout all this, said nothing at all. Her expression was that of a sphinx.

The next morning we hailed Thowintha on open circuits and explained ourselves, using the translator. Some hours later, an answer came back—from Inspector Troy: ''We have approved whatever action you wish to pursue, Professor. Here is your best landing plan. . . .''

But though she gave detailed instructions, complete with coordinates, her concern struck some of us as off-handed.

Shortly the *Ventris*, its tanks topped off by the lock's half-sentient machinery, was released in an equatorial orbit and began a slow descent into the thick carbon-dioxide atmosphere of primordial Mars.

Our destination was the shore of a desert sea whose margins were expanding by the hour. Floods of silt-laden water were still pouring in, carving wide channels through sand and rock on their way from the highlands where the nearest icy fragments had struck.

The tug settled on a handy butte, in a mess of smoke and fire and sand—landing tail first on two of its three legs, then falling over in a kind of controlled crash to come to rest on a sturdy tripod, a horizontal orientation which left the cargo and equipment holds readily accessible from the surface. It seemed an awkward system, but it had been devised for the wildly varying gravities and surface conditions of Jupiter's moons, and it worked well enough for Mars.

I could scarcely bear imprisonment in the tug, seeing only what the flatscreen and the narrow windows could show. McNeil bore the brunt of my impatience to get outside, to see the world-ship come down and watch the Amaltheans set to work.

The phlegmatic engineer humored my attempts

at inspiring him with a prefiguration of great events. "It won't be hard to patch something together, Professor," he told me. "I've already been at work on it."

We didn't need pressure suits. The atmosphere of ancestral Mars was thick indeed—at our present elevation, a pressure of more than one bar, that of Earth on a planet only one-tenth the mass of Earth—but the dominant gas was carbon dioxide. What we needed was a supply of oxygen.

McNeil pointed out that while the Martian pressure suits of our era were equipped with breather units to recycle respiratory gases and thin atmospheric carbon dioxide, extracting pure oxygen by means of artificial enzymes, we had no such suits handy; we'd certainly never contemplated visiting Mars. On the other hand, the ship's kit included a broad selection of biologically useful artificial enzymes; the fresh air recyclers specifically included the catalysts needed to break down CO_2. He'd set our biosynthesizers to work making more of the needed mix.

Meanwhile he'd been at work himself, on a prototype breathing system. He showed me the unit, a compact thing consisting of a filter intake, a mask and hose, and a pair of bottles to be worn on the chest.

Privately I marveled that this compact and beautifully crafted assembly, with its lathe-turned parts so lovingly polished and joined (from his description I had expected a real Heath Robinson), was the product of McNeil's large and curiously neat hands. Within that bulky man resides the soul of an artist.

Soon McNeil had Groves and Walsh and me busy rigging our own breathing systems. (Even Hawkins showed interest, despite himself.) The task was quickly done, and—although none of us produced so beautiful a piece of machinery as McNeil's—one certainly takes the necessary precautions when one's own life depends on the quality of the work.

The moment for testing arrived; Tony Groves insisted on being the first out of the lock. He took a few steps away from the main air lock, holding his breath. We heard his cautious exhalation and the bold indrawn breath that followed. Walsh had volunteered to stand by in the lock in full spacesuit regalia, ready if necessary to rush out and drag Groves back in. But his next breath sounded steadier, the next steadier yet.

"Works fine," he reported. "And a lovely view."

One by one we tested our gear. When my turn came I found my initial nervousness passing quickly. I looked around to appreciate the view that Tony Groves had recommended.

It was high noon, under a small hot sun in a transparent purple sky; a cold wind was blowing, but the sunlight was warm on my skin. Above me, a handful of stars winked like distant signal lanterns. More numerous still were the dozens of pale streaming comets that streaked the daytime sky, thin smudges of chalk on a celestial blackboard.

I allowed myself only a few moments to savor this day on ancient Mars. We had very little time to prepare for the coming of the aliens.

Walsh and I were out on the rim of the bluff with photogram cameras to record their arrival. They appeared almost twenty minutes earlier than we expected; we had to hurry and grab what we could.

The world-ship descended obliquely on streamers of fire, an immense diamond moon soaring in over mounded black volcanic peaks and plains of rusty sand, gliding across the wide valley that meandered toward our sparkling equatorial sea. Several kilometers off our shore, which was sharply defined by flat red buttes and mesas, the ship settled into the wind-whipped blue water. Far off we could see clouds of steam rising where the mirrored egg sat in the bright water; the steam quickly dispersed, leaving the ship resting delicately on its bottom. Its arching top stood high above us—over twenty-five kilometers high. A formation of ranked cirrus clouds formed spontaneously above it, drawn to it like a school of curious fish.

Then *they* came out. By the thousands.

High on the shining ellipsoid the equatorial locks spiraled open; like a pregnant guppy swollen to term, the world-ship expelled its offspring in clouds. Their disembarkation was militarily precise, as if rehearsed to perfection. Fleets of transparent medusas—hundreds of squadrons of vessels which must have been synthesized by the living machinery of the world-ship—rapidly deployed to all points of the compass, flying outward in ordered formations to take up their far-flung positions around the planet.

Their enemies would put up no active resistance to the invasion, I reflected. For their enemies were sterile seas and dead sands. The assault on Mars had not in fact been rehearsed: among members of a species who aspire to consensus and coordinated action from birth, near-perfect communication more than compensates for rehearsal.

Alas, humans do not mesh with one another so easily.

13

This, from my journal:
00.02.14.15

Shortly after the first descent of the world-ship—our New Year's Day, our Year Zero—exotic constructions appeared in many places on the planet. "Cities," if that is not too misleading a term—clusters of gleaming structures, partly underwater and partly onshore, their visible parts bone white against the pink sands at the margins of the narrow blue seas. Seeing them from a distance now, I catch myself daydreaming of the "chess-bone cities" that the writer Raybury, I think his name was, set down from his imagination before anyone had the slightest notion of the truth of matters on this planet.

The Amaltheans are going very smartly about the business of customizing Mars to suit themselves. *These* chess-bone cities—centers of transformation—incorporate immense processors which break down carbon dioxide into oxygen and carbon. Atmospheric pressure remains high, but at the rate these bone-white gleaming refineries remove carbon and spill oxygen into the atmosphere, we will soon be able to breathe the air as easily as scuba divers breathe bottled air a few meters underwater. It's the sort of atmosphere in which the Amaltheans must feel quite at home.

Where does the carbon go? A mystery. . . .

Meanwhile bacteria swarm; orange and gray lichens cover the rocks everywhere; green mosses spread into every sheltered cranny. Columns of algae cover the sandy floors of ubiquitous shallow lagoons. To visit the shores of the sea near our basecamp every few weeks or days is like watching a film of evolution speeded up a million times. Today I noticed that the clear waters were teeming with tiny shrimp, and the salt-encrusted shores were buzzing with swarms of black flies.

00.08.01.08

The purple skies are crossed by fleets of gravity-defying medusas, busy with their ecological errands. The transformation of Mars continues. (I can not help thinking of it as the "cruciforming" of Mars, after the Amaltheans' homeworld in Crux.) What is striking is the degree to which the Amaltheans have evidently abandoned their original goal.

Primordial Venus, what little we glimpsed of it, may have been a close analogue of the Amalthean homeworld, but Mars could hardly be more different—smaller and colder and drier by far. The narrow seas are alive now, but most of the surface remains an austere desert. Surely the few creatures that live in the dry lands, eking an existence from the watercourses or braving the dunes and lava plains, are novel inventions, not importations from some exotic oceanic world—*viz* those delicate, lively, ferocious windspiders that roll like miniature fanged tumbleweeds over the sand! This may be paradise, for like the first paradise it is a carefully tended garden in the sand, but if by heaven one means the race's once and hoped-for future home, Mars cannot be even a pale copy of Amalthean heaven.

Or of human heaven. I think of these things when I join my colleagues, wearing our breathing masks, to tend the struggling desert shrubs in the decidedly human-scale gardens near our basecamp, our dry miniature paradise.

00.08.27.22

Still we live aboard the *Ventris*. On this night another sad but inescapable occasion for eavesdropping. . . .

"My whole life I've been going from one place to another without knowing why," I heard Marianne say. "People never took me seriously. They wanted sex, or they were like Blake—he ignored me, he couldn't wait to get away from me. You didn't take me seriously either."

Hawkins sounded as miserable as usual. "I *did*, Marianne, I . . ."

"You *didn't*. You wanted to impress me; you definitely didn't want to *include* me." Her laugh was bitterly self-deprecating. "And I thought Nemo was different."

The events they were rehearsing had happened long ago on Ganymede, before our expedition had left for Amalthea; Marianne had been a tourist who had made Hawkins's acquaintance quite accidentally. But Hawkins had puffed himself up and subsequently made a fool of himself in front of her and the urbane Sir Randolph Mays.

Nemo had "included" her indeed, made use of her youth and eagerness and spirit in the most cynical way imaginable. In trying to wreck our expedition he had deliberately put her life in extreme danger, and he'd been prepared, should she survive, to let her take the blame for the crimes he himself had committed.

Soon I heard the soft, familiar sound of Marianne in tears (she spends hours a day weeping, despite the antidepressants Jo Walsh insists that she take). "I don't know why I'm here," she said. "I don't know where I'm going, or what's happening to me."

"You want it to be like it was before."

"*No*." Her vehemence must have startled Hawkins as much as it did me. ''I want what I never thought I would want. I want to be in one place, with people I know. I don't want to go anywhere strange. I don't want to think about getting myself killed because there's no air or gravity or whatever—I want to be safe. I want to be loved. I don't want to deal with any more strangers. I don't want to have to deal with those . . . those . . . *creatures.''*

''I love you, Marianne. I want what you want. If there's anything I can do to help you get it, I will. I swear.''

Hawkins's dilemma is as accute as any we face. How can he keep his promise to this lost girl? How can he restore to her a world she has never really known, but has only created from wishful memories?

00.11.26.19

My ethnographic notes on the Amaltheans now fill almost an entire chip. My mineral collection enlarges every day, as do my collections of plants, animals, and microorganisms. The Amalthean lifeforms are disturbingly Earthlike; often, even when I have never seen anything like a particular specimen on Earth, one or more of my colleagues has. At other times, none of us knows the species but the general type is familiar. At still other times, what we behold is truly alien.

And I do have exquisite specimens; whenever an even more exquisite example of something already on hand is found, I ruthlessly throw out the old and replace it. Anyone who finds these homemade wooden and paper crates and boxes, these crude pottery vials and plastic jars, will marvel at what they contain and think that ancient Mars was a place of perfection unparalleled in the Galaxy.

Unless, of course, there exist places of *real* perfection.

Angus is of extraordinary help in this work. The man is possessed of odd stores of knowledge, informational tastes of astonishing catholicity, among them the apparent memorization of numerous catalogues of the natural world. When he cannot name something—a fish, a flower, an ore-bearing rock—he can often suggest an analogue. Among the six of us who are willy-nilly sharing out the tasks of Adam and Eve, he has taken on the naming. Thus we evolve a peculiar Martian taxonomy, half fantastic and mythological, half prosaic and Linnaean, a novel *Systema naturae*, viz, *Bufo elephantopus* (a big frog) and *Lebistus McNeilis* (a guppy-like fish) on the one hand, *Puccinia pandorae* (a wheat-like plant, with unfortunate side-effects if badly cooked) and *Raphanus novus* (a radish) on the other. I might add that, even among those who once studied the subject, none of us seriously pretends to remember his or her Latin. I include myself, for I have much less Latin than Greek.

00.21.07.08

The medusas have sown the barren fields of Mars with a cornucopia of seed, which has exploded into life. The plants have grown riotously: I have watched amazed as blue seas like rivers grow borders with grassy meadows, as the slopes of the low pink hills cover themselves with a sort of chaparral or maqui of low bushes, as the ridges of the valleys sprout spiky lines of bent trees. What were sterile seas are now wide swaths of green, as green as the "canals" of the old science-fiction writers.

The proportion of oxygen in the atmosphere has increased faster than anyone could have predicted. The manic growth of plant life, feeding on carbon dioxide, excreting oxygen, accounts for only a small part of the oxygen increase; those white factories are everywhere on Mars, all over the globe—immensely scaled-up versions of our artificial-enzyme breathers. I have found what becomes of the carbon. Conveyor lines of flying medusas feed the carbon into the throats of massive volcanoes—directly into the ground, through great shafts the Amaltheans have sunk to magma chambers deep below the surface, there to be stored up for eventual recycling by geologic processes. What is the logic of this? It is manifold, I think, and will be revealed in time.

With the heady rush of oxygen has come a swarm of animal species. Insects enliven the meadows: stick-like dragonflies, as blue as neon with black button eyes; clouds of gnats and mosquitos; ants and spiders teeming among the roots. And at night, locusts singing to the bright stars.

Beetles everywhere! According to Angus McNeil, there was a noted 20th-century biologist named Haldane who, having been questioned what inference about God one might draw from a study of His works, replied, "An inordinate fondness for beetles." On Mars we glimpse a foreshadowing of that fondness, if not its rationale.

The Martian seas teem as thickly. Following the infusion of oxygen into the waters, the portals of the world-ship have opened and emptied their living reservoirs of plankton and coral and worms and jellyfish and crustaceans and cephalopods. Captain Walsh and I have been down in the Manta to see for ourselves; the sunlit blue-water scenery is reminiscent of the Red Sea, the richest sea on Earth. We could not move the submarine without encountering life in myriad shapes and colors—and frantic, fantastic behaviors.

Today, for the first time since we landed on Mars, I walked on the surface with the mask of my breather dangling unused in front of me. With every step, succulent ice plant squashed under my boots. Today for the first time I saw a flock of birds, or something like birds, moving against the horizon.

The Amaltheans are masters at this; surely they are the gardeners of the universe. And Mars is the Garden of Eden.

00.21.13.19

My friend Angus tells me that Paradise cannot last.

INFOPAK
TECHNICAL
BLUEPRINTS

On the following pages are computer-generated diagrams representing some of the structures and engineering found in *Venus Prime:*

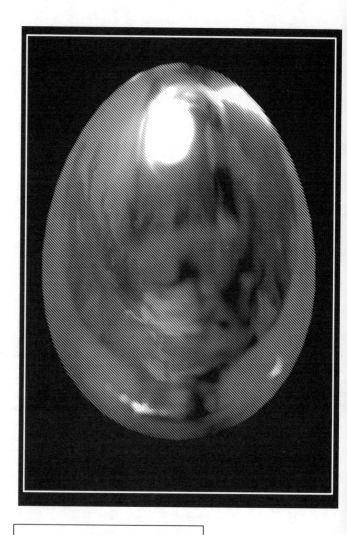

WORLD-SHIP

EXTERIOR VIEW
LONG AXIS

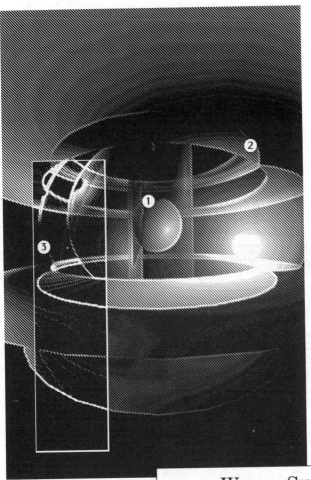

WORLD-SHIP
INTERIOR VIEW

1. TEMPLE BRIDGE
2. SPIRAL PLATES
3. INNER CHAMBER SHELL

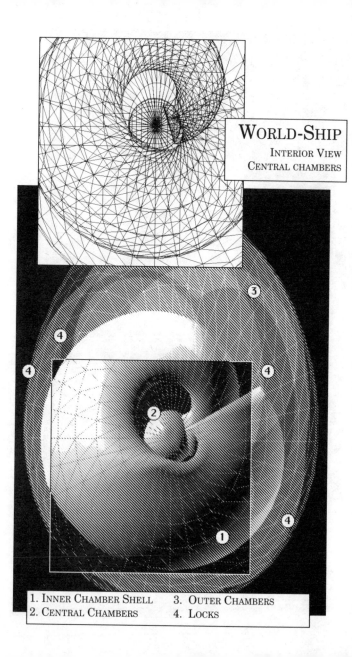

WORLD-SHIP
INTERIOR VIEW
CENTRAL CHAMBERS

1. INNER CHAMBER SHELL   3. OUTER CHAMBERS
2. CENTRAL CHAMBERS   4. LOCKS

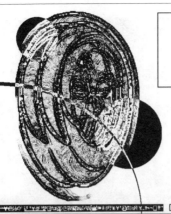

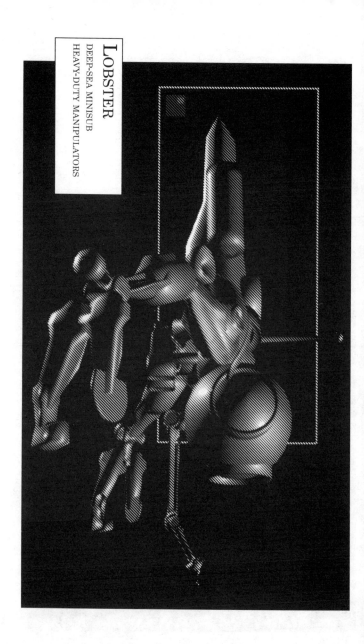

LOBSTER

DEEP-SEA MINISUB
HEAVY-DUTY MANIPULATORS

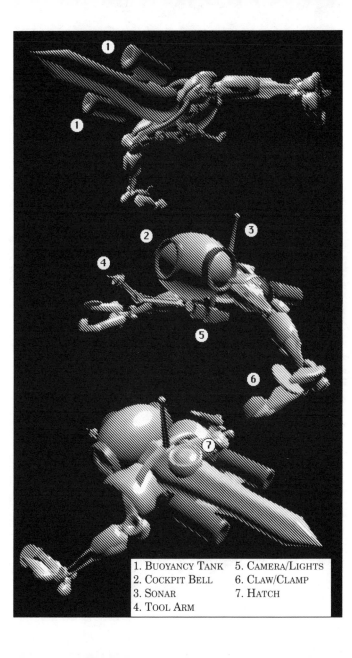

1. BUOYANCY TANK   5. CAMERA/LIGHTS
2. COCKPIT BELL   6. CLAW/CLAMP
3. SONAR   7. HATCH
4. TOOL ARM

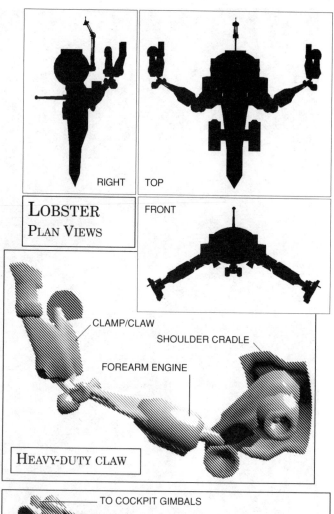

RIGHT   TOP

LOBSTER
PLAN VIEWS

FRONT

CLAMP/CLAW

SHOULDER CRADLE

FOREARM ENGINE

HEAVY-DUTY CLAW

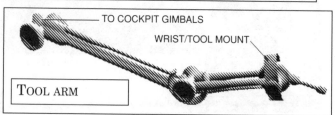

TO COCKPIT GIMBALS

WRIST/TOOL MOUNT

TOOL ARM

THOWINTHA

AMALTHEAN AMBASSADOR

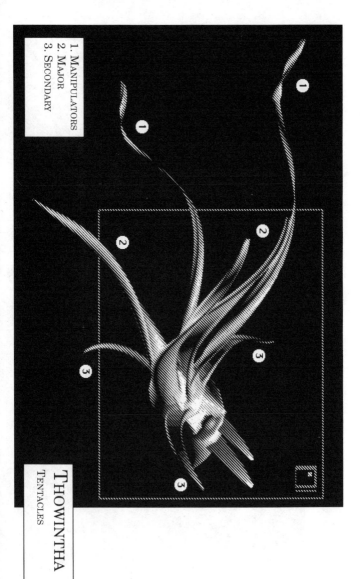

1. MANIPULATORS
2. MAJOR
3. SECONDARY

THOWINTHA
TENTACLES

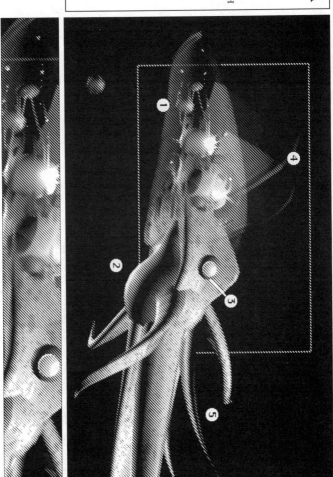

Thowintha

Detail of hood
and head

1. Hood-Organs
2. Digestive pouch
3. Eye
4. Hood Fins
5. Tentacles

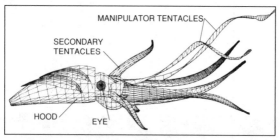

MANIPULATOR TENTACLES

SECONDARY TENTACLES

HOOD

EYE

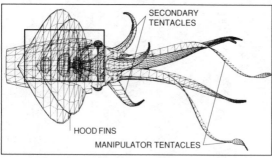

SECONDARY TENTACLES

HOOD FINS

MANIPULATOR TENTACLES

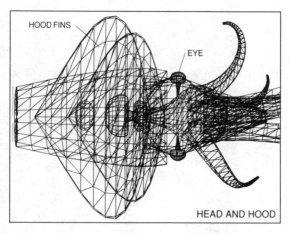

HOOD FINS

EYE

HEAD AND HOOD

THOWINTHA
HEAD AND HOOD SCHEMATICS

MEDUSA
AMALTHEAN VESSEL

MEDUSA

1. CORE TENTACLES
2. INNER MANTLE
3. CORE SPHERE
4. CORE SPHERE SCANS

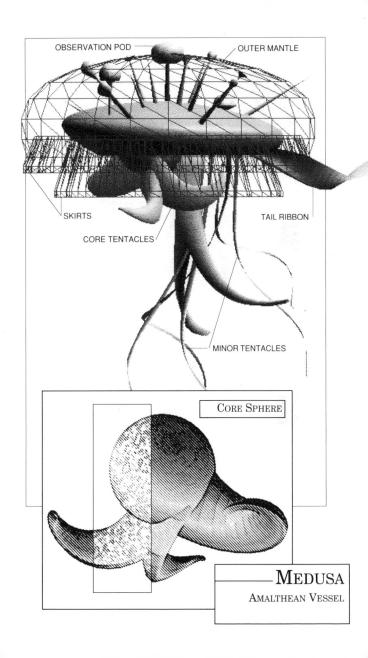

OBSERVATION POD

OUTER MANTLE

SKIRTS

CORE TENTACLES

TAIL RIBBON

MINOR TENTACLES

CORE SPHERE

MEDUSA

AMALTHEAN VESSEL

existed a Martian year ago. The ultimate source of these waterfalls was visible on the purple edge of the desert a hundred kilometers away, in a line of rainstorms rolling sublimely across the sands.

"Rain constantly dissolves atmospheric carbon dioxide to form carbonic acid," Angus explained, "and the acid eats at the rocks where the rain falls and the water runs, and the carbon is locked into them." He bent down and picked up a shard of sandstone, prying at its water-blackened surface with his thumbnail. "If the carbon in this rock should fail to return to the atmosphere—if the carbon in enough weathered rocks like this does not return to the atmosphere, and if the carbon the Amaltheans are shoveling into the volcanoes never returns to the atmosphere—Mars will freeze.

"Carbon is released when the rocks are heated. But Mars has no plate tectonics to carry slabs of surface rock deep into the interior," he went on. "For now, and for the last billion years or so, the planet is recycling such rocks by burying them under immense layers of lava and volcanic ash. Granted, Mars has, or anyway will have in our era, the biggest volcanoes in the solar system. But as they cool—and they must—carbon will be removed from the atmosphere and locked in the rocks, water will freeze, the animals will die, and the plants will dry up and roll away on a cold, cold wind."

Although Angus painted this disastrous picture perhaps too graphically, I saw his point. Yet I cannot believe the Amaltheans have not anticipated these events and planned some means of forestalling the inevitable.

14

00.22.06.13

What is Troy up to? What has become of that once-genial fellow Redfield? Their communications with us are infrequent and brief. Of course they never expected us to be here with them. Their alien friend tried to leave us in our own era, among our own kind. But did *they* expect to come here? What role do they have to play in all this?

And I wonder about that cult of theirs, of which the late—and, I confess, little missed—Sir Randolph Mays was apparently some sort of figurehead. Nemo now, wherever he's gone to, and well named.

As for Troy and Redfield, they claim never to have been believers in the Free Spirit—unlike Troy's parents. But I wonder. Perhaps I will never know. We on the *Ventris* are not privy to their councils. We know what they tell us, and that only, and we do our best—like obedience-trained media-hounds—to cover the pre-announced news.

There has been much of it.

After that long ago and thrilling first landing on Mars we kept ourselves busy to the point of exhaustion merely by attempting to keep up with the swift work of the Amaltheans. We could not hope to document everything they did—there were too many of them for that, and they were too widely dispersed over the surface of the planet. But Troy's infrequent bulletins notified us of the more spectacular events—the melting of the southern ice cap and the flooding of the Hellas depression, the sowing of the waters with a thousand species of fish numbered in the billions, the planting of the Scandia highlands with conifers (a million trees in a week, with wildflowers and mosses and all the rest to sustain the ecosystem, an instant taiga!)—and we moved the *Michael Ventris* as necessary in order to capture them with our cameras as they unfolded.

We dropped the tug's clip-on holds, of course, and the equipment bay too, except when we needed it to transport the Manta. The little submarine was an invaluable tool; so much of what we wanted to see happened underwater. Other than the Manta, the hold had carried only the battered Moon Cruiser in which Mays and Marianne had arrived on Amalthea, and for which we had made room by abandoning our ice mole. We'd dragged the cruiser with us as evidence of Mays's misdeeds, evidence intended to be used in some eventual Space Board inquiry—which seemed, as the months passed, increasingly unlikely ever to convene (at least with any of us present to testify). So the cruiser's gone now, torn apart, recycled, serving useful purposes.

Even stripped, the *Ventris* is an awkward craft for flying in the thick atmosphere: it is wholly dependent upon its rocket engines for lift; its flight paths are suborbital parabolas. It needs too-frequent refuelings from the world-ship's immense reservoirs of liquid hydrogen and oxygen. Therefore Tony and Angus are planning a sailplane to carry on our explorations, one modeled on the graceful marsplanes of our own era. At the moment it's a spare-time labor of love for them; all of us are busy with full-time work. We have been building a home on Mars.

We walk freely in the warm, oxygen-rich air, having discarded our breathers long ago. What was our basecamp has become our settlement, our village. We have a nearby fresh-water spring in the shelter of a high sandstone bluff to the west, to windward. Less than half a kilometer to the north is the sea, which (on another Mars?) will someday drain into the vastness of the Valles Marineris.

The old *Ventris* is parked half a kilometer in the opposite direction, a skeletal vehicle perched in the dunes, surrounded by cast-off holds like rusting boilers that make it look like a gutted steamship, although in this case our ship, however rarely called upon to demonstrate its spaceworthiness, is in fact still capable of getting up steam.

Rocket engines make a fine foundry fire, and the rocks of Mars are rich in iron ore. Rockets are also quite capable of melting sand to pure silica, although we have lately fashioned solar mirrors that do the job almost as well. We have made a variety of implements of glass and iron and crude steel, but the principal product of our steel mill is reinforcing bar. Here and there, at the margins of our narrow sea, the crumbling red bluffs are seamed with gypsum and limestone (the presence of limestone was a surprise to me, for I had thought it a product solely of life)—all the makings of a cement industry.

Our houses are made from reinforced concrete and glass. We shape them as if we were happily patting sandcastles on a beach, scooping out the sand and mounding it, pouring water on the mounds to hold, temporarily, whatever whimsical shapes we might wish to carve in them, then emplacing our glass slabs and securing the mounds in a net of iron bars.

The right recipe for concrete was not easy to find. In our first attempts the sandy mixture never set but merely crumbled to powder. We recalibrated our chemical programs—not without some grumbling from a ship's computer program that thinks itself above such mundane business. Now the smooth, heavy mud sets quickly· and, over the course of a week or so, cures nicely, whereupon we dig the sandy mold from beneath it. *Voila*, a graceful domed structure, much higher and more boldly vaulted in this planet's low gravity than any corresponding structure could be on Earth, the intricacy of its intaglio limited only by the imagination and patience of its builders (and of course by the speed of evaporation). Even the first crude results gave us pleasure more intense than I could have foreseen.

Because we seek protection from the wind—our mound-building is easier if we dig holes in the sand rather than make exposed piles of it, which the wind too rapidly dries and resculpts—our settlement is more than half buried; only the very tops of the domes show above ground level. Shrubs and trees and ground-hugging flowers borrowed from Amalthean plantations grow in the cool and sheltered pathways among our houses and work-rooms. Angus tells us they are remarkably like the desert plants of some parts of our Earth—the man's fund of odd knowledge is a continual delight and surprise, the more so because he never thrusts it upon us—and he has taught us their names: pepper trees, oleanders, ocotillos, chollas, barrel cactuses, palos verdes, sago palms, desert primroses, shooting stars, a hundred other species of tiny bright flowers whose names I quickly forget (all of them carefully recorded, of course). Angus knows them as well as the names of his friends.

Some of the fruit trees are also familiar; the original apple of Eden is here. But many are unlike anything on Earth. We named the "whiteglobe" for the fruit it bears copiously, for several months at a time—fruit as spherical as oranges, as smooth as melons, as pale as eggs. Yesterday I came upon Marianne as she was pruning the too-vigorous growth from the whiteglobe trees, lopping off shiny wands of wood that were erupting with pink and purple blossoms from what had been hard green fuses only a week ago, and carefully setting the more perfect cuttings aside to use in the floral arrangements with which she often graces our rooms.

Although the days and nights here are only a few minutes longer than Earthly days and nights, the

year and the seasons are twice as long. Just now
the cool Martian spring is slowly lengthening into
the long Martian summer. Marianne was dressed
only in a tapa chiton, enjoying the sun on her bare
limbs. Like all of us, her skin was deeply tanned
and there were lines around her still-young eyes
from staring into bright distances.

She was crying—she cries easily—but not from
sadness. She told me, after we had talked about
this and that while the small sun set in a moonless
sky, that she is pregnant.

So the last roles are filled; we truly have our
Adam and Eve.

00.22.29.19
In a little more than a month we will have been
a year here—a Martian year, which is a little less
than two Earthly years. (The Martian days, on the
other hand, are not much more than twenty-four
hours long.) We have devised a twenty-four-month
calendar, alternating twenty-nine-day months with
twenty-eight-day months and tacking on a couple
of extra days at year's end. It is not the system they
use on Mars in the era we came from, when dates
throughout the solar system refer to standard dates
on Earth, but ours works better for us. It reminds
us that we really are on Mars—that that other
Earth, and the times of our origin, are inaccessible.

The names of our months will come later—we've
decided not to hurry tradition, or impose artificial
order on what should be a spontaneous process. It
makes little difference that New Year's Day does
not happen to fall in midwinter in the north of Mars
(in fact it falls in the northern summer), for our
base camp is not far from the equator.

Troy occasionally favors us with one of her commlink bulletins, but otherwise we see little of her
or Redfield. She keeps us in mind—we never seem
to need to remind her when goods and supplies
that only the aliens can provide are low; we have
been able to contact her as we wish, even to have

occasional access to Amalthean vessels and facilities; but she does not seem to concern herself much with the minutiae of our welfare.

We have, I think, accepted what we had earlier wished to avoid, what some might call our fate. Although I think it decidedly unclassical that the Fates, those stern goddesses, would have entangled themselves in so antisymmetric a state of affairs. We ill-matched, ill-chosen representatives of the human race are hardly suited to play primogenitors, any pair of us. All Africa is carried in Jo's well-stirred Caribbean ancestry, all Asia in Redfield's genes from his Chinese mother (and for that matter, Redfield is seen among us less often than Troy).

If fate has not brought us here, what has? Chaos? The second law of thermodynamics? These go equally against the grain. A man of my age (however one counts the years) should be prepared to accept the meaninglessness of the universe, I suppose. And be happy merely to comprehend some small part of it.

In the quotidian, acceptance means only that we do not look forward to another miraculous change of affairs. Weird and unlikely as it seems, we are here upon the surface of the planet Mars some billions of years before the era in which we were born. We watch the planet being transformed before our eyes. We record the transformation, laboring to produce documents we hope will be uncovered by some distant generation of our descendants or other relatives, or even by some version of ourselves.

Of course, in history as I have lived it so far, *I* did not find the record we are making—nor did anyone I know of. Why not? It has often been suggested that this is an *alternate* history.

As for our present selves, or "real" selves, it seems very likely that we Martian pioneers will die here. But no time soon, I hope.

15

00.23.03.19

Tony and Angus have finished their airplane at last.

Test flights in the neighborhood have been wildly successful. Oh it is a lovely sight, this ruddy, long-winged craft—to my eye, much more graceful than the Martian sailplanes of our era which inspired it. Its stringers are bamboo, its ribs a kind of willow or poplar, its fabric covering our finest tapa, which is really more like a thin paper made from the fibrous stems of reeds and painted (''doped,'' Jo says) with a strong-smelling red vegetable lacquer cooked up by Angus.

The plane carries two people, one behind the other; both have controls. Its main instruments are a portable altimeter and an inertial compass, adapted from a now-useless deep-space suit system.

Tomorrow, Jo, our best pilot, and Tony—not only our navigator, but the lightest of us—are to set out on the first long-range flight.

Where to, no one can say for sure. The motive power of this airplane is wind, nothing more; the pilot flies it where the wind carries it. Whoever is not driving has even less to say about the itinerary. Perhaps all this is less tricky than it seems; I am no aeronautical engineer. It has been pointed out to me that in our low gravity, only a third of Earth's,

139

it is not only easier to get an airplane into the air, it is certainly much easier on the flyers if it fails to stay there.

But what makes the whole project practical is that this Mars, not unlike the Earth of our own era, has thick ionized layers of atmosphere which serve to reflect radio signals over the steep curve of the planet. So if there is a crash landing—even thousands of kilometers away—we can come to the rescue in the *Ventris*.

00.23.06.12

Jo radioed us at the scheduled time:

"Wind's still carrying us northeast. In three days we've covered seven thousand kilometers on the ground, practically in a great circle. Crossed over Eden, west of Arabia. It's beginning to look like we're being sucked into a huge weather vortex over the north pole."

00.23.07.12

"We're almost over the pole. Cold as a banker's heart—good thing these old pressure suits still work, or we could have been forced down just to keep from freezing. There's lots of medusa activity going on here. Something our friend Troy hasn't bothered to tell us about. A couple of curious medusas came over to give us a look—we saw those friendly fishy faces peering out at us, but they went away without saying hello."

00.23.08.12

"There's definitely something strange going on over the pole. They're building an enormous silver tower right on the pole itself. And the weather in the upper atmosphere isn't natural; somehow they're controlling it."

00.23.10.12

"We crossed forty degrees north latitude this morning, headed south again; the inertial puts us at about two-forty west, over a stretch of sand Tony tells me is called Aetheria on the map. At this rate, on this heading, we may make it back to within a few hundred kilometers of base. We may *even* . . . but never mind, I'm too superstitious to say it out loud.''

00.23.11.20

They're safely back.

After flying a ragged arc a third the circumference of the planet, Jo and Tony managed to come down less than a hundred kilometers to the west of us; Jo probably could have brought the plane all the way in, but as she explained, the last stretch was fifty kilometers over open water with little hope of thermals, and she didn't think it was worth the risk.

Angus, with my eager if useless attempt to help, made a quick, fuel-intensive hop in the *Ventris* to bring them and their paper airplane back home.

Having been gone a week, Tony and Jo were delighted to get out of their pressure suits (their waste-disposal systems having been overtaxed, as I probably do not need to mention even for these, my own records). But as soon as they'd freshened up and put down some solid fare, they told us as much as they could of what they'd seen of the activity at the pole.

Jo said, ''We decided not to transmit everything we saw. They didn't tell us what they're doing; maybe they're hoping we didn't find out.''

We were siting under the olive trees on our patio, the table still littered with the remains of supper. The low, red sun cast restless intricate shadows of olive leaves on the rough rounded sides of the nearest domes.

''We encountered a gravitational anomaly up there,'' Tony said. ''Noticeable to big. At first I didn't want to trust the readings—the gravimeter's just a scrounge from a deep-space rig, after all, not what you'd call a precision instrument.'' Having

teased us, Tony sipped at a beaker of juice, waiting
for someone to ask for details.

"What exactly did you find out?" My impatience was all too obvious.

He smiled at me rather languidly; he is our map-
per and the nearest thing we have to a geophysicist
(although Angus has committed more geological
knowledge to memory), and he was clearly enjoying our attention. "It was a *negative* anomaly. At
the time we crossed the region, therefore, gravity
was distinctly *less* than average over the pole."

"How can that be?" Bill asked.

"The lithosphere must be significantly less dense
over the pole," McNeil put in.

"Not in *our* era," said Bill. "It almost sounds like
something was pulling *up*."

Tony didn't contradict him. In fact, for the rest
of the evening Tony said very little, while the rest
of us heatedly argued theories we made up—out of
thin air, so to speak—to explain the strange obser-
vations of our aerial explorers.

01.01.01.20

New Year! By consensus we celebrated at sun-
down. A fine party—I note that there's no shortage
of fermented stuff, even a year after the last of the
expedition's supplies were exhausted. No surprise,
given a biological kit as well supplied as ours.

But before it was dark, before we'd fairly gotten
started, Bill stood up with an odd expression on his
face, swiped at his schoolboy hair, and nervously
cleared his throat. "Marianne and I have something to say."

"Go ahead," said Jo. "No ceremony here."

Bill blushed and glanced fondly at Marianne. Her
face was newly scrubbed and sleek with youth, a
beautiful face—now creased around the mouth and
brows. She smiled, but she seemed wistful. Bill
said, "I . . . we, I mean . . . we've decided we want
to get married." His square-fingered hand groped
for her small, slender one, encouraging her. "Right,

Marianne?'' he said anxiously. She surrendered her hand but still found no words.

Jo said lightly, ''So the guy's in love with you. Not exactly news to the rest of us. You gonna let him talk for you too?''

That seemed to rouse her; we'd always known her as an independent young woman. ''Yes.'' Her green eyes flashed. ''It's what we want.''

''No problem,'' said Jo. ''I can still claim to be the captain of that hulk of a ship over there. Two hours of counselling first—Space Board regs,'' she growled, mock seriously. ''I should be real good at that.''

''I take it that congratulations are in order,'' Angus said, ''in which case, I've waited long enough for a drink.''

Were our young lovers happy or bereft? Or perhaps a bit of both? After much convivial back-pounding and hugging and tears, we managed to put the question behind us, substituting for it a serious appraisal of Angus's latest barrel of home-brew. But I find myself thinking—and hoping—that it is a happy and a sensible thing for Marianne and Bill to have done. Why do I say that? Because Marianne has at last accepted—not her fate—but the reality of her situation and ours. And her own needs and desires. Because she no longer holds against Bill that for which he had too long foolishly blamed himself, our mutual predicament.

And because Bill and Marianne are young. Perhaps only the old know that there is no joy in coupling without belief in the future. Jo put it well to me (and I urged her to put it the same way to them): that Marianne could let go of her unhappiness and marry the man she loves (even a little) gives us all confidence.

Also it was a sensible thing to do because it partly solves a complex equation. I suppose Angus and Tony will now be competing with each other (and with me?) for the attentions of our captain.

Sometime during the night I giddily proposed that we name the first month of the year "Marianne."

01.03.13.20

"I've been watching the gravimeter every day. The readings have shifted considerably." Tony paused halfway through the grilled catfish that was the centerpiece of our luncheon. "Anyone here feel . . . *heavier* than usual?"

"Heavier?" Marianne said, amused. "Definitely. Every day." She patted her abdomen. Although her internal changes were as yet invisible to us, she was accutely aware of them.

The rest of us considered one another, trying to recall complaints of fatigue in recent days. Tireder, maybe—nothing unusual about that, we're all getting older, and with Marianne out of the schedule, there's been more than the usual amount of work to do.

"Actually, I too feel heavier every day," Angus allowed. "My imagination, no doubt."

"Not entirely," said Tony. "If my crude instruments are not completely worthless, this whole planet is more massive than it was two weeks ago."

"Weren't you telling us the planet was *less* massive—at least at the pole?" Bill succinctly expressed our confusion.

"That was temporary. We—Jo and I—think the additional mass approached from space along the polar axis, then was somehow inserted through the north pole within the last few days," Tony said, satisfied with himself.

"And we suspect something symmetrical has happened at the south pole," Jo said.

Tony nodded. "The reason being that you can't add mass to a spinning top—or a planet—without throwing the whole thing into a crazy spiral, anywhere except at the poles."

"What sort of mass?" I wanted to now.

"Most probably . . . black holes," replied Tony. "Small, with event horizons no bigger than molecules, I'd guess, but with the mass of whole mountain ranges, maybe whole subcontinents. We know the Amaltheans have some control over the vacuum, and they appear to be using it to plant black holes in the core of Mars. When the two meet, they'll coalesce into a single hole.''

''Good Lord!'' Bill's dudgeon came complete with pink nose, ears, and scalp; very English. ''Why *would* they do such a thing?''

''Elementary,'' Angus grumbled, ''in the long view.'' He glanced at Tony, asking permission to steal his thunder, I think, and Tony nodded the go-ahead. ''All the marvelous progress that's been made in the years we've been here is ephemeral, unless there are fundamental changes in the geology of the planet,'' said Angus. ''Mars has a thick atmosphere now, but it needs enough mass to keep the air from eventually escaping. *And* it needs internal heat to maintain the carbon cycle. A black hole in the center of Mars solves both problems: it increases the planetary mass, and it heats up the core.''

''How does it do that?'' I wondered. ''Heating the core?''

''Radiation.'' Tony again. ''Paradoxically, the smaller the radius of the hole, the greater the tidal forces at the Schwarzchild radius—the edge, that is. The greater the tidal force, the greater the amount of radiation coming from the hole.''

''Where does the radiation come from?'' Marianne asked. ''I thought there was *nothing* inside a black hole.''

''Nothing's where the radiation comes from,'' Tony replied. ''From the vacuum. The vacuum is seething with particles that come and go too quickly to detect. Pairs of virtual particles—protons and antiprotons, electrons and positrons, all kinds—are constantly flashing into existence and vanishing again, instantly—everywhere, all around us, all the time. If that should happen right on the edge of a black hole, one of the pair can be caught; the other escapes as, well, *real* radiation.''

''Why won't this hole just eat the planet up from the center?'' Marianne asked.

''Maybe it will,'' Jo put in. ''But it will take a long time to feed all of Mars into a hole the size of a molecule.''

''Well, but the more mass it absorbs, the faster it grows, right?'' Marianne's native intelligence had clearly been engaged by this fascinating new question.

''Right. Given a handy source of matter—the core of Mars—the hole will tend to grow from the infall,'' said Tony. ''But the radiation we've been talking about offsets that tendency. Indeed, a hole as tiny as the one indicated by the gravimeter radiates a tremendous amount of energy—so much so that, in a vacuum, it would evaporate in a short time.''

''I take it you're saying that at some point the two tendencies cancel, and the system achieves a sort of equilibrium?'' Bill sounded dubious.

Tony nodded. ''I can have a go at the calculations if you want a precise answer—not a simple task—but in essence the matter inside Mars will be converted to energy with extreme efficiency— enough to warm the planet without a noticeable reduction in mass for at least a couple of billion years.''

Warmth lingered in the air and light lingered on the horizon, although the sun was down and the wind had stopped stirring the olives. Marianne stood up to light the lamps, moving herself carefully. The worried call of a quail came from somewhere off in the shadowed dunes, now overgrown with stiff grass.

I traded glances with Angus. His dire prediction that Mars would freeze had indeed been anticipated by the Amaltheans, in a fashion that none of us could have predicted.

''A fascinating supposition,'' I said to Tony. ''But

I wonder why Troy didn't bother to alert us? Why, having invited us to record all the magnificent achievements of the Amaltheans until now, did she try to suppress this greatest of their feats?''

16

01.01.15.03

Midsummer on Mars—the four-
teenth of Marianne—and Bill and
Marianne have done the sensible
thing. At dusk, that hour when the
wind fails and the warmth of the day
lingers in the still air, the ceremony began with
music.

Tony did most of the work, providing a hum-
ming melody and a perhaps rather moody bass line
on his rigged-up version of a Synthekord, with Jo
accompanying him on pottery drums stretched
with polymer skin. Angus banged out a very re-
spectable rhythm on what looked like oversized
iron castanets. Torches fueled with oil from a shrub
Angus calls creosote bush fluttered at the edges of
our little central plaza. We'd all pitched in to do
the decorating, principally garlands of leaves strung
among the huts and the saplings.

Bill came forward shyly to stand in the center of
the little courtyard, in a space heavy with the scent
of autumn-flowering vines and warm with light
from flickering yellow flames, wearing his best, the
scrubbed remnants of a pair of twill trousers and a
white cotton shirt that he had brought with him to
Ganymede uncountable years ago. His bright English hair was slicked down against his long skull,
his bright English face was pink with embarrassed
happiness in the torchlight. Here was a man who

had got what he wanted at last, and he was un-critically thankful to his friends for it.

Marianne and I were waiting in the domed hut I used for a workplace; I held the door ajar and peeked out, awaiting our cue. There were no lights on, but I imagined her happiness was enough to shed a soft glow through the place. She wore layers of silk-fine tapa and wore white-flowered vines, both as a coronet and in layers of fragrant neck-laces.

The sound of the little orchestra, augmented by synthesized strings and brass, now swelled boldly in the desert night, echoing from the sandstone walls of the buttes. After a while Jo left off the high-pitched patter of the ceramic drums—by then Tony had sampled her playing and kept her rhythms alive on his Synthekord as she went to take her position at the pottery bench that had been cleared to serve as an altar.

It was time to present the bride. The music fell silent as I escorted Marianne the few steps across the flagstones to stand in front of the "altar"; Tony took up the best man's position beside Bill, and Angus stood by, approximating the maid of hon-or's place with a solemnity that would have been comic had we not all been touched by the moment. Jo addressed us, standing easily with her hands clasped behind her back, talking no more formally than at any crew meeting. But there was enough expectancy in the air to lend a touch of solemnity.

"We're here to celebrate with Bill and Mar-ianne—celebrate not just the fact of their marriage but the boost it gives us all. Seems they've decided that life is worth living."

"Here, here," Angus muttered with feeling.

"And since we're not standing on ceremony," Jo went on, "I think it's okay to mention that they obviously think life is worth *giving.*"

Which drew a serene smile from Marianne and an intense blush from Bill—expressions we hon-ored with rowdy applause.

"We've had to face what no one could have fore-seen." Jo became serious. "We've disagreed, gotten mad at each other, stepped on each other's toes. Sometimes we've pulled in different directions. But we've made a home and a life together. And our first major event as a . . . *society*, I think we've got to call it . . . isn't a funeral, as it might have been. Nobody's gotten sick, nobody's had an accident. Nobody's killed anybody else or themselves. Instead, we've got a marriage to celebrate and a child on the way. Maybe we're the only humans in this place and time, but we've made a start. So thank you, Marianne, and thank you, Bill, for making it official." She nodded at Tony. "Speaking of official, if you guys can find those rings, I'll read the words."

Tony and Angus produced rings of forged iron, Jo's work. Bill trembled as he tried to force the braided black band over Marianne's finger. She had to help. Her hand was steadier than his, and she got his ring over his callussed knuckle with less difficulty.

Jo said, "Marianne, do you take Bill as your lawfully wedded husband, to work out your life together however you two see fit?"

"I do." Her voice was filled with conviction.

"And Bill, do you take Marianne as your lawfully wedded wife, with the intention of being her partner in all things needing partnership and otherwise minding your own business?"

"I do," Bill said fervently.

"Then, by the authority vested in me as captain of the *Michael Ventris*—of which for purposes of making this legal I consider you two part of my crew—I pronounce you married. You can kiss each other."

They did, tentatively and very gently.

Simple, but oddly touching. I may even have shed a discreet tear. I find these things easier to admit as I grow older.

At this precise moment the thin, sweet sound of

a flute echoed from the wall of the nearby buttes. We looked at one another in surprise; no one had planned this.

The melody of the distant flute repeated the melody Tony and the others had played earlier, an irreverent but pretty rendition of the march from Mendelssohn's *Midsummer Night's Dream*. The single strand of music seemed to float like cottonwood silk on the still desert air. As it approached we peered into the night, but the torchlight interfered with night vision; besides, our little village was sunk below the ground level, and even in daylight we could have seen only narrow patches of the surrounding dunes.

We felt rather than saw the shadow that passed over the stars. One of the Amalthean's huge, semi-transparent medusa ships was edging across the spangled Milky Way to hang over us, its interior dimly alight with a faint purple glow.

The flute music was close now. Troy and then Redfield emerged from the darkness at the edge of the firelit circle. Redfield was the one playing the flute; he perched himself on a convenient slab of sandstone looking the perfect figure of Pan, bare-limbed and sun-blackened, wearing only a scrap of cloth about his loins. His glossy auburn hair fell over his shoulder and across his chest almost to his thin waist, but despite his rakishness he no longer looked, I thought, quite like a young man. Rather he seemed thin and tough, dried out, almost salt-cured, his eyes burning darkly under black brows. Purple scars striped the sides of his chest, and for a moment I did not recognize them for what they were, his organs of breath under the water.

Nor did Troy look young. She was wearing as little clothing as Redfield and was as dark as he was; her blond hair had been bleached to the color of driftwood by sun and salt, had grown long and fell in a slant across her sinewed, small-breasted chest. In the sides of her chest the gill slits, once hardly noticeable, were pronounced, no doubt developed by constant use; they stood out as parallel purple scars that striped her rib cage, like Redfield's. Overall, her appearance was wild, alien—slightly incongruous with her cheerful smile.

She carried a bundle wrapped in silvery cloth. ''A wedding present,'' she said.

With a liquid flourish of notes Redfield brought his playing to a close. Troy descended the short steps to the sandstone court and laid her bundle on the altar bench. ''For the parents of the first Martian.''

Marianne held back, regarding Troy warily. As for Redfield, she'd hardly glanced at him; I knew she had disliked him since she'd met him.

A tense moment: it had been easy at times for all of us to blame Troy for our fate, or at least to resent her and Redfield for not sharing their program with us. When at last Marianne stepped forward to tug at the silvery wrapping of the bundle on the bench, it was without a smile or a nod of acknowledgment to her unexpected guests.

A set of black chips lay revealed in their nest of soft silver. Marianne studied them a moment, puzzled.

''They're books,'' Troy said. ''Book House Books. For reading to the child. And other books, encyclopedias and so on—a few things not in the *Ventris* library—for parents and friends.''

''Where did you get them?'' Bill asked, and half a beat later said, ''Sorry, I mean, thank you very much. We're grateful.''

''Yes, thank you,'' Marianne murmured, her eyes fixed on the trove. We all knew what she was thinking: if the book chips were loaded to capacity, they might very well contain more than the entire library of the *Ventris*. Books, more than anything else in her involuntary exile, were what Marianne had longed for.

Where did Troy get them? I thought I knew. I had pondered what Jozsef Nagy had told me about his daughter, during our short interview on Ganymede; I knew what she was. She had gotten the library from her own memory.

For a moment the silence threatened to grow awkward. Jo and I started making murmuring, clucking sounds, the content of which, if any, I don't recall. Tony began playing his homemade Synthekord again, producing languid, plangent sounds, halfway between an organ and a bass flute, and a chant-like rhythm that could have been made by Red Indians softly thumping big tom-toms, for all I knew. Angus took up the same rhythm with his strange rattles and sussurating bean-shakers, and Redfield joined in on the melancholy Pan pipes.

Marianne looked up from the books, her green eyes gleaming with tears. Troy watched her with a look pale and knowing. Marianne said, ''Thank you, thank you,'' in a fervent whisper—

—but when she took a step toward Troy, intending perhaps to embrace her, Troy was not where she had been, having translated herself farther back into the shadows in a movement so subtle and flowing I had hardly noticed it.

Redfield, on his feet now, still playing, nodded to the rest of us with glistening eyes and turned, mounting the steps with a springy step worthy of the goat god. A moment later he was gone into the darkness. Perhaps he had deliberately drawn our attention to himself, or perhaps Troy, like a silent desert djinni, was gifted with invisibility, for when we thought to look, she was no longer there.

Then I felt fingers brush my shoulder and turned to find her beside me, beckoning me silently with her eyes. I glanced at the others: they were rapt, listening to the sad, sweet melody of Redfield's flute drifting from the dunes. I backed away from them and followed Troy deeper into the night, among the huts. She was a wraith, a spirit who came and went without warning, and I could not be sure whether the apparition boded well or ill.

''We didn't know if it would work,'' she said

without preamble. Her accent was odd in the still air, the accent of one who, like a person grown slowly deaf, remembers the sound of words through the air but has not heard them that way for a long time. "If it had not worked, there would have been a cataclysm to tear this world to pieces."

"Has it worked?"

Close up, she was as gaunt as a dry ocotillo, a blackened stick that has not flowered since the last rains, who might or might not ever flower again. "We are doing more than rebuilding a world, Professor. We have altered time. We have remade reality."

"These days the others call me plain Forster. If anyone's the professor here, it's your old friend McNeil."

"Awfully informal, Forster. . . ."

"The J, Q, and R don't stand for anything, you know," I was surprised to hear myself admit. "Actually, the honorable parents couldn't agree on a name. Instead they settled on what they hoped would be an imposing string of initials." I had rarely confessed this failure of the progenitive imagination; certainly in recent months I had lost much of my former reserve.

For reply Troy put out her thin, strong right hand and rested it on my arm, and I thought I detected the ghost of a smile when she said, "Little did they know."

Seeing the truth of that, I laughed. What did an imposing string of initials amount to, under present circumstances? "So," I said, "you and your alien friends have given us this whole new world, this whole new history. If we'd been given access . . ."

She cut me short. "What you have not been able to record, no amount of access would have helped you understand. The devices of the aliens are far beyond our grasp." Her mood was mercurial, now lighthearted, now irritable, as if darting about in some multidimensional psi space.

"What do you want to tell me?" I demanded.

"I believe that the success of what we do here will determine whether Earth evolves—as we comprehend that process." Her eyes were like glowing sparks. "If we are to share our solar system with the Amaltheans, we must be sure that they are content to remain here on Mars."

"You do not trust them?"

"I do not understand them."

"This is a fine paradox," I said after a moment's thought. "If Earth evolves as we knew it, presumably *we* will be born. But if we must make Mars an Amalthean Paradise in order to insure that, then the solar system into which we will be born will be a very different place."

"Whether we personally are born into the same cosmos a few billion years from now hardly makes a difference. What makes a difference is whether human beings evolve on Earth."

"Why is that in doubt?" I asked, puzzled by her concern.

"Are we alone here, circling the sun?" she asked, her voice husky with intention. "On Venus, there were Amaltheans who would settle for nothing less than a perfect reproduction of their homeworld. Nemo insinuated himself into their company, as we insinuated ourselves into Thowintha's."

"Perhaps they left Venus, left our solar system, traveled on in search of new worlds. . . ."

"My last sight of Nemo was of him urging them to cut us off," Troy replied. "They seemed readily swayed by his passion."

"Why have you chosen to tell me these things now?" I asked. "For a Martian year you've avoided us."

"Survival," she answered. "For now, at least, Bill and Marianne need to believe that what we and they are building here will last forever. Tony too."

"Angus and Jo . . ."

"They're adaptable. Even so, I've never known them more content."

''And me?''

''You may not realize how much they all still think of you as their leader,'' Troy said.

My reply to that was a derisive snort, which I attempted to muffle, too late.

She smiled. ''You are a changed man, Forster. One might almost think you had learned humility.''

''I say . . .''

''You *are* their leader, whatever you think. I leave it to you to decide how much to tell, and when, and to whom. But I warn you—keep your flock together. At any moment the universe may change.''

Above us, the myriad stars came out again, uncovered by the movement of the hovering medusa. I looked up, and when I looked back to say something more to Troy, she was gone.

Bemused, I rejoined the others. No one remarked on my absence—with all the wine we'd drunk, a brief trip to the bushes was hardly unusual.

Angus put down his cymbals and rattles and pressed a new-filled beaker into my hand. ''Cheer up, friend. There are no ghosts in those sands.''

At that moment, to our astonishment, fireworks began in the heavens. Huge balls of glistening white flame. Streaks of blue and gold. A bright ball of green fire trailing a thin thread of smoke, whiffling audibly overhead as it went.

''Comets again.'' Angus peered at me gravely.

I was agape. ''I thought that was mostly done with.''

''They've steered a few bits into collision courses to give us a show''—Tony greeted the spectacle of the exploding heavens with crescendos of synthesized sound—''All in aid of our celebration.''

The display continued, long after we'd gotten tired of watching it. With all the excitement, it seemed to take Bill and Marianne forever to decide they wanted privacy. At last they slipped off with shy smiles in our direction—to the same domed hut they'd been sharing for years.

As I record this, lying on my own bunk (a little drunk, I confess) and peering into the darkness occasionally lit by the silent flares of wrecked comets in the night sky, I brood upon the future. I resented Troy for not confiding in me. Now I resent her because she did.

01.01.19.17

Marianne and Bill are doing their part. Am I doing mine?

I long regretted that I never learned where the Martian plaque was found. Now I have another reason to regret my ignorance: we cannot put the extensive records we are compiling there to be found with it.

Of course there is no Martian plaque as yet. Likely we humans will have been long buried in the sands of Mars when (and *if*, in this reality) the plaque is crafted. Nor do I have any hope that I personally will return to Venus—to put in place the Venusian tablets I discovered there, recording the languages of Bronze Age Earth. That task will evidently be left to some other man or woman. Or more likely to some nonhuman creature.

01.01.21.04

The display in the sky goes on without stopping. Perhaps we were too ready to think it put there for us. The far horizon is clouded by storms, and lightning plays constantly across the desert; the sea level is rising. . . .

17

The date I recorded this is uncertain. . . .

Troy came to us this evening to invite us to a grand occasion. The first stage of the transformation of Mars was complete, she said: the Amaltheans had seeded an entire world with microorganisms and plants and animals, creatures of the land and sea and air, of the interstices of the rock, and of the crevices deep beneath the surface of the ice. Having seen that the ecology was stable, they had determined to mark it with permanence.

This was a world as congenial to humans as to Amaltheans—although, according to Troy, we neighborly Galactic races were likely to see even less of each other from this time on. Given a choice, the Amaltheans preferred the ocean depths; we, possibly having inherited a tendency to climb the tallest handy tree and peer around (and as our adventure with the paper airplane had confirmed), preferred the heights.

But a new world! A new Crux! A new Earth! A novel *plenum organum!* The Amaltheans, not wholly unlike humans (though in fact they are very unlike humans), planned to observe the occasion by dedicating a memorial. They graciously invited us to attend the ceremony.

Before Troy left, she took me aside again. It would be prudent, she said, if everyone came along together. It would be prudent, in fact, if we stayed together from now on into the foreseeable future. She managed to imply without saying so that it was up to me to shepherd our little flock.

So it was that, when the time came, I had persuaded all but one of my colleagues into joining the expedition. Bill opposed me (as usual) by urging Marianne to stay, but she insisted she would not miss what promised to be an extraordinary sight. And since it was plain that Bill wanted to go, he gave in rather easily; I didn't need to interfere. Only Tony, whose suspicion of the aliens had grown into an obsession with the passage of time, insisted upon staying behind. The best I could do was extract a promise that he would not leave the neighborhood until we returned.

Redfield called for us in a splendidly fringed and tentacled medusa. By now Redfield was only a little less alien to us than the Amaltheans themselves; we treated one another cordially enough, but the chance of renewing our old comradeship was long gone. He accompanied the five of us from our equatorial home to the frigid pole.

In a few hours the medusa covered, by a shorter route, the distance the paper sailplane had taken five days to traverse. From its transparent bubble we saw, piercing the sky above the frozen horizon, the needle-thin bright structure Jo and Tony had described, and soon we were hovering near its snow-drifted base. It was a diamond tower, the gleaming axis of the world, rising a kilometer or more out of the frozen mists and pointing straight up into a whirlpool of clouds overhead.

A dark inverted funnel opened in the milky vortex of the snow-burdened sky above, a tunnel into space, at the top of which a star-strewn patch of dark sky could be seen. The whole formation was apparently motionless—which meant the deep cloud structure was rotating at the same speed as the planet.

Redfield said the clouds were expected to dissipate within a day or two. "It's a cyclone induced by the black hole," he told us, "an artifact of gravitation. They synchronized the hole's spin to the planet's, to eliminate effects on planetary rotation. When it was drawn down out of space, it spun up the atmosphere."

"What *is* this tower, then?" Angus asked. "Some sort of black hole generator?"

"No, just a sort of fancy drill rig," Redfield replied. "The top of a shaft that goes to the center of the planet."

"And I suppose there's an identical drill head at the south pole," Bill said. "For symmetry."

"Of course."

"What keeps the shafts from collapsing?" Angus asked.

"They're cased with synthetic crystalline matter—stronger than the crystal structure of the condensed interior. It's the same stuff the world-ship is made of—harder than diamond and transparent to heat."

"So what's the origin of these black holes? How do the Amaltheans steer them where they want them to go?"

"I wish I knew the answer to that. The holes were made locally, but as to how the aliens handle them . . ." Redfield shrugged. He simply did not understand, he said, how the Amaltheans could alternately wrinkle and smooth the local fabric of spacetime.

We could have asked endless questions about these apparent miracles, but Redfield gently put us off, claiming that in all the years he had had to study Amalthean technology, he had grasped only a few minor practical matters. "Mostly, what not to touch when," he said. His grin briefly reminded me of our old days together. He seemed quite sincere.

The hovering medusa slowly circled the great tower. Fleets of other medusas were arrayed on every side in loose formations, thousands upon thousands of the half-living vessels that had done the work of transforming a world. We came to rest, barely brushing the ground.

Redfield invited us to dismount and inspect the tower more closely. Only Marianne declined; she was far along, and thought it better not to brave the cold. He produced capes of fluffy white material, which we wrapped around our shoulders and clipped to our wrists and ankles. The medusa's tentacles set us down in wind-glazed snow.

Trudging away from beneath the craft, I looked up and gazed directly into the strange cyclone over us, the windless eye of a static hurricane. The air was cold enough to take my breath away.

We walked quickly toward the tower, watching our distorted selves in its mirrored surface, and soon we knew what it was that Redfield had wanted us to see.

There were inscriptions and low-relief sculptures covering the base of the diamond tower, most of them reaching a little higher than human eye level and some of them already drifted with snow— pictures of animals and plants and landforms and machines. And maps, and what appeared to be treatises on geology and biology and mechanics, and philosophical essays, and gossip and graffiti. Much of it was incomprehensible, even at first glance.

We had arrived in front of an oval area, like a kind of appliqué, reminiscent of the ceramicized photographs sometimes found on tombstones on Earth in our era. This one was made of the strange bright metal, however, and applied next to what was certainly a map of our solar system. It was a long text, very finely engraved—

—and it attracted me instantly. It was as if I could read it even before I was close enough to clearly make it out.

. . . *After we left our home we came first to a system in the Black Smoker, whose planets we had believed to be habitable but which proved barren by virtue of the pri-*

*mary's excessive ultraviolet emissions. We journeyed on-
ward, sleeping long, awaking to investigate each star listed
in the Catalogue of Possible Manifestations. None were
suitable, until at last we reached the star designated Plain
Yellow 9436-7815.*

*It was a Manifestation such as might have been created
from our very dreams—a young sun like the primary of
our home with a planet whose size and mass and orbit
were like our home world itself, blessed with a saline ocean,
a quiet geology, and an atmosphere thick in oxygen and
carbon compounds. It was a good-tasting world, a fine-
smelling world. We called it New Home. To our joy, New
Home was without a trace of life, beyond the precursor
molecules common to us all throughout the universe. Thus,
our great work began and long persisted. But we had not
detected the existence of a companion to the primary, a
dead and deadly companion. . . .*

What I once thought of as the language of Culture
X, I now thought of as classical Amalthean—a flexible and musical speech quite unlike the stilted
translations I had once constructed on Earth (for
those were derived inescapably from the human
Bronze Age languages recorded on the so-called Venusian tablets, which for Culture X was the equivalent of the Rosetta stone).

What I read here on the side of the towering
North Pole was a flowing and simple account of the
Amalthean Odyssey, embellished with the sort of
details that might appeal to later generations of
Amaltheans. The words and phrases sounding in
my head were like nothing I had heard or read before, but I knew I had often seen and studied it—
or rather a small part of it. . . .

*It was Thowintha consciousness that infused itself among
us then, and brought us to this least promising place. How
far it was from a Manifestation! Yet life is various and
abundant. How much more abundantly life embraces itself
in the manifestation of an unexpected multitude of forms!
Perfection is mutable. That is Thowintha consciousness.
The designated heralds of future alien life honored us with
their responsive feeling and sharing of consciousness. They*

tasted with us and smelled with us, and with them we tasted the new and the strange. They sang with us; we shared stories of mutual delight. Our vessels flowed outward like a current surging in the sea, and where we went, life arose. Life strange and familiar, life old and new—one arising from the other, the many arising from the few. In Mutation is Manifestation. That is Thowintha consciousness. . . .

I bent closer. My breath frosted the writing and as quickly cleared away, for the diamond tower was warmer than the air. I became aware of Bill beside me, peering at the writing as closely as I was.

"What have you found there, Professor?"

I mumbled something wordless in reply. My mind's eye laid a template over the shining mass of this writing and found within it a rounded irregular shape—imaginary, for no such shape had been contemplated by the makers of this text—a shape consisting of a thousand or so characters stacked a couple of dozen lines high, nesting near a corner of the shining plaque.

Bill gasped. "Is that . . . ?"

"Yes. The Martian plaque."

Other designates are our guests, living happily among themselves in their way, a way hardly comprehensible to us, a way which nevertheless persists and gives occasion for optimism and play. Many plants and animals are not of the Manifestation but of the designates' home, made as they have suggested. We live together on this new home, in intricate cooperation. Thus we have named it: Harmony.

For the way that can be exhaustively understood is not the mutual way. That is Thowintha consciousness. . . .

The Martian plaque. Its translation had been the greatest triumph of my career. "Can you read it, Bill?"

He leaned closer, then shook his head. "I guess I haven't kept up, Professor. Like you have."

"How laughably I misinterpreted what I read!" A fever had taken me; the old fire of academic priority was upon my brow. ''Not that my rivals came any closer to the truth; how could any of us have suspected that the plaque's oft-mentioned 'designates' were *human beings*—a billion years before their time! That one of the designates was *myself?''*

As was Bill, I might have added, but didn't. He chose not to respond to my diatribe, and I read on, eagerly.

In shared joy at the enlivening of this tiny planet, now truly our home world, we who work from the far-flying, half-living vessels have made these story-songs and story-pictures on the axis of the world. Our comrade, our sibling, our great and living ship of Manifestation, imbued with Thowintha consciousness, goes forth from here to seed the clouds of the greatest of the nearby planets with undying half-life. The ship of Manifestation has done its work. Let Thowintha consciousness lapse into long sleep until we shall call upon it again. Meanwhile we remain here. Our comrade's awakening will come in the fullness of waiting at the great world. Then the designates shall reappear. Then the final acts shall be undertaken. Then all will be well.

As I read the plaque's last words I was transfixed by the most extraordinary clash of emotions. Fierce delight at learning the richness of its complete and correct text. A certain amusement at how far afield my well-meaning attempts to reconstruct its meaning had led me.

And fear. Were we really living in an alternate universe, as we had rather complacently decided? Or were we after all living in our own past—a past in which some unimaginable blow would shatter the plaque in front of me, leaving only a single scrap of it to survive into our own era?

Bill peered at me, his nose red with cold, his face innocent of my worries. ''I wonder what could possible smash *that* up?'' he said cheerfully.

I could only shake my head in ignorance.

Jo called from a few meters away. ''Cold's getting to us. We're going back to the medusa.''

Bill pulled his cloak tighter around his shoulders. ''I guess I'll be joining them, sir.''

Sir? He hadn't called me that in a while; something in my manner had touched him. We—all of us—knew one another too well for formality. Or perhaps Troy was more right about my role than I had been willing to admit.

I watched the others trudge through the crusted snow toward the strange ship that waited under the frozen sky, a ship whose graceful swelling membranes and trailing tentacles were forms that had evolved in warm seas—at first glance so weirdly out of place in an arctic landscape, yet grown so familiar to us "Martians" that it seemed no more exotic than a skimobile.

A last look at the mirror-bright Martian plaque . . . perhaps this *was* a different reality, and the plaque would last forever. Or even if it did not escape its fate, perhaps a billion years would pass before the blow fell. Perhaps we happy few humans would never know, would never need to know.

I turned and made my way toward the medusa. Between it and the far horizon fleets of other medusas drifted against the gray clouds, shifting as if on currents of ocean. Beyond them a gray and white sun was rising. . . .

The sun was the world-ship, lifting itself upon columns of white fire. I knew then it was on its way to Jupiter, the Great World, carrying with it Thowintha—"Thowintha consciousness," rather. My brain seethed with questions I knew would never be answered, and some that soon would be. Were Troy and Redfield going with the world-ship, to await the awakening—to be awakened, a billion years from now, by us and themselves? Or were they planning to stay here—join us—grow old and die on Mars? Would they expect to be welcomed among us, who had once been their friends?

Fleets of medusas bobbled and moved aside as the gleaming world-ship approached, an immense convex mirror almost brushing the snow below and curdling the clouds above. I looked up and saw, reflected in the huge mirror, the spectacle around me—the snow and the tower and the massed medusas—but all turned upside down, overwhelmed and overwhelming.

In our own era, some silly would-be linguist once queried, "When you are overwhelmed, where is the whelm you are over, and what exactly does it look like?" He should have stood *here*, I thought. Overwhelmed, you are *under* the whelm—the curling wave of wholeness. Have a good look, while you can.

Hypnotized by these thoughts, and perhaps nearer to being frozen than I knew, I stood immobile, hypnotized by the approach of the world-ship across the polar snows of Mars—

—when the surface of the planet was suddenly wrenched from beneath my feet.

18

Troy had been right to be concerned
for us, but the danger did not come
from any mismanagement of the black
holes. Not directly.

I record this uncounted hours (perhaps weeks?) later, hoping to recall in
rough outline the principal events which drove us
from our home, the second Eden. Yet I must ask
how many paradises the aliens have tried to build
for themselves? And from how many have they
been driven?

The ground shook and I was thrown to the snow
in front of the great tower the Amaltheans had
erected at the north pole of Mars. I felt as if I was
riding an ice flow in a sudden thaw. The frozen
surface beneath me tilted and heaved; I dug my
bare hands into the snow and clung to it for my
life.

Just then, in a flurry of snow, I was snatched
into the air: a tentacle had descended from our medusa, and within seconds it had pulled me into the
aerial machine. But I was thrown down again immediately, this time by sudden acceleration—the
medusa was rising up and away from the tower,
high into the atmosphere, making swiftly for the
oncoming world-ship.

All of us in the medusa—we humans I mean—
had fallen to the floor, but because the whole machine was flexible and transparent our view of the

outside was not cut off. I landed on my back; I could see right up through the clear roof of the vessel. Strangely, I was seeing the ground!

The whole landscape below was reflected in the vast mirror of the world-ship looming above. It was a landscape in upheaval, with waves like ocean swells traveling across the snowy plains to crash against the base of the tower in torrents of white surf. Gouts of steam erupted in rows across the snow like the impacts of machine-gun bullets; they collapsed almost as suddenly into pits like bullet holes, but big as volcanoes. Far off, a long fissure split the plains, exploded with steam, then filled with fountains of lava that glowed dull orange against the bleak waste.

When enormous, perfectly round voids opened in the landscape (I had to remind myself that it was, after all, only a *reflection*) I was slow to recognize the world-ship's locks spiraling open. On every side the great fleets of medusas, assembled about the north pole in the tens of thousands, were streaming toward the open ports.

''What's happening?'' somebody next to me— Angus, I think—croaked in a ghastly half whisper.

''We're under attack,'' said a voice I recognized as Redfield's.

''Who . . . ?'' Angus said.

''The *Doppelgangers.*''

It took me longer than it should have to comprehend Redfield's remark. Meanwhile our medusa flew swiftly toward the nearest lock and crowded into it, jostling skin to skin with the nearest other medusas.

Acceleration abruptly ceased. The huge lock was filled with shimmering medusas, close-packed as fish eggs. As the skin of the lock healed itself and the wintry sunlight was cut off, to be replaced by the world-ship's ubiquitous inner blue glow, water rushed into the lock and we were submerged in the primal sac.

Where we stood in our pressurized bubble, our

tailored microenvironment, the air was cool and fresh—maintained by the osmotic controls of a living machine that was able to sense our needs. What the machine could not do was overcome the strange, intensely queasy sensation induced in us by the proximity of numerous spacetime-warping nodes in the other medusas that crammed the lock. To take a step was to pass through subtly shifting gravitational fields.

The medusas began to move past us, jostling and sliding over one another, letting themselves be sucked into the interior of the great ship. Poor Marianne became violently ill. She began to groan, then cry out. Jo and Angus crawled to her aid; Bill struggled to reach her. I was late coming out of my nausea, and by then she needed air more than she needed another useless onlooker.

Just then we felt the universe move again, massively—the world-ship itself was accelerating.

"Where are we going?" Jo demanded of Redfield; she was the first to ask the urgent question.

"To pick up Tony. Then away from Mars."

"She can't take it. She's in contraction."

Marianne was writhing in pain. Sweat stood out on her pale forehead.

"I'll do what I can," he said. But he made no immediate move, and never had he sounded more detached.

Marianne's crisis was at its peak when the world-ship lurched again. The great lock had emptied of medusas; its dome now spiraled open. Our own medusa shot into the sky. . . .

In retrospect I suppose our medusa floated free with as much tenderness as it could manage—balancing what was, in human terms, a cold equation: urgency versus pity, the fate of all against the fate of one—or two. For Marianne was giving birth prematurely.

We were over our little settlement beside the sea. The medusa coursed swiftly back and forth over the buttes and dunes, but Tony was not to be seen. The sailplane was gone.

Redfield had disappeared into the lower parts of the hull; I could see his vague outline as he swam through the watery spaces below, conversing in streams of thin bubbles with the tentacled creatures who presumably were the crew of our vessel. Shortly he reemerged into our sector, his long hair streaming with water. "We must go back."

"Not without Tony," Angus roared. "I won't let him die."

"We can't stay. *All* of us will die."

Angus lunged at Redfield, who did something to him, so swiftly I could not see it—and Angus cried out and fell to his knees. I am ashamed to confess that I was paralyzed with indecision. Redfield stepped away from Angus, and in the same moment Jo made the decision for us: "No fighting. Save who you can, Redfield. But please save Marianne and her baby."

He went away again, and by the time he came back the medusa was inside the world-ship and the world-ship had begun to move. And by then it was too late for the baby.

"Oh *why?*" Jo cried out as the grief washed over her. Beneath her comforting hands, Marianne was unconscious, lying in a pool of blood, and Bill was near shock, cradling a bloody child who was hardly bigger than his own hands.

"I'm sorry," Redfield said flatly. I looked for any hint of emotion in him and saw none. He knelt beside Marianne, checking her pulse, looking into her eyes. "It's not too late for her." It was a clinical judgment, devoid of feeling.

"Are we being taken to Jupiter?" I asked. "Are they planning to freeze us in the ice with you?"

"I don't know where we're going."

"The plaque," I said. "It clearly states that the world-ship will wait at the Great World . . . until the Awakening."

"I don't know where we're going," he repeated

coldly. "Ellen and I were committed to Mars. We were planning to stay."

"What's happening outside?" Angus whispered. I could hardly hear his hoarse whisper.

"The world-ship's double," Redfield said. "It was spotted minutes ago, inbound from Jupiter. Just as on Venus. It's tearing up the work they've done, trying to remove the singularities they've implanted." Redfield's glance flickered past me and the others, lingering upon Marianne. He said, "We'll have to go into the water."

Bill looked away from his wife. "What will happen to . . . ?" His voice was hardly a whisper; it was the first thing he'd said since we were snatched from the surface.

"She'll be fine once she's in the water. I'm sorry about . . . the others."

"Are none of us to be allowed our preferences?" I was startled by my own anger.

Redfield recoiled, surprised and defensive. "Groves made *his* choice. He promised to stay until we returned—instead he deliberately flew away. He could see what was happening."

"He prefers to die a free man," Angus said.

"Pardon my presumption, but *you* want to live, don't you?"

"You were our friend, Blake," Angus said heavily. "We've seen too little of you."

"Within a year Mars will be a freezing, uninhabitable waste—everything we've striven for destroyed. But do what you think best." Redfield's face was a dark and expressionless mask. "The Amaltheans will come for you soon. Perhaps there's still time to drop you off. Tell them your decision." He turned away, his long black hair swinging behind him; I saw the gill-slits along his ribs flare as he descended into the watery depths of the medusa.

Moments later the floor membrane heaved and the mucous-protected mantle of one of the Amaltheans emerged into our air-filled space. A chorus of voices seemed to issue from the walls as the alien spoke: *You must tell us now. Shall we place you in the water?*

We all looked to Jo, letting her speak for us.

"Yes."

"What then?" Jozsef asks, appalled. The fire has burned low, and the misty night sky seems to glow with phosphorescence outside the tall windows of the dark, empty library.

"Why then, we drowned," Forster says quietly. "We went gently into that dark and fluid good night, taking only our fears and sorrows with us. We had no hope of a morning to come."

"And Mars?" the commander whispers, his voice as dry as the Martian winds.

"Oh yes, of Mars I dreamed most vividly. Now these visions must have been based on informed imagination—this is what I tell myself—but later the rough truth of it was confirmed. . . .

"I dreamed I saw the planet bulge, that the immense Tharsis plateau, which had not previously existed on Mars, now heaved up and burst into gouts of flame and smoke along great seams, that through its gigantic volcanoes the planet hemorrhaged and poured out thick magmatic blood, into heaps so vast in extent—a lava flow that could have covered northwestern Africa—that they caused a severe gravitational anomaly which persists into our own era.

"Somewhere deep within the planet's surface, submicroscopic black holes were stirring and wandering. Eventually they tore their way out of the planet's heart, dragged by some competing force that grew stronger by the second.

"I dreamed that the shining polar tower I had studied so recently suddenly splintered and vanished, partly vaporized, partly scattered as dust and debris high into the still-thick atmosphere. Most of the debris was sucked right out into space. Glittering motes of it settled back into the churning snow, all of them but one—that fragment we call the Martian plaque—to be lost forever. The black holes had escaped, destroying the devices that controlled them; they constituted perhaps the only force in the universe that could have destroyed those indestructible objects.

"The skies themselves flashed into a roof of rolling flame.

"I saw the sudden end of our settlement. Our gardens and orchards were no more than a quick puff of ashy smoke on a hurricane wind. Our concrete domes were baked to the color of bronze; our glass windows slickened to greasy blue before they shattered; nets of iron reinforcing bar stood naked when the concrete shells they had supported turned to powder and dropped away, and only a moment passed before they too melted and the iron puddled in the arid dust.

"The *Michael Ventris*, with our little Manta submarine still in its belly, was shattered by the explosion of its fuel tanks, and the wreckage was strewn upon the sands, then swallowed forever in a flood of lava that swept down from the highlands and obliterated the last sign that humans had ever walked those buttes and hills.

"I saw poor Tony's paper airplane blown across heaving deserts, climbing higher on fountains of superheated air until finally it was ignited by lightning and its tattered scraps swallowed in the black anvil of a thunderhead.

"The meandering oceans boiled. I heard the dying agonies of countless millions of creatures. Forests exploded. Birds fell flaming from the skies.

"We fled Mars on a swerving course, pursued by our double. My dreaming brain plotted the path of evasive action. We plowed through flights of oncoming asteroids and comets, shattering some, smashing others into new orbits. Mars acquired moons—broken, blackened, retrograde moons.

"Not for the first time I wondered what interference in the continuum of matter or fields would constitute the 'reduction of the wave function' we dreaded. Our world-ship and the other could simultaneously inhabit spacetime, it seemed, perhaps even communicate, so long as we did not inhabit the same local region of spacetime. But where were the boundaries of sameness of locality? What made our doubles think that *they* would be the ones to survive an encounter?

"Perhaps they had no such confidence. Perhaps they did not care whether they lived or died. Who could say what evil genius now influenced their acts? But their purpose was plainly to destroy. The alien inhabitants of our own world-ship, however, remote as they might be from human affairs, were nevertheless passionately committed to life; tact and judgment and hope dictated that *we* must be the ones to flee.

"We humans slept in the waters. In my dreams the red-gold planet Mars receded, like a golden apple of paradise now lost to us forever."

Forster falls silent. A brief sputter of flame is the only sound of the room; black shadows swell and waver upon the ceiling.

Ari, uncharacteristically reticent, asks, "My daughter? What of her?"

Forster smiles. "My acquaintance with her, so recently renewed, was to be elaborated under circumstances more intimate—and more peculiar—than any I had yet imagined."

19

Drowned again, I dreamed a while.

I heard a whispered voice close beside me. "You wanted to be privy to our plans." It was Troy, bringing me out of the waters into the air-filled bubble of a medusa.

"What about the others?"

"Better to let them sleep. We woke you to witness a crucial event. Whatever happens, win or lose, you are here to record it."

The medusa floated out of the world-ship's open lock. The setting was familiar: a night sky smudged with hazy lines among the stars. I took them for comets. . . .

"Life on Venus was destroyed by a natural greenhouse, primed by periodic cometary bombardment," Troy told me. "On Mars, our efforts to *start* a greenhouse with the help of cometary ice were frustrated by the traditionalists whom we fled on Venus, those who follow the Mandate. Only one terrestrial planet remains. Thowintha's group—the adaptationists—have left it undisturbed."

"Why?"

"Because it possesses indigenous life forms."

"Because you have persuaded them, I think."

She did not answer. Troy is, I think, the best liar I have ever known; she does it by telling only the truth. She was concealing something from me, so obviously I think she meant me to guess at it, but she was too subtle; I have never been able to decide what she wanted me to know.

"Both factions were in doubt," she pronounced, as if lecturing. "Had the organisms that were known to inhabit the seas of Earth—and known to resemble Amalthean lifeforms in startling ways, particularly the primitive forms like medusas and krill and such—accidentally been sown there by the Amaltheans themselves during their earliest survey of our solar system, or were these creatures already present, their resemblance merely chance, examples of convergent evolution?

"Whatever the answer, our adaptationist friends felt that evolution on Earth should be allowed to proceed unchecked. There is no inevitable outcome to any evolutionary contingency. Looking back, evolution is history, a very particular history with innumerable branch points, always obeying laws of physics and probability but, in its particulars, ruled only by chance.

"Earth's dark companion, the singularity called Nemesis, is an agent of that chance. Every twenty-six million years it sends comets hurtling toward the sun. Often one or more of them strike Earth—radically altering its environment, extinguishing some species, allowing others to move into new niches from which their daughter species evolve even further.

"We have come to Earth to ward off a black contingency. We have seen the traditionalists—Amaltheans who clung to their Mandate religiously and abhorred and rejected adaptation to any pre-existing ecology—deliberately destroy our work on Mars. By their own belief they should have moved onward, seeking another star; in losing Venus they lost their only chance to fulfill the Mandate in *this* solar system. But perhaps they have shied from the awful prospect of another billion-year odyssey. Certainly they have chosen to regard our friends as heretics—and they have stayed behind to eradicate us all, Amaltheans and humans alike.

"To destroy humanity it is sufficient to alter evolution on Earth. The simplest way to do that is to alter the pattern of comet impacts caused by Nemesis. The Whirlpool."

"Where are we?" I asked her. "*When* are we?"

"The final moments of the Cretaceous," she said.

The time of the most famous of all cometary impacts . . .

Our medusa emerged from night into daylight. Soon we were floating low over the Earth's globe. Its seas and continents were rather differently arranged then, but I guessed that we were in mid-North America. The rolling plains of what would be Montana looked much as central China or eastern Oregon does in our era.

I knew that a warm, shallow sea had covered the region a couple of million years earlier and had since retreated south and east. Now, lazy rivers drained the plain. To the west, the Rocky Mountains were nothing but low volcanic hills, airy uplands covered with pines and desert shrubs. The swampy lowlands sprouted ferny forests of bald cyprus and metasequoia—a dark and feathery tree called dawn redwood, which was thought to be extinct in the 20th century until a few specimens were found in a Chinese temple garden. Along the gravel levies of the braided riverbanks the forest was semitropical, a tangle of flowering plants and hardwoods, huge sycamores, persimmons, *kadsuras*, palms, magnolias. . . .

Where we could do so—without risk of disturbing anything but the lightest draft of air (for while there must be a limit to the delicacy of perturbations that can alter whole evolutionary pathways, we did not want to approach that limit even distantly)—we came within a few centimeters of the swamp. We observed frogs and turtles splashing in the shallows, hunted by immense, horrific crocodiles. Lizards scurried through the woods, and boa constrictors slid along the tree branches.

Oh and there were dinosaurs! Herbivorous *Tricer-*

atops, horned and frilled, built like a battle tank; *Tyrannosaurus*, that awesome carnivore, fifteen meters of teeth and tail balanced on two legs (and with a brain more adequate than most people think).

We found what we were most anxious to find: mammals, managing to scratch out a living. Some of them would look quite familiar today, including our own ancestors, tiny shrew-like creatures, and others such as opossums who have changed little in millions of years—while others would seem odd indeed.

Condylarths in particular. They were square-nosed creatures about the size of fox terriers, with clumpy, five-hooved feet and square teeth capable of grinding up vegetation; we were delighted to see a herd of them, for they were the ancestors of all hooved placental mammals—horses, cows, hippopotamuses, elephants. . . .

It was across the skies of this teeming Eden that we expected the fatal (and vital) comet to approach, a streak of pale light that could hardly be apprehended until the very end, when—the likeliest scenario, though no human before us had been there to confirm it—it would pierce the ocean at a velocity of some ninety thousand kilometers per hour, releasing a hundred million megatons of energy to raise tidal waves eight kilometers high, to bowl over dinosaurs and blow down forests everywhere, to punch a hole through the atmosphere and spew a quadrillion tons of liquified and vaporized matter—its own stuff mixed with the Earth's—into the highest regions of air . . . some even into orbit, where it would hang for months to blacken the sun.

But upon our return to the world-ship we learned there was no evidence of what we had most hoped to find. The ship's systems had calculated the vectors of all visible comets in the swarm then converging upon the inner solar system. None were on a collision course with Earth.

Our conversation paused—Troy was there with

me, Redfield was there—while I strived to appreciate our uncertainty. . . .

If no comet were to hit the Earth at the end of the Cretaceous, it would be a different world indeed. What was to prevent some smart descendant of the dinosaurs from assuming the position we smart descendants of apes held so proudly?

But how was one to interpret the absence of the dinosaur-killing comet—as a sign of interference on the part of Amalthean traditionalists? Had they been here before us? Or was the true natural history of the solar system here revealed? If this were the true course of history, with no interference from outsiders, what was to be done?

Troy waited until I had a grasp on our fine ethical dilemma, then made hash of my indecision.

"I have conferred with Thowintha. We picked the likeliest candidate. It had the right size—nine kilometers on the semimajor axis—and its orbit is highly unstable. Clearly it has recently been perturbed, whether deliberately or by chance."

"You think Nemo has persuaded them to perturb it?" It was, I believe, the excuse she wanted me to grasp.

"It will take only the barest nudge from our world-ship to send it straight into Earth."

That was the only moment during our discussion when I indulged myself in irony. "You seem to have made great efforts to insure that history would live up to its prior billing," I said.

She went ahead and did what she had intended to do all along.

Later, she told me what happened. "The comet nucleus struck the Caribbean plate—as knowledge from our era confirmed. That sort of accuracy was utterly beyond our control. We would have been happy had it hit anywhere in the North Atlantic." She smiled at me, a smile I had learned to be leery of. "The mathematics of macroscopic quantum theory is intriguing, but in the final analysis there is only one reality, Forster my friend. Since it presently includes us, history will surely have provided for our evolution—whatever course we or the Amaltheans take."

"Certainly it has done so," I replied, "at least until now."

Troy inclined her head microscopically. "Just so." She held her smile, although it had grown thin and faint, and I thought she showed her age at that moment, even as I was beginning to. "With or without quantum theory, there is no way of predicting the future," she said. "Even in principle. The future will have changed by the time we get there."

PART
4

THE MIRROR
OF APHRODITE

20

This time, when I woke up, the medusa was flying a few feet from the planet's surface. Had they drowned me again? My skin was white and wrinkled, but I was warm and dry and breathing surpassingly sweet air; I could actually identify the aroma of thyme and oregano. Hot sunlight poured through the medusa's clear canopy. I wiggled my fingers and toes and stretched my limbs. Delicious!

Gravity seemed Earth normal, or close to it; I was shaky, but I didn't seem wasted or weak, as I had upon being revived from the previous drowning session. I had been under only a short while, or else something had been at work to restore me to good physical condition. Still, I was in no hurry to sit up. I studied what I could see of the view, reflected in the glassy curve of the canopy over my head.

The craft was skimming foam-edged blue wavetops at what was, for a medusa, a moderate pace, gliding toward the towering clouds and sunlit gray peaks of the sea-girt peninsula or island. I saw living shapes in the reflected water, and with delight I recognized them for what they were—we were so near the waves that sleek dolphins paced us, leaping and curving through the transparent water, sparkling wetly in the sun.

In my confused state it took me a long time to

notice that a man and woman were standing beside me. I sat up at last. I noted first their physical appearance, and especially their very long hair—hers a tarnished gold, his a kind of blackened bronze—intricately braided and bound up on their heads. They wore robes of some loose and snowy white material, draped with negligent elegance over their bare limbs.

Troy and Redfield, standing tense and watchful as the medusa approached the shore, resembled nothing so much as archaic statues of the kind once thought to represent Persephone and Apollo. They were perfect Greek *kore* and *kouros*.

I found that I was wearing the same sort of garment. I felt my head and discovered that I had been provided with a hat, a wide-brimmed floppy thing made of felt, almost like a sombrero. Under it, I found that my own hair, of a rather lusterless pale color (some have called it "gingery") had apparently grown very long after my last stay in the drowning chamber, and someone had gone to the trouble of carefully braiding it into a fashionable Bronze Age arrangement.

"Hello, Forster." Troy had seen that I was awake.

"Where are the others?" I asked. The question had become a habit with me.

"Still asleep. This time we need your knowledge of languages."

"Where are we?"

"Ahead of us are the mountains of eastern Crete. If we've timed things correctly, the time should be about three centuries after the decline of the Mycenaeans."

I counted centuries. "Then it's the Dark Ages. The Dorians will have overrun the place. Is my . . . ?" I groped for my translator and immediately discovered that I had no pockets. But I did have a pouch—it seemed to be made of leather—and inside it was my precious translator and vocal synthesizer. Not that the machine could understand an unknown tongue, of course, but properly programmed, it was an essential aid to communication. ''Why in the world do we want to talk to Dorians?'' I asked—exhibiting a bit of snobbery, I'm ashamed to confess.

''We're not particularly interested in Greeks, of whatever tribe. It's just that we needed a period when we had some hope of understanding *some* language. Or at least of *you* understanding a language,'' she said. ''On this trip we're looking for Eteocretans.''

''Natives of Crete!''

''They still inhabit strongholds in these mountains. Presumably they still speak the lost language.''

It was my turn to raise a brow. ''And we are here . . . ?''

''To record it and decipher it.'' She smiled. ''Here's your chance to do what your hero, Michael Ventris, never had the chance to do. He solved Linear B; you can solve Linear A.''

I thought about that stunning possibility a moment—a daunting prospect. But my first words on the subject were not precisely humble: ''Well, of course I am better qualified than the only other candidate,'' I said, getting slowly to my feet and peering dubiously at my chiton, which came only to mid-thigh. ''I don't believe Bill Hawkins went in much for Minoan studies.''

''Don't be modest, Forster,'' said Redfield. ''You're our expert on the Bronze Age.''

I left off mourning my bony knees and faced the man and woman before me. They were golden creatures, if a bit weathered. ''Delighted as I am to be here, I'm inclined to ask why this trip is necessary. What urgent connection do these philological studies have with our program?''

Her smile was distant. ''You will see the connection soon enough.''

The medusa had entered a wide blue gulf edged with a curving strip of tawny sand, broken by eroded headlands. We were flying south, just high enough to see across the narrow isthmus ahead, a neck of land that connected two parts of the great island that extended to our right and left. To the west a mass of mountains rose from hills carved with cultivated terraces; another block presented itself in sheer cliffs to the east.

The medusa gained a few meters of altitude and veered to the left, eastward, entering a smaller, satellite bay, where a trickle of creek bisected a wide beach. We passed low over the masts of half a dozen fishing boats and one graceful fifty-oared ship just putting ashore. The surprised men aboard stared up at us in undisguised alarm.

We crossed the beach and proceeded inland above thorny wild scrub and isolated groves of silvery olive trees. Flocks of goats were startled into flight as our shadow crossed over them. At the foot of the mountains we slowed and began to climb.

Before us rose sheer mountains of gray limestone riven by breathtaking vertical gorges, their lower slopes terraced in grapevines and corn (what the North Americans call wheat). Straight ahead of us stood a spire of rock perhaps seven hundred meters high, upon which one could discern threads of smoke and the flat roofs of houses built into the stone, like the Hopi villages on the mesas of the American Southwest. Immediately beneath us was a village on a high hill, fallen into ruin.

"I know this place," I said. "This is *Vronda*." Thunder Hill. It was the modern Greek name for the abandoned village, halfway up the mountainside; in our era the spire of rock that towers above it is known as the Kastro, the Castle. "Why don't we land up there, where the people are?"

"We don't want to startle them into attacking us." She touched my arm. "We brought you here without asking. This first stage could be tricky. You don't have to go with us right away."

I saw her hot eyes, set in a seamed and sunburned face. What could I say? I was a xeno-archaeologist, but first of all an archaeologist—and a philologist. This was the sort of experience I had consigned to unrealizable fantasy; what in fact I had *lived* for, if only in imagination. I had named our exploratory ship *Michael Ventris* after the man who had deciphered Minoan Linear B, who had proved that the script was indeed Greek; all my work—before an accident of history had removed me from my own space and time—had drawn its inspiration from Ventris. What would *he* have given for this chance?

"Let us go to meet them together," I said.

The medusa put us down on red soil studded with boulders of pitted limestone. The conical roofs of low round tombs pressed upon the borders of the abandoned village, where piles of gray stone marked collapsed houses. Stalks of purple asphodel drooped in the fields, past their first bloom; thus I knew the season was late spring.

We walked uphill, following a road that skirted the village. The shimmering medusa followed at a discreet distance, hovering incongruously a meter or so above the dry weeds and bright wildflowers. I stubbed my toe viciously within the first few meters, suppressing a curse, and thereafter walked with a limp that I tried to hide from my companions.

We had walked perhaps half a kilometer before we saw people hurrying down the mountain to meet us—at least a dozen nervous young men with oiled black hair, tall, broad-shouldered and narrow-waisted, brown as raisins and naked except for tight loinstraps around their middles. They carried long shields of cowhide and brandished iron-tipped spears. Behind the men were others, women and children, who seemed shy of us. I could not see them well.

I was impressed by the discipline of these young men—they stood firm in the face of a sight that what would have terrified me, a 21st-century Englishman! For as harmless as Troy and Redfield and

I might have appeared in person, we were backed by the apparition of the medusa, bigger than a bireme, shimmering in midair. Then I reflected that to these people the miraculous was, if not routine, at least real.

They shouted at us, something incomprehensible. I replied in Greek, the language of their enemies.

What else could I do? Greek was the only language we could possibly share—although classical Greek (and who is sure of *its* pronunciation?) was no more like the Doric of their time than demotic is like the language of the New Testament. (To tell the truth, for all my supposed expertise, it had been decades since I had studied *any* language without the aid of electronics.)

I had said, "*Eimaste fili sas*," which I hoped meant, "We are your friends." And meanwhile I fiddled desperately with my translator.

My words had no noticeable effect on the armed young men, whose spears were tilted at a uniform angle in our direction. Clearly they had not understood me, and they were becoming increasingly tense. There was movement behind them; one of them glanced backward and said something, and there was a sudden hurried scuffle aside. The soldiers hastily transferred their weapons to their left hands and struck their foreheads with their right fists, arching their backs in exaggerrated poses of attention.

Through the gap in their ranks a woman stepped toward us. She was perhaps thirty years old, a natural beauty but heavily made-up: her green eyes were boldly shadowed and outlined, her full lips reddened, her high-boned cheeks rouged. Her dress was of fine wool dyed in reds and yellows, with short sleeves and a flounced skirt—it was a costume familiar from the statuettes and seal impressions and frescos of an earlier age, most striking in that it left her breasts bare. Her sleek black hair was in ringlets, and on her head was a tiara of flat gold that looked very ancient.

"*Poia eiste? Apo pou?*" she demanded in a voice ringing with authority. Her accent was strange indeed, filled with sibilance and hard vowels, but the words were simple Greek, and plain enough: "Who are you? From where?"

She had not addressed me, however. Her words and her attention were directed wholly at Troy.

"*Apo 'ouranos kai 'thalassa,*" said Troy, in a voice remarkably like the woman's own. "From heaven and the sea."

At that I must have gaped a bit, and not just at the bad grammar, for Troy whispered harshly at me, "Be prepared to do your bit. And don't flinch when Blake does his."

"*Eiste i Aphrodite? Eiste o Posidon?*" The woman's voice was full of skepticism bordering on scorn.

"*Nai, eimaste,*" said Troy firmly, just as Redfield thrust out both his hands and lofted something small and silvery into the air over the heads of the little party who faced us—as if tossing coins.

First to the left and then to the right the morning sky was ripped by flashes of lightning, followed instantly by ear-splitting crashes and searing pyrotechnic screams. Despite Troy's warning, I flinched. Indeed, without her firm grip on my arm I might have flung myself upon the ground. Which was no pose for a god—the role we had undertaken to play.

No matter. None of the Eteocretans noticed my behavior. All but their priestess (she was clearly that) had wheeled to face the new threat behind and beside them. Despite their terror, they shouted as bravely as they could and brandished their spears at the sky.

A diffuse shadow moved over the ground from behind us, and I guessed that our medusa had come up to hover closer above us. The priestess lifted her eyes to it, studied the thing for a long moment, then lowered her gaze to Troy. "*I Aphrodite,*" she said dryly, and raised both arms over her head. She shifted her attention to Redfield, and moved minimally in his direction. *"O Posidon."* Then she glanced at me. *"Kai . . . ?"*

"O Ermes," Troy said. She glanced at me. "What's the word for messenger?"

"Try *mandatophoros,"* I whispered, bemused. Perhaps Troy was persuasive as "the Aphrodite," the Foam-Born, and Redfield convincing as "the Poseidon," the Earth-Shaker, but I found it difficult to picture myself as the winged-sandaled Hermes, Messenger of the Gods.

"O Ermes enai mandatophoros mas," Troy said loudly.

The priestess looked at me sidelong and said, *"O Ermes"*—was that a wince?—then lowered her arms, rather hastily I thought, and turned back to Troy. *"Emai i Diktynna."*

Troy immediately raised her own arms. I hastily followed suit, and Redfield was even quicker than I. *"I Diktynna,"* said Troy, and lowered her arms slowly. Redfield and I repeated the name, or title— *"I Diktynna"*—and did as Troy had done.

This tribute evidently placated the Diktynna, for she graced us with a cautious smile. Then, in strange and rapid Greek that I could barely follow, she addressed me. I consulted my translator. After a long moment it spoke—and I realized she had invited us to dinner.

A further difficult exchange of sentences established that dinner was to be atop the seven-hundred-meter spire of rock that thrust out of the mountain before us. My long-unexercised legs, already wobbling after the short walk from our landing place, wobbled more severely at the mere thought of an hour of climbing to come.

"Offer her a lift in the medusa," said Troy. "Make it sound good."

I did my best with the translator, using lavish (and I hoped understandable) references to the comforts of our heavenly chariot. After much discussion among Diktynna and her escorts, the Cretan priestess—a woman of curiosity and evident intelligence—accepted our invitation with great dignity . . . and with barely disguised excitement.

The medusa took us aboard and instantly lifted us into the air. In the translucent cells below the observation chamber moved the shadows of its fishy alien crew. What would Diktynna possibly make of them?

Ahead were pine-clad mountains riven by a vertical gash, a deep ravine through which poured a crystal stream. We climbed toward the steeply rising cliffs. From terraced vineyards and gardens a few women and young children looked up at us gape-mouthed as we passed over them; men and boys watched us from the precipitous goat pastures above.

Then we were soaring straight up the crag beside the deepest of the shadow-filled ravines, to the falcon's eyrie upon which perched the living village—its houses barely distinguishable from the dark rock, were it not for a dozen fragrant threads of woodsmoke that rose from its stepped crest.

Far below us I saw the blue gulf (its name in our era was Mirabello) studded with graceful ships and caiques, and the strips of wagon road that followed the coast to the east and across the narrow isthmus to the south. White towns stood out on a few hilltops, but even whiter were the bones of long-abandoned Minoan villas, moldering among olive groves and vineyards and cornfields gone to wildflower.

Diktynna stood upright in the observation dome of the medusa as it lifted us ever higher into the clear island air. She maintained a stern and bright-eyed demeanor, superbly aloof from her extraordinary circumstances.

What passed through her mind? She spoke Greek, a form I suspected was closer to Mycenaean than Doric, and surely she was familiar with Mycenaean beliefs. The Mycenaeans worshipped Poseidon, even Hermes, and Aphrodite as well, who was a manifestation of the Great Goddess.

But on Crete, Diktynna was the Great Goddess herself, a deity of trees and mountain peaks and wild animals. Although the woman with us was no more supernatural than we were, she was holy. Thus the name of the goddess was a title; it had come down to her, I was sure, from the great Minoan civilization which had been crushed by earthquake and volcanic eruption . . . and corrupted by the invasion of foreigners.

21

Night and fire.

In the flaring light of rude clay lamps the rough walls were even harder to distinguish from the weathered rock of the pinnacle upon which the village perched. The stars and a gibbous moon in the velvet heavens above us were as bright as the stars of our lost home on Mars. Somewhere out of sight, over the rooftops, hovered the medusa, our sky-borne chariot.

The Diktynna had managed to disappear shortly after we landed upon the rock, but her villagers had taken good care of us since. While the sun was still above Mount Dikte to the west they brought sheep down from the pastures and slaughtered lambs for us on a killing floor at the edge of the cliff. The carcasses now roasted on spits; the entrails, cleaned and stuffed with wild greens, boiled merrily in water jars set upon piles of coals. We were seated outdoors (no inner room could possibly have accomodated all who insisted upon seeing us) on benches covered with rugs of tightly-woven wool, dyed red and blue and embroidered with flowers and birds. Soon (its rich aroma had long advertised it) hot bread emerged steaming from beehive ovens, and from giant storage jars came handfuls of black olives shining with oil, and chunks of strong white cheese dripping with whey, and wine by the jugful, strong and young and tasting of herbs.

Wide-eyed children brought us these things in clay bowls and stood close in front of us, peering at us as we ate. I could almost hear their thoughts: ''Do the gods eat thus? With fingers and lips and teeth and tongues? Exactly like our parents!'' Old men thrust especially tasty morsels at us, which we consumed with much lip-smacking and nods of pleasure, and old women pressed us with fragments of oozing honeycomb, watching us as avidly as their children.

At first I understood not a word of what was said to us, except when some oldster, stating the obvious, essayed the Greek word for ''bread'' or ''meat'' or ''wine.'' But even without my translator we communicated: they made us understand we were the best entertainment they had had for a long time, a grand excuse for a party. I entered what words I could catch into the machine, all the while questioning our hosts closely for equivalents, and thus began assembling a primitive vocabulary of a tongue of which I had previously seen only a few fragments and a single skimpy example, long ago.

At last, to the evident disappointment of our hosts, we could eat no more; soon thereafter, musical instruments appeared. An old man struck a lyre made of horn and tortoise shell, strung with gut, and someone else shook a rattle much like an Egyptian sistrum, and two young men pounded vigorously on drums made of polished cedar wood stretched with spotted hide. After the rhythm section had gotten well started we heard the sound of a flute, skirling dizzily above the hiss and thump of the rattles and drums.

A shaft of yellow light fell into the little *plateia*, one edge of which was a cliff. A curtain had been moved aside in a nearby house, and in the backlit rectangle of the doorway an adolescent boy appeared. He held a double wooden flute to his lips, and his fingers did a rapid dance on the stops.

We had not met this boy before. Perhaps fifteen years old, he was slender, black-haired, and wild-eyed—a beautiful creature, clad simply in a brief linen loincloth, with a golden dagger at his belt. The people of the village seemed to be fascinated by him, and watched him with respect. For a moment he stood rimmed in the light from the doorway, enjoying their attention; then, without interrupting his playing, he moved to join the other musicians. An urgent memory took me, as I recalled Redfield coming out of the darkness on Mars, playing his reed flute to celebrate the wedding of Bill and Marianne; Redfield and the boy were well matched, each as wild and dangerous as the other.

From the same house, which I knew must be the shrine of the Goddess, four young women now emerged. Although none of the other village women we had seen affected this style, they wore flounced skirts and open bodices like Diktynna's, echoes of the ancient civilization. The women linked arms and began to dance, while the musicians played even more energetically.

The music, rapid and piercing but pitched true, spilled out in sinuous rills. It was like nothing I had heard before. At the same time it hinted teasingly at the music of half a dozen Middle Eastern cultures of our era—at once restless, tireless, hypnotic, provocative, rococo.

The music slowed. The women were suddenly joined by four young men in the minimal ancient costume that, it seemed, ritual demanded—embossed leather straps like codpieces, and not much more. The men and women held hands and formed a circle, and for a few minutes did an intricate and stately dance together. Painted eyes flashed, red lips smiled, black ringlets flew.

Memory teased me: there was a passage in the *Iliad* . . . but I could not bring it to mind. After all,

this was not some high ceremony from the age of
the great palaces; this was a simple village dance.

The tempo picked up again, and shortly the
women ran off. Someone tossed a leather ball into
the circle of men, who caught it with laughter and
shouts and began throwing it back and forth. Their
feats of spinning and leaping, of balance and
sleight-of-hand—even if they seemed more impressive than they really were, in the tricky light—were
a dazzling, well-practiced routine.

Now memory pressed upon me more strongly:
this was not a scene from the *Iliad* but was straight
from the *Odyssey*. During Odysseus's visit to the
Phaeacians he had been entertained by ball-playing
young men who "moved in their dance on the
bountiful earth, while the other youths stood at the
ringside beating time, till the air was filled with
sound." Just so.

The dancing continued with changes of tempo
and melody and an occasional change of cast. Finally, the original dancers all vanished, to be replaced by less skillful if no less enthusiastic
volunteers from among the villagers, men and
women and the littlest of children. And the most
daring by far were the oldest, no doubt remember-
ing their glory days.

We visitors "from heaven and the sea" were
thoroughly lulled by food and drink. When the
music abruptly ended, the silence startled us awake
again.

The curtain of the simple shrine opened and for
the first time since the festivities had begun, Diktynna appeared. Her dress was a new one, of the
same pattern; her golden crown was gone, and her
hair was tied at the nape of the neck with a com-
plexly knotted scarf. The boy who had been playing the flute was by her side.

The little procession moved a few steps to the
middle of the lamp-lit square; the boy and the leading dancers, male and female, were carrying small
painted clay chests. Diktynna briefly raised her

arms in the ritual gesture of worship. Looking first around her and then at us, she said—in Greek that now sounded limpid to my ears—"My friends, we have been honored by the presence of these heavenly guests. Therefore let us make them friendly donations, as is only proper."

She eyed me, and the expression on her face can only be described as mischievous. "First, to Hermes, the Ambassador of the Gods, whose feet—so sure, so swift when treading upon the clouds, as I have often heard the Achaians claim—were sorely taxed by our rocky paths today."

One of the women stepped forward and placed a small clay chest upon the ground in front of the bench where I sat, lifted its lid, and stepped back. I hesitated—then reached in and drew out a pair of embossed high-laced sandals, beautifully made of supple golden cowhide. I held them up for the appreciation of the crowd. The gesture was greeted with a murmur of approval; I heard a name repeated and several people looking at a gnarled man, the one who, I supposed, had made them.

After a few seconds of urgent consultation with my translator, I came forth with a speech I hoped would be adequate: "Blessed hosts, I thank you for these beautiful sandals, and I promise I will never be without them in time of need. Moreover, so sturdily and cleverly are they fashioned"—I gave the suspected craftsman a nod—"that I hereby confer upon them the property of extended life, so that they shall remain in perfect condition so long as I have need of them—which, judging from past experience, may well be for hundreds or thousands or even *countless* numbers of years to come."

Diktynna received this pronouncement with her eyebrows raised to new heights of skepticism (I also caught sidelong glances from Troy and Redfield), but the villagers responded with murmurs of wonder and, I thought, appreciation. "Most eloquently spoken . . . Giant-slayer," Diktynna remarked, applying to me yet another of the titles of Hermes—the least apt yet.

She turned her wide gaze upon Redfield. "O fearful Poseidon, Earthshaker, ruler of wind and wave"—to my ears, her cool tone seemed to convey even richer irony—"on this visit, if not always in times past, you have displayed benign restraint in the exercise of your undoubted might. For which of course we are most grateful. Now in the days of our glory, we would naturally have sacrificed hecatombs of oxen in your honor and presented you with whole ships full of treasure. Alas"—she allowed herself a dry and diffident cough—"times and circumstances change. What we can give you, you do not need . . . but who better than you can appreciate its uses?"

A youth came forward and set a chest down in front of Redfield. From it Redfield withdrew a fishnet, the kind made for throwing. Even at first glance, it was an exquisite thing; its threads were of some fiber as hard and shiny as silk, and its mesh was so fine he could not have put his little finger through it. The sinkers spaced along its hem were of carved white stones, which I recognized as Minoan sealstones from an earlier time, adapted to the purpose.

Redfield held his gift up, as I had done; at first the silence that greeted his gesture was a little ominous. This clearly was a treasured object, extraordinarily expensive in hours of labor and in the ancient treasures that had gone to decorate it; no doubt it had been an offering dedicated to the village shrine.

Again the murmurs and glances of the people identified the net's maker, a shrunken old man. (I say old, but who from our era of saving medicines could tell if these wizened elders were ninety or fifty?) I had noticed him performing a few tottering ritual steps in the dance after the young women had retreated, although he had not given himself to the general giddiness.

Diktynna saw that we recognized who had made the gift, and that was no doubt as she had intended. In this I sensed her reply to the easy tricks with which Redfield had earlier challenged her authority. Does cheap magic make a god? We are all humans here, she seemed to say. If you cannot properly honor simple humanity, what right have you to our respect?

Redfield was silent a moment, studying the net. I did not envy his dilemma. While no words of his could justify his accepting the offering—thus taking it away from the village—he could not possibly refuse it.

Then Redfield—to my astonishment, for after sitting so long I was virtually paralyzed, and he had been sitting with his legs tucked under him as long as I had—bounded to his feet. The watchers gasped in surprise. He stood still a moment, the focus of every pair of eyes in the *plateia*. Then he began to dance.

For almost a minute there was perfect silence. Redfield danced slowly, to some perfect inner rhythm. His dance mimicked some of the steps he had seen performed for us, but for the most part he danced an eclectic modern Greek sort of dance— a few steps this way, then a kick and a fancy back step, then onward about the circle—until gradually he had danced an orbit around Diktynna and her contingent. All the while he held his arms high; instead of another dancer's hand or a scrap of handkerchief he held up the gleaming net, first draping it over his shoulders, then sliding it along the length of his arms.

First the drummers, then the other musicians— all but the boy—began to play. They began softly, but Redfield's energy encouraged them, and theirs encouraged him, and soon he was leaping and wheeling in the flickering light in a display that delighted me and all his audience. The music entwining us soon whirled Redfield to heights of frenzy. I saw Diktynna's boy fidget as if itching to take up his flute, or perhaps to join the dance; with a squeeze of his wrist Diktynne brusquely discouraged him.

As Redfield turned, he let the net slide from his shoulders into his hands: it bloomed about him like a flower, like a coral, golden in the lamplight, as soft as a vision under the sea. His long hair, glossy black and flaring with coppery highlights, became unraveled and flew out loose around his head. His black Asian eyes were half closed in ecstasy. His loose chiton became disarranged. Gradually his deep breathing expanded his lungs—and caused the gill slits under his ribs to open.

Everyone watching saw it. Diktynna's expression faltered, as if she were suddenly a little less certain what sort of creature she was dealing with, but she recovered nicely. Her world was populated with nymphs and sprites to whom she must routinely address rites of propitiation and control; she was still confident that none of us were gods and therefore, I think, at some deep level she was truly unconcerned.

Redfield ended his dance almost as suddenly as he had begun it. He stood quietly a moment, then finished nicely with a deep bow to the old man, the netmaker. Although the sweat ran in rivers and his chest still heaved, he walked back to his place between Troy and me and with easy dignity sat down, having said not a word. The crowd buzzed with sudden awe and approval.

Diktynna held his eyes a moment; her acknowledgment was as wordless as his tribute had been.

She turned to Troy—assessing her more cautiously than she had Redfield and me. "Aphrodite, born of the sea-foam, Great Lady: we search within ourselves for the reasons you and your divine friends have chosen to honor us." This time her words sounded sincere. "We cannot fathom your mystery. Naturally it is wholly fitting that a goddess should contain herself—until whim or strategy leads her to choose another course."

Diktynna's boy stepped forward, bringing the last chest to lay before Troy. His black-outlined eyes were fixed upon her, bold as a man's. That he was barely more than a child, paradoxically, made him seem dangerous.

I dredged up from memory the information— only a hypothesis, really—that the boy-god so often depicted with the Cretan goddess was identified with Zeus. Or sometimes with Dionysus.

The challenge in his mascaraed gaze was indeed dangerous, and explicit. If Troy looked away from him first, she would lose the staring game. Perhaps that particular game did not carry the same charge as in our era, but what we had seen so far suggested it might. On the other hand, if she held his gaze too long, who knew the implications?

Troy solved the dilemma effortlessly. As she watched him, her chest swelled. His eyes flickered, then dropped.

Redfield's gill slits had been revealed when he danced, but since he had not been breathing with his gills, their intakes had remained closed. For a bare second, Troy deliberately opened the gashes that paralleled her collar bones. She extended her flesh.

The village boy looked straight down into those blood-rich orifices. He stepped back quickly, solemn and pale, and managed a bob of his head before resuming his place beside his priestess. No one else had seen what made him flinch.

Troy reached into the clay chest and withdrew a mirror, its handle of ivory carved with flowers, its reflecting surface a circle of polished bronze. She studied her reflection a moment—in the flame-light, in the soft unfocused bronze, it must have been a flattering portrait—and she smiled.

Meanwhile, I studied the back of the round disk, held toward me. It was incised with naked gods and goddesses, lively figures—bluntly sexual, angular, and to my eyes distinctly Picassoesque. Troy held it up high so the people could see. From their cranings and polite murmurings it was apparent that like the other gifts the object was valuable, but unlike them it had been made by no one in the village. It was a mirror, a sophisticated thing requiring not only the technical facilities but the self-conscious sensibility of a palace or city. It was several centuries old.

"In these beautiful depths I see those who came before us," said Troy. She held the mirror to her own face, then to Diktynna's. "Goddess, you are one with us," she said. "You and your companion and your people are one with us all."

She rose up swiftly and before Diktynna could react she took the priestess's hand. With her other hand she gestured to the musicians, then beckoned Redfield and me to join her—and in a few seconds, it seemed, all of us were dancing, everyone in this tiny village, which clung to its tower of rock, thrusting itself at the stars.

Now, I had heard rumors that Troy had been a dancer, although I had never believed them. An Inspector of the Board of Space Control a dancer? But I was mistaken. I do not have the words to describe what I saw that night, but I do know that Troy first managed to wrap all of us in a web of communal movement—in which the distinction between gods and humans dissolved almost completely—and then broke away into a performance of athletic grace that, while it took nothing from Redfield's earlier exertions, was of a different order of art.

She was beautiful indeed.

22

A snake was sliding over my leg.

For a moment time seemed suspended. The room was filled with indirect morning light, diffusing from gray stone walls and the beaten red earth floor. Hadn't Troy and Redfield gone to sleep beside me? They were nowhere in sight. I heard the soft chortle and lament of doves; a pair of the slender gray-brown birds had perched in a narrow window above statuettes of the goddess. From some crevice of memory came the supposition that the arrival of doves meant the presence of the goddess herself.

Her shrine was a single low room, divided into two spaces by a squat pillar in the center, and in the inner space there was a low bench that held two short, cylindrical clay portraits of her—not good likenesses. Offering stands set on the ground in front of them were decorated with sinuous snakes.

The live snake moving over my bare leg seemed to me a huge thing, although I suppose it was no more than a meter long—but very round and sleek, its scales glistening with a lovely rose color. I had inadvertently positioned myself between the snake's hole in the corner of the wall and the birds' eggs and day-old mullet and dishes of milk set for it before the altar. It was on its way to breakfast, and clearly unconcerned with me; people must sleep here all the time.

I wish they'd warned me. I shivered as it slithered away.

The whole village would have stayed up to watch us talk last night, but when Diktynna showed us into the shrine the villagers gradually dispersed and went to their houses. Inside we palavered for hours with the goddess and the boy-god, peering into each others' faces by the light of rough clay lamps, exchanging stories, while the man with the lyre, the only other person in the room, continued his playing. There was wine from a seemingly bottomless jar, new and harsh, not watered as was the Greek custom. I recorded everything I heard, every trivial anecdote, every marvel. Before long my translator/synthesizer spoke and understood Hephtian—so-called Minoan—like a native of Crete.

The story that transfixed us was told by the harper himself, whose name was Tzermon. It was a tale of Proteus, the Old Man of the Sea, and in it I recognized, centuries closer to the source, another incident that would someday find its place in the *Odyssey.* Tzermon placed his tale off the east shore of Crete; Homer put it on the island of Pharos. There was of course a Pharos in the Nile delta—a lighthouse—but "a day's sail out for a well-found vessel with a roaring wind astern" makes Crete seem the more likely. At any rate, Menelaus and his crews, marooned after leaving the mouth of the Nile, were desperate to escape the windless, waterless place.

"They were on the point of death from starvation when the goddess Eidothe approached Menelaus and told him he could escape the windless place only by forcing Proteus to do his bidding," chanted Tzermon, to the low thrumming of his lyre.

" 'How can I force him? It is not easy for a man to get the better of a god,' Menelaus complained.

"Eidothe replied, 'Each day about noon he comes

up from below, shadowing the surface of the sea as if with a light breeze to conceal his coming. If all is safe he walks up onto the beach and enters a shallow cave, whereupon a flock of seals, children of the brine, heave out and follow him and settle themselves to sleep all piled around him. When he has counted them and seen they are all there, he will lie down among them like a shepherd with his sheep. That is your moment. . . .' ''

According to Tzermon (and to Homer), at the appropriate hour Eidothe helped Menelaus and three of his crew to wrap themselves in the skins of seals she had flayed and to lie down in nests in the sand. She also smeared aromatic ambrosia on their nostrils to kill the awful stench. Proteus came out of the water.

In Tzermon's version he had the shape of a man, but his skin was white and wrinkled like an octopus's, and he was covered with seaweed which seemed to grow out of his head and body. He accepted the disguised Menelaus and his companions as members of his flock of seals, and paying them little attention, he went into the cave. After giving the sea-god time to settle down to his siesta, Menelaus and his men threw off their odious cloaks and rushed him.

Here Homer and Tzermon diverge markedly.

In Homer, Proteus was caught in a sound sleep, and a terrific wrestling match ensued. Menelaus had been warned that Proteus was a shape-changer, and would try anything to escape. He started by turning into a bearded lion, then a snake, then a panther, then a giant boar. He even changed into running water—wrestle with that!—and a huge, leafy tree. ''But we set our teeth and held him like a vise.''

In Tzermon's version, however, ''They came upon the god in colloquy with priests of Zeus. Upon seeing them, the priests vanished into the interior of the grotto. The Achaians hesitated, terrified that they had profaned a sacred rite. The god turned upon Menelaus and demanded of him, 'Who are you, to interrupt these solemn proceedings?' His voice was a horrible whisper, filled with the hiss of the sea.

"Menelaus explained his belief that Proteus had killed the winds and detained him and his men because he had inadvertently angered some god. He prayed forgiveness. Proteus was astonished. 'Who told you this? Who conspired with you to waylay me and capture me?' The truth was that he held them no grudge, nor did he know of any god who did. 'Then what shall become of us?' Menelaus cried hopelessly.

" 'Do not despair, your wish is granted,' said Proteus. 'Soon I will send the *meltemi*. Then you must return to Egypt. Inquire there what god you have offended. Then attend to your purification.' "

"Menelaus professed thanks but proposed to stay with Proteus until the god should keep his word and raise the northwest wind. At this, Proteus grew angry and bid them begone, but Menelaus and his men drew their swords and refused to leave. Proteus raved at them in many unknown tongues but at last said that if they would withdraw and stand back a few steps—far enough to see but not to hear—he would conclude his offering to Zeus. Then he would come out with Menelaus and his men.

"Menelaus agreed, but when he and the Achaians had retreated, Proteus hurled himself deeper into the interior, just as the priests had done. Menelaus dashed after him, but was soon lost in a maze of stony passages. In despair he retreated; he and his men returned, dejected, to the beach.

"To their profound surprise they found Proteus himself already in the surf, trailing green ribbons of seaweed behind him as he swam hard for the open sea. The Achaians dashed after him, and swam hard in their turn. As they drew near him, an immense creature rose out of the sea. It was bulbous, like a giant jellyfish, and purple in color, and the light shone through it; a thousand tentacles dangled from its underside.

"Yet Menelaus was close enough to grasp for Proteus. But at the very moment that his hand closed upon the god, the god changed. He became an enormous sea creature, slick and gray and wreathed with many arms like an octopus. Menelaus lost his grasp. There was a great boiling of surf. The giant sea creature Proteus had summoned from the waves sank back into the waves and vanished."

Tzermon paused then, and I thought he spent a moment studying Redfield—"Poseidon"—before he quickly concluded his tale. "Soon after the escape of Proteus, the strong northwest wind rose. Menelaus doubted whether the god had kept his promise, for in truth the season of the wind had come. Nevertheless, he returned to the heaven-fed waters of the Nile with the *meltemi* behind his black ships and, after appeasing the deathless gods, made his way to his native land, on a favorable wind sent by the immortals."

Troy and Redfield and I found we had nothing to say; the implications of Tzermon's tale were disturbing. Our conversation faltered shortly thereafter. We bedded down to spend the remainder of the night here in the shrine—the most capacious guest-house in the village.

A shaft of bright daylight split the soft haze and Redfield came in through the curtained door, followed by Troy.

"If your god-like bladder or any of your other organs is distended, you'll find a handy place to relieve yourself down the path to the left. Too bad we forgot to bring deodorant ambrosia with us from cloud-topped Olympus."

"Oh, and don't mind the audience," Troy remarked as I stepped through the doorway. "They're remarkably easy to please."

Very funny. I did what I could to maintain my privacy from the crowd of children who followed me to the place. Still, audience or none, there was a certain wild joy to be found in pissing vigorously into the cool blue morning, a sheer seven hundred meters above the sea. . . .

Returning to the shrine I spied a small flock of *agrimi* cavorting on the higher slopes beyond the spire of the Castle—*kri-kri*, the Cretan ibex, the wild goats worshiped by the Minoans, rarely seen outside zoos in our era. From the male's massive curving horns, according to some, came the legend of the cornucopia. And the female was the inspiration for the goat-nymph who nursed baby Zeus—the original Amalthea.

Troy and Redfield and I were relieved to find ourselves alone in the shrine. We compared notes of the previous day. Tzermon's tale of Menelaus and Proteus told us plainly enough that Nemo was here—or had been here, perhaps as much as a century or two ago, or even longer ago than that. But perhaps more recently. No description could have been more explicit. In this, it was plain, the alien traditionalists were his accomplices.

How had he survived? What was his intent? Who were these "priests of Zeus" with whom he was communicating? Troy had already guessed the answers to these questions, but my sluggish brain, congenitally reluctant to deal with conspiracy theories, did not readily see the implications.

"Nemo has been ahead of us again—in this as in so many things," she said.

"And he could still nip us in the bud," said Blake.

"What do you mean?" I asked, alarmed.

"Our world-ship—the key version of it, the source of all that has to happen later—is sleeping in the ice around Jupiter. It's been there for thirteen million years, since the last approach of Nemesis. Defenseless. Vulnerable."

Briefly I wondered what ship *we* had been traveling in. But I was distracted by Blake's dire intimations. "You mean Nemo and the Traditionalists could simply destroy it?" I was aghast.

"Perhaps they already have."

"*Destroyed* the world-ship?"

"Perhaps many times," said Troy.

"But not in *this* reality," Blake added—rather complacently, I thought.

"Yes and no," Troy corrected him. "There are many potential realities. There is only one reality. It's apparent that Nemo himself has realized this by now—realized that no attempt to change the past can possibly succeed, and that the only path to success is to join us. Despite himself, he has become our conspirator."

"What can you possibly mean by that?" I asked, all agape.

But just then Diktynna arrived with her acolytes, bringing platters of bread and yogurt and figs. In the morning light she looked less like a goddess than like a woman of thirty who had lived a hard life. All of us must have looked ourselves that morning. We understood each other well enough: without men and women to impersonate them on appropriate occasions, deities would lose all their influence over human affairs. . . .

We left the village of the Hephtiu, the Eteocretans, at midday, our medusa bearing us sedately into the blue sky as the people waved madly from atop their rocky fortress.

In the weeks that followed, our medusa coursed swiftly here and there over the wild and fertile lands of late Bronze-Age Earth—and how clean, how blissfully empty of people they were! How precious, by contrast, the tiny nodes of civilization scattered in these sublime wildernesses!—I became more accustomed to the thinking of Troy and Redfield, my rediscovered friends. I began to appreciate the work they had undertaken and the danger still to be faced. . . .

For Nemo had been to Egypt before us, appearing in the company of 'veiled god-messengers' to do honor to Pharaoh, bringing the priest-king gifts of knives made of 'god-metal' and intoxicating liquor in clear glass bottles, diagramming for the Egyptian priests precisely where he and his companions had come from. From Crux.

Nemo had been to the land of the Israelites before us. The arrival and departure of his medusa had been noted, by the oracular *nabi*, who described them in visions of fiery wheels in the sky.

Nemo had been to Ethiopia, and to Arabia, and to Babylon, and to the Indus, and to China before us. . . .

While we were here to collect Bronze Age languages and texts, Nemo was busy creating the Knowledge, the ancient corruptions that would one day justify his existence. And all the horrors upon which his existence floated.

With this realization I comprehended the Amalthean program at last—the program of *our* Amaltheans, I mean, those who espoused adaptability and had chosen to exercise restraining, flexible, and responsive stewardship—and more significantly I began to grasp Troy's personal program. It was a program to save the universe as we (or at least she) understood it.

"Nemo meant to catch us here, to wipe us out," she told me. "He missed."

"How did he miss? Were we just lucky?"

"There's little precision in using world-ships for time travel—a minor mistake could cost months or even years to rectify. He may have tried more than once, but sooner or later he realized that our world-ship was there all along, waiting for us around Jupiter. Yet even if he did persuade his friends to destroy it, it would soon have occurred to him that nothing really had changed. As many world-ships as he destroyed, as many more still exist."

"How is that possible?"

Her answer struck me as surpassingly strange.

"Because we are all still inside the time loop," she said. "Perhaps I should have seen it sooner. Obviously he *has* seen it."

My open mouth, my soundless questions were enough to elicit more from her.

"A wave packet of potential realities has been generated which cannot finally be reduced—not yet." She hurried on to avoid bogging down in a fuller explanation. "Meanwhile, Nemo understands as well as we do—perhaps better—that his only hope, and *our* only hope, is to restore the universe as precisely as possible to its *former state*. We must leave his business to him. He will do it well, I think. We must finish our own task—our own Mandate."

She left me then, with my mouth still open.

A few weeks later there came a moment when I found myself dictating the content of our Bronze Age researches to intelligent machines, watching as they inscribed the strange characters upon tablets of adamantine crystal, alongside their Amalthean equivalents. As the tablets took form I recognized their shapes; on impulse, I added a few key signs. With those terminal characters—an elegant Hebrew aleph, ink-brush style, a few quick wedge-shapes, like Sumerian clay—the Venusian tablets had fully formed themselves in front of my eyes.

I understood Troy at last. We *had* to create the world we knew. Having recorded the Bronze-Age languages, we must now preserve them. I knew where it would be done; after all, I myself had discovered the Venusian tablets. I was as yet unsure how it *could* be done. . . .

Then our medusa lifted us straight into starry heaven, where our world-ship—or one of its Doppels—waited. Two days later we were diving into the poisonous sulfur-dioxide clouds of Venus.

23

Beneath us, coral reefs had once thickened and spread in an uneven plain of branched and knobbed structures, having grown there at a level much deeper than in the oceans of Earth—

for while coral loves warm water, in those days the oceans of Venus were near boiling at the surface.

Those days were long ago. Nowadays the air at ground level was as heavy as the sea, and hot enough to melt lead. The atmosphere was dark, ruddy, so thick it bent the horizon like the inside of a bowl, only a few hundred meters ahead of us.

Beyond the ancient coral plantations (burnt lumps, unrecognizable to any but those like us, who had been there) we came upon a shelving beach. It could have been a moonscape, for lava flows and primordial wave action had not fully erased the rims of the craters, many of them overlapping, which gave evidence of continued bombardment by celestial objects of all sizes. Still, certain clues were accessible to the trained and sensitive eye. Here undersea organisms had once fed on bits of detritus that had followed a lazy current seaward; the scouring of the outflow was still faintly visible in the rock.

We were in what had been a submarine canyon, a river channel. Over our heads, waves had surged toward the land in parallel lines of surf, overriding the outflowing current. On either side, uncountable chalky shellfish had clotted the rocks that rose up steeply, forming the base of high cliffs.

I knew these cliffs; I knew them well indeed. With my friend Albers Merck—the same who later tried to murder me—I had crawled into these very mountains in an armored Venusian rover. Here we had been trapped by earthquake and rockfall, and here our lives had almost ended before Troy rescued us. To die then would have suited Merck well, I suppose; the only thing he accomplished in his later attempt on my life was his own death, plus the destruction of a great many valuable records.

Contrary to my expectations, I had restored them. And now I brought them with me in their original form, as forged in the depths of the worldship.

The medusa in which I rode was not quite like the others I had grown so used to. Its inner walls glowed with ruddy light, the color of salmon roe; downward, through story upon story of what looked like giant foam—an aerosol frozen in place— the mass of the vessel was divided into countless sacs or chambers, a nest of tough-walled bubbles in graduated sizes, and in each chamber, dark shapes against the diffuse light. All different. Each a specimen.

Not all were sea creatures, although there were hundreds of these, some familiar from Earth— jellyfish and nudibranchs and clams and urchins and sponges and corals and worms and snails and a thousand species of fish—but others never seen on Earth, even as vanished fossils. There were land creatures and creatures of the air as well, amphibians and reptiles and a dizzying collection of insects and arthropods, and here and there a leathery winged creature or a tiny thing that, like the medusas of the sea, apparently floated freely upon the rain-soaked winds. And there were mosses and ferns and algae, some big enough for the coal swamps of Earth, others too diminutive to make out clearly. . . .

I had no doubt that our alien ark contained a complete collection of microorganisms as well. Among the immensity of the collection, there were many things that were never seen and never would have been seen on Earth. With one exception. *I* had seen them before. They had been in the cave—

—the cave the mining robot stumbled upon and that Merck and I had gone to investigate. We had been interested in the tablets, principally. The plants and animals had been a bonus.

The medusa began slowly to ascend. The skies reddened and dark cliffs rose narrowly on either side, so close the medusa brushed against them. I tried to imagine this place as it might have been three billion years ago, with rain driving against the canopy and numberless waterfalls streaming from the cliffs above. Below there would have been a rushing stream, silvery with the reflected light of blue-white clouds, pouring over coal-black rocks and pooling behind dams of choked vegetation— giant log dams, tangled piles of palm logs and tree ferns and huge fibrous horsetails, dams chinked with black mud and fronds and mosses torn from the flooded walls of the arroyo, the steaming pools behind them silting up with spongy vegetation.

Already the river would have been cutting its way through these vine-draped basalt cliffs for a thousand million years or more, hauling down boulders to do the heavy work, then breaking the boulders to gravel, then grinding the gravel to sand, then pushing the sand out to sea. Already the river would have cut its way down through beds of older organic stuff, coal and dead coral from when the sea had been higher still.

Here, somewhere near. You must show us the place. . . .

Staring at the ruined watercourse twisting between narrowing walls of reddish-black rock, gleaming with the slick metallic patina of ancient rainwater, my mind had played me a trick. Now I tried to recall when and where I really was.

"This is the place," I said. "Beyond that turn, beneath that cliff."

The Amaltheans did not query me again. The medusa moved swiftly to the spot and stopped there. Beneath us there was vigorous invisible movement—I felt its vibrations, but could see nothing of what was happening.

They were making a cave and putting the specimens into it, and with them the diamond-metal tablets, inscribed with the ancient texts in the forty-three signs of the Amalthean alphabet. They were putting everything where Merck and I would find it, three thousand years from now. The Venusian tablets that I had deciphered, and that I, more than anyone, had been responsible for writing. . . .

Soon I was back aboard the world-ship. Which world-ship? Which *me?* Of all contesting realities, which would win? We drove at high acceleration through swarms of oncoming comets, toward the singularity. As the presence of the comets suggested, our target was close to the sun, near perihelion. Within two light-months the world-ship dived into the tiny bright sphere of distorted space-time—

—and instantly re-emerged.

24

"I don't understand where the world-ship was during these adventures," the commander says. "At one point you've got it orbiting Jupiter, a minute later it's waiting to pick you up at Earth." He has joined the others on the rug-strewn floor, around the litter of their picnic supper.

"A fascinating question, one with several answers," Forster replies. "You see, by now our own world-ship had divided . . ."

"Divided?" Ari seems amused.

"Doubled, tripled, multiplied itself."

"Multiplied itself!" Jozsef is astonished.

"Oh, for practical purposes, the world-ship was just where it always was. While we were busy exploring the Dark Ages of the Aegean, one copy was orbiting Earth at the fourth Lagrangian point. But the original ship orbited Jupiter, covered with ice—long since having assumed the identity of Amalthea in which we were to discover it."

"How could this happen?" Jozsef persists. "This second Doppelganger?"

"Just as it happened before, or so your daughter informed me. Nemesis—the Whirlpool—visits us every twenty-six million years; our era happens to be in the middle of this cycle. Thirteen million years ago we dived into the spinning Whirlpool and came out again—shortly before we had gone in. We went in again, and when we emerged, there were two of us. And then again . . . well, you can work out the details.''

Already Jozsef has seen the implications. ''But the humans! Do you mean to say . . . ?'' He cannot put the increasingly awful thought into words.

Forster makes the thought explicit. ''We did not meet ourselves when we first explored the world-ship. Perhaps because we had never been to that particular ship, or perhaps only because it is a very large vessel—certainly we did not find the thousands of Amaltheans who inhabited the world-ship when I saw it last. But I'm sure that your daughter, and Blake Redfield as well, understood what was coming. I suspect they planned it with Thowin-tha—the one or the many versions of him'er—who knew that sh'he, they, would forget almost everything in their long sleep to come. But they would not forget that humans would come again, or that your daughter would be among them.''

Ari shakes her head angrily. ''Linda was with you in the Bronze Age. One of her, not a multitude. Your account has become fantastic.''

''I sympathize with your confusion,'' Forster says coolly, pondering the last traces of liquid in his glass. ''Imagine my own confusion when I realized that *realities*, for want of a better word, had begun to proliferate uncontrollably. We had made a loop within a loop of time. And we were not the first to do so.''

''Tell me this,'' says the commander. ''Did Nemo destroy the ship at Amalthea, or did he not?''

''If he did, it was replaced by another. And if that one was destroyed, it was replaced by another. Inside the loop, there is no resolution.''

Forster looks to the commander. The tall man has turned suddenly away and now seems to be ignoring him, busying himself rebuilding the fire. When the last the fresh flames are leaping, he straightens his spare frame almost painfully. ''We know what the man you call Nemo did," says the commander.

Forster smiles. "No doubt there are people in your organization who would place him at the death of Moses, of Siddhartha, of Alexander and Jesus and Lincoln and Gandhi."

"A very great boon to humanity, in that case," says Ari sharply. "Who would have paid those people any attention if they had lived out their lives?"

"Sympathy for the devil," Forster remarks.

The commander keeps his steely gaze focused upon Forster. "Not a rare emotion among the Free Spirit. Or in Salamander. Tell us why *you* are here, why *you* survived. Tell us why we should believe that you are . . . real, as you put it."

Forster shrugs, feeling no threat. "As for myself, the singular me, even at the climax I still had only the dimmest understanding of those events in which apparently I played an important role. Or roles. I have done my best to reconstruct what actually happened on Earth while we were gone—if I may be permitted to use the word *actually* under these circumstances. . . ."

PART
5

THE SHINING ONES

25

"And so we approach the present. A hundred world-ships fill the skies. Or a thousand. Or an infinity of world-ships." Outside the empty library, the pre-dawn sky dazzlingly confirms Forster's description. "Of all my researches the personal account by the Swiss diving engineer, Herr Klaus Muller, touches me most closely. *'Don't call me a diver, please,'* he told me, *'I hate the name. . . .'*"

I'm a deep-sea engineer, and I use diving gear about as often as an airman uses a parachute. Most of my work is done with videolinked, remote-controlled robots. When I do have to go down myself, I'm inside a minisub with external manipulators. We call it the Lobster because of its claws; the standard model works down to seventeen hundred meters, but there are special versions that will work at the bottom of the Marianas Trench—which may not be the deepest place in the solar system, if you count some of the watery moons, but certainly makes for the greatest water pressure you'll find anywhere. Now I've never been down there myself, but I'll be glad to quote you terms if you're interested. At a rough estimate it will cost you a new dollar a foot, plus a thousand an hour on the job itself. You won't get a better deal elsewhere.

There is no other firm in the world that can live up to our motto: ANY JOB, ANY DEPTH.

So when Goncharov interrupted my holidays, I knew we had a problem with the deep end of the Trincomalee project—even before he told me that the site engineers had reported a complete breakdown.

Our firm was covered, technically, because the client had signed the take-over certificate, thereby admitting that the job was up to specification. However, it was not as simple as that; if negligence on our part was proved, we might be safe from legal action—but it would be very bad for business. Even worse for me, personally, for I had been project supervisor in Trinco Deep.

The morning after my rather melodramatic conversation with Goncharov—complete with ominously repeated deadlines and strangling noises from his end—I was in a helicopter over the Alps, with only a short stop in Bern on the way to La Spezia, where our company kept the heavy stuff.

After settling affairs at Spezia I commandeered the firm's executive suite there. I had a phonelink conversation with Gertrud and the boys, who were not delighted at my sudden departure, which made me wonder why I hadn't become a banker or a hotelier or gone into the watch business, like any other sensible Swiss. It was all the fault of Hannes Keller and the Picards, I told myself moodily: why did they have to start this deep-sea tradition, in Switzerland of all countries? Then I shut off the commlinks and settled myself to four hours' sleep, knowing I would have little enough in the days to come.

I took the company rocket plane; we approached Trincomalee just after dawn. Below the plane I caught a glimpse of the huge, complex harbor, whose surface geography I've never quite mastered—a maze of capes, islands, interconnecting waterways, and basins large enough to hold all the navies of Earth. I could see the power project's big white control building, in a somewhat flamboyant architectural style, on a headland overlooking the Indian Ocean—the site was pure propaganda, although of course if I'd been North Continental staff I'd have called it "public relations."

Not that I blamed my clients; they had good reason to be proud of this, the most ambitious attempt yet to harness the thermal energy of the sea.

It was not the first attempt. There had been unsuccessful ones, beginning with the Frenchman Georges Claude's in Cuba in the 1930s, and later ones in Africa and Hawaii and in many other places. All of these projects depended on the same interesting fact: even in the tropics the sea a couple of kilometers down is almost at freezing point. When billions of tonnes of water are concerned, this temperature difference represents a colossal amount of energy—and a fine challenge to the engineers of power-starved countries.

Claude and his successors had tried to tap this energy with low-pressure steam engines. The North Continentals—and particularly the Russians, who were foremost in the work—used a much simpler and more direct method. For a couple of centuries it has been known that electric currents flow in many materials if one end of a sample is heated and the other cooled, and ever since the 1940s Russian scientists had been working to put this *thermoelectric effect* to practical use. Their earliest devices had not been very efficient—though still good enough to power thousands of radios by the heat of kerosene lamps! But late in the century they had made the crucial breakthrough.

The technical details were outside my expertise, and though I installed the power elements at the cold end of the system, I never really saw them, covered as they were in layers of shielding and anticorrosive paint. All I know is that they formed a big grid, a bit like lots of old-fashioned steam radiators bolted together.

As I stepped from the plane I recognized most of

the faces in the little crowd waiting on the Trinco airstrip. Friends and enemies, they all seemed relieved to see me. Especially Chief Engineer Lev Shapiro, who greeted me with a dark scowl. . . .

"Well, Lev," I said as the robot station wagon drove us away, "what's the trouble?"

"We don't know," he said, remarkably frankly. He spoke like an Oxonian but he was one of those Russian Jews whose ancestors had bucked the odds and decided to ride out the troubles when the Soviet Empire started coming apart in the late 20th century; I always speculated that that was one of the reasons he was more of a nationalist than was fashionable these days—indeed, more of a Russian chauvinist than most of the other Russians I knew.

"It's your job to find out," he growled at me, "and put it right."

"Well, what *happened*?"

"Everything worked perfectly up to the full-power tests," he answered. "Output was within five percent of estimate until oh-one-thirty-four Tuesday morning." He grimaced; obviously that time was engraved on his heart. "Then the voltage started to fluctuate violently, so we cut the load and watched the meters. I thought some idiot of a skipper had hooked the cables—you know the trouble we've taken to avoid *that* happening—so we switched on the searchlights and looked out to sea. There wasn't a ship in sight. Anyway, who would have wanted to anchor just *outside* the harbor on a clear, calm night?"

I couldn't answer that, so I said nothing, waiting for him to go on.

He let go a frustrated sigh. "There was nothing we could do except watch the instruments and keep testing. I'll show you all the graphs when we get to the office. After four minutes everything went open circuit. We can locate the break exactly, of course—and it's in the deepest part, right at the grid. It *would* be there, and not at *this* end of the system," he added gloomily, pointing out the window.

We were just driving past the solar pond, the equivalent of the boiler in a conventional heat engine. This was an idea the Russians had borrowed from the Israelis (Russian-born Israelis, no doubt— I sometimes wondered if Lev appreciated the irony). It was simply a shallow lake, blackened on the bottom, holding a concentrated solution of brine; it acted as a very efficient heat trap, so that the sun's rays bring the liquid nearly to the boiling point. Submerged in it were the hot grids of the thermoelectric system—every centimeter of two fathoms down.

Massive cables connected them to my department, about a hundred degrees colder and a thousand meters lower, in the undersea canyon that descends from the entrance of Trinco harbor.

"I suppose you checked for earthquakes," I said, not hopefully.

"Of course." Lev's tone implied that I had called him an idiot. "There was nothing on the seismograms."

"What about whales?" More than a year ago, when the main conductors were being run out to sea, I'd told the engineers about a drowned sperm whale once found entangled in a telegraph cable a kilometer down off the coast of South America. "They can be big trouble."

About a dozen similar cases were known but this, apparently, was not one of them. "That was the second thing we thought of," Lev growled. "We got onto Fisheries, and the navy and air force. No whale sign anywhere along the coast."

It was at that point that I stopped theorizing. I'd overheard something from the back of the station wagon that made me a little uncomfortable. Like all Swiss I'm good at languages, and in the course of the job I'd picked up a fair amount of Russian— although one didn't need to be much of a linguist to recognize *sabotash*.

Dimitri Karpukhin has said the dirty word. Karpukhin sported some unconvincing title on the organization chart, but he was in fact a political agitator and spy, one of the old-style Russian supremacists who wanted to see that other S in USSR changed back to Socialist—moreover, who believed the Soviets deserved a bigger role in the North Continental Treaty Alliance. Nobody liked Karpukhin, not even Lev Shapiro, but since he worked for one of the biggest Russian consortiums he had to be tolerated.

Not that sabotage was out of the question, in fact. There were a great many people who would not have been brokenhearted if the Trinco Power Project failed. Politically, the prestige of the North Continentals was committed, and to some extent the prestige of the Russian Republic, but more important, billions were involved economically. If hydrothermal plants proved a success, they would compete with Arabian and Persian and North African oil (not to mention relieving the pressure on Russia's reserves), as well as with North American coal, with African uranium. . . .

But I could not really believe in sabotage. Espionage, maybe—it was just possible that someone had made a clumsy attempt to grab a sample of the grid. Even this seemed unlikely. I could count on my fingers the number of people in the world who could tackle such a job—and half of them were on my payroll!

The underwater videolink arrived that evening. By working through the night we had cameras, monitors, and over a mile of cable loaded aboard a launch. As we pulled out of the harbor I thought I saw a familiar figure standing on the jetty, but it was too far away to be certain, and I had other things on my mind. (If you must know, I am *not* a good sailor; I am really happy only *underneath* the sea.)

We took a careful fix on the Round Island lighthouse and stationed ourselves directly above the grid. The self-propelled camera, looking like a midget bathyscaphe, went over the side. We went with it in spirit, watching the monitors.

The water was extremely clear and extremely empty, but as we neared the bottom there were a few signs of life. A small shark came and stared at us. Then a pulsating blob of jelly went drifting by, followed by a thing like a big spider with hundreds of hairy legs tangling and twisting together (I know these creatures have names; I've been told what they are, dozens of times, but they don't stick in my memory, which seems to store only technical matters). At last the sloping canyon wall swam into view. We were right on target, for there were the thick cables running down into the depths, just as I had seen them when I made the final check of the installation six months ago.

I turned on the low-power jets and let the camera drift down the power cables. They seemed in perfect condition, still firmly anchored by the pitons we had driven into the rock. Not until we came to the grid itself was there any sign of trouble. . . .

Have you ever seen the radiator grille of a robocar whose guidance has failed and driven it into a lamppost? Well, one section of the power grid looked very much like that. Something had battered it in, as if a madman had gone to work on it with a sledgehammer.

There were gasps of astonishment and anger from the people looking over my shoulder at the videoplates. I heard *sabotash* muttered again; for the first time I considered it seriously.

The only other reasonable explanation was a falling boulder. But the slopes of the canyon had been carefully mapped and, where necessary, recontoured against this very possibility.

Whatever the cause of the damage, a section of the grid had to be replaced, which would not be done until my Lobster, all twenty tonnes of it, arrived from the Spezia dockyard where it was kept between jobs.

"Well?" Lev Shapiro demanded, when I had finished my visual inspection and stored the videoplate's sorry spectacle on chip. "How long will it take?"

I refused to commit myself. The first thing I ever learned in the underwater business is that no job turns out as you expect. Cost and time estimates can never be firm because it's not until you are halfway through a contract that you know exactly what you're up against.

My private guess was three days. So I said, "If everything goes well, it shouldn't take more than a week."

Lev groaned audibly. "Can't you do it quicker?"

"I won't tempt fate by making rash promises. Anyway, if I do it in a week, that still gives you two weeks before you're scheduled to come online."

He had to be content with that, though he kept nagging at me all the way back into the harbor. Then, when we arrived onshore, Lev found he had something else to think about.

"Morning, Joe," I said to the man who was still waiting patiently on the jetty. "I thought I recognized you, on the way out. What brings *you* here?"

"I was going to ask you the very same question, Klaus."

"You'd better put that through my boss. Chief Engineer Shapiro, meet Joe Watkins, science correspondent for *US Newstime*."

Lev's response was not cordial. Normally there was noting he liked better than talking to newshounds, who showed up at the rate of about one a week. Now, as the target date for the commencement of power production approached, they would be flying in from all directions—including from Moscow. At the present moment, *Tass* would be every bit as unwelcome as *Newstime*.

Karpukhin was on hand, of course, and it was amusing to see him take charge of the situation, blitzing Joe with assurances that we were merely reconfirming the superb preparedness of the Russian-designed facility, etc., etc. And from that moment on, Joe found that he had permanently attached to him as guide, philosopher, and drinking companion, a smooth young PR type named Sergei Markov. Despite all Joe's efforts, the two were inseparable—or more accurately, Joe realized he could not separate himself from Sergei.

That evening, weary after a long conference in Shapiro's office, I caught up with the two of them. We had dinner at the district government's resthouse, where I was staying while onshore—actually a rather posh hotel and club.

"What's going on, Klaus?" Joe asked, managing to sound pathetic. "I smell something interesting, but no one will admit to a thing."

I toyed with my curry, trying to separate the bits that were safe from those that would take off the top of my head. "You can't expect me to discuss a client's affairs," I replied, stagily glaring at Sergei, who grinned back at me like the idiot he wasn't.

"You were talkative enough when you were doing the survey for the Gibraltar Bridge," Joe reminded me.

"Well yes—and I appreciate the write-up you gave us. But this time there are trade secrets involved. I'm, ah, making some last-minute adjustments to improve the efficiency of the system." And that, of course, was the truth; I was indeed hoping to raise the efficiency of the system, from its present value of exactly zero.

"Thank you very much," Joe responded sarcastically.

"Enough about this—you know the project as well as I do," I said, trying to head him off. "What's *your* latest crackbrained theory? Aliens still doing surgery on cattle in the American west? UFO's still cutting circles in English hayfields?"

For a highly competent science writer, Joe has an odd liking for the bizarre and the improbable. Perhaps it's a form of escapism; I happen to know that he also writes science fiction, though this is a well-kept secret from his sobersided journalistic employers. But while he has a secret fondness for poltergeists and ESP and flying saucers, his real specialty is lost continents.

"I *am* working on a couple of new ideas," he admitted. "In fact they cropped up while I was doing the research on this story."

"Go on," I said, not yet daring to look up from the analysis of my curry.

"The other day I came across a very old map—Ptolemy's, if you're interested—of Sri Lanka. It reminded me of another old map in my collection, and I turned it up. Sure enough, there was the same central mountain, the same arrangement of rivers flowing to the sea. But *this* was a map of Atlantis."

"Oh, no," I said with a groan, risking a glance at him. "Last time we talked, you had me convinced that Atlantis was in the Mediterranean. Rhodes or Crete or someplace."

Joe gave me his most engaging grin. "I could be wrong, couldn't I? Anyway, I've got a much more striking piece of evidence. Think about the name of this island."

"Yes? Sri Lanka?"

"Sri *Lanka*," he said with a vigorous nod. "That name was around a very long time, you know, long before the Sinhalese adopted it in place of Ceylon."

"Good Lord, Joe, you can't be serious," for I saw what he was driving at. "Lanka—Atlantis?" Although I had to admit that the names did roll smoothly off the tongue.

"Precisely," said Joe. "Two clues, however striking and persuasive, don't make a theory, of course."

"Hm, quite. So?"

"Well . . ." He looked uncomfortable. "Two clues is all I've got. At the moment."

"Too bad," I said, genuinely disappointed. "But

you said you were working on a couple of ideas. What's your other project?''

"Now *this* will really make you sit up," Joe answered smugly. He reached into the battered briefcase he always carried and pulled out a folding flatscreen, which he proceeded to unfold. "This happened only a couple of hundred kilometers from here, and just over two centuries ago. The source of my information, you'll note, is about the best there is.''

He called up a document on the flatscreen and handed it to me: it was a page of the *London Times* for July 4, 1874. I started to read it without much enthusiasm, for Joe was always producing bits of ancient newspapers.

My apathy did not last for long.

Briefly—I'd give you the whole thing, but if you want more details you can call it up on your own flatscreen in about ten seconds flat—Joe's clipping described how the hundred-and-fifty-ton schooner *Pearl* left Ceylon in early May 1874 and then fell becalmed in the Bay of Bengal. On May 10, just before nightfall, an enormous squid surfaced half a mile from the schooner, whose captain foolishly opened fire on it with his rifle.

The squid swam straight for the *Pearl*, grabbed the masts with its tentacles, and pulled the vessel over on its side. It sank within seconds, taking two of the crew with it. The others aboard were rescued only by the lucky chance that the P. and O. steamer *Strathowen* was in sight and had witnessed the incident.

"Well," said Joe eagerly, when I'd read the piece through for the second time, "what do you think?''

I'm afraid my Swiss-German accent was a bit thicker and stiffer than usual as I said, "I don't believe in sea monsters," and handed him back the flatscreen.

"The *London Times* was not prone to sensationalist journalism, even two hundred years ago," Joe answered smugly. "And giant squids certainly exist, though the biggest we know about are feeble, flabby beasts that don't weigh more than a tonne.'' He added slyly, ''Even if they *do* have arms fifteen meters long.''

''Again, so? An animal that size—impressive as it is—couldn't capsize a hundred-and-fifty-ton schooner.''

''True. But there's a lot of evidence that the so-called *giant* squid is merely a, hm, well, a *large* squid. There may be decapods in the sea that really are giants. Why, only a year after the *Pearl* incident, a sperm whale off the coast of Brazil was seen struggling inside gigantic coils which finally *dragged it down into the sea*. . . .''

''Could it possibly have been the same whale later found drowned in the telegraph cable?'' I murmured, too softly.

''What?'' Joe said, distracted from his argument.

''What's your reference?'' I asked brightly.

''Um, you'll find it . . . um, the incident is described in the *Illustrated London News* for November 20, 1875. . . .''

''Another impeccable source,'' I said, rather too dryly, perhaps.

''And then of course there's that chapter in *Moby Dick*.''

''What chapter?''

''Why, the one aptly called 'Squid.' We know that Melville was a very careful observer, but here he really lets himself go. He describes a calm day when 'a great white mass' rose out of the sea 'like a snow-slide, new slid from the hills.' And this happened *here*, in the Indian Ocean, perhaps fifteen hundred kilometers south of the *Pearl* incident. Weather conditions were identical, please note.''

''So noted.'' Here I snuck a glance at Sergei, to see how Karpukhin's operative was taking all this. Alas, the poor lad had been working too valiantly at his vodka—but who could keep up with a journalist of the old school like Joe?—and seemed to have gone to sleep sitting up.

"What the men of the *Pequod* saw floating on the water," Joe continued, as if he'd been on the scene himself, viddiecorder in hand, "was a 'vast pulpy mass, furlongs in length and breadth, of a glancing cream color, innumerable long arms radiating from its center, curling and twisting like a nest of anacondas.' "

"Just a minute," said Sergei, suddenly awake. His expression was that of a sleepwalker; Joe and I regarded him with alarm. "What's a furlong?" he said, with exaggerated clarity.

Joe and I exchanged glances. "It's an eighth of an English mile, actually," Joe carefully explained.

"Oh," said Sergei, "in that case . . ." and, after a momentous pause, his eyes closed and his head declined.

Joe looked at me, embarrassed. "I'm sure Melville didn't mean that literally. A creature over two hundred meters in length and breadth? But remember, here was a man who met sperm whales every day, who was groping for a unit of length to describe something a lot bigger. So he jumped from fathoms to furlongs. That's my theory, anyway."

I pushed away the remaining untouchable portions of my curry and looked up at Joe with curiously mixed feelings. "I'm a busy lad—I'm afraid I've got to get my beauty sleep." I nodded toward Sergei, whose blissful snores were getting louder by the moment. "If you want a taste of the local nightlife, old friend, get going. It may be your last chance to escape."

I rose and excused myself. Joe remained seated, studying me. "If you think you've scared me out of my job," I said carefully, "you've failed miserably. But I promise you this. When I do meet a giant squid, I'll snip off a tentacle and bring it back as a souvenir."

26

Klaus Muller's account continued:

I didn't have time for the viddie news that morning, although I gathered from my crew that it was filled with news of the approaching alien ship that my boys had been so eager to find in our telescope. Seems it was right on schedule, still due to cross Earth orbit at a distance described tersely as "arbitrarily close," right at the spring equinox.

Well, I had more urgent things to worry about than the end of the world.

Less than twenty-four hours after Joe Watkins's disquisition upon the squid I was settled into our company's Lobster, sinking slowly through cold black water toward the damaged power grid. There was no way to keep the operation secret: as we went under, Joe was an interested spectator, watching from a nearby launch (with Sergei watching Joe, indeed trying frantically to distract his attention with who-knows-what comic monologue, but to no avail). Apparently my own feeble effort the night before to tempt Joe with the local flesh-pots (of whose existence I had no real evidence) had come to nothing.

That was the Russians' problem, not mine. I had tried to persuade Shapiro to take Joe into his confidence, but Karpukhin had vetoed the notion. One could almost see him thinking—*why* should a North

American newshound turn up at this very moment?—ignoring the obvious answer that Trincomalee was about to be big news in any event.

There is nothing in the least exciting or glamorous about deep-water operations, if they're done properly. Excitement means lack of foresight, which means incompetence. As one of the early Antarctic explorers, a survivor when others courted death, had put it, "Tragedy was not our business." The incompetent do not last long in *my* business. Nor do those who crave excitement. I went about my job with all the pent-up emotion of a plumber dealing with a leaking faucet.

The grids had been designed for easy maintenance, since sooner or later we knew they would have to be replaced. Luckily none of the threads of this section had been damaged, and the securing nuts came off easily when gripped with the power wrench. I switched control to the heavy-duty claws and lifted out the damaged grid without the slightest difficulty.

It's bad tactics to hurry an underwater operation; if you try to do too much at once you're liable to make mistakes. (And if things go smoothly and you finish in a day a job you said would take a week, the client feels he hasn't had his money's worth.) So, although I was sure I could have replaced the grid that same afternoon, I followed the damaged unit up to the surface and closed shop for the day.

The thermoelement was rushed off for an autopsy, and I spent the rest of the evening hiding from Joe Watkins, whose curiosity was relentless. Trinco is a small town, but I managed to keep out of his way by visiting the local cinema, where I sat through several hours of an interminable Tamil epic in which three successive generations suffered identical domestic crises of mistaken identity, drunkenness, desertion, death, and insanity, all in full Sensovision—vibrant color, too-realistic smells, and Surround-sound turned to earthquake level.

Thus, I managed not only to avoid Joe, I also avoided learning anything much about what was going on in the skies above us.

Next morning, despite a mild headache, I was at the site soon after dawn. (So was Joe, and so was Sergei, the two of them all set for a quiet day's fishing. . . .) I cheerfully waved to them as I climbed into the Lobster; the tender's crane lowered me over the side.

Over the other side, where Joe couldn't see it, went the replacement grid. A few fathoms down I lifted it out of the hoist and carried it to the bottom of Trinco Deep, where by the middle of the afternoon I had it re-installed, without any trouble. Before I surfaced again, the lock nuts had been secured, the conductors spot-welded, and the engineers on the beach had completed their continuity tests.

A quick and easy success: by the time I was back on deck the system was under load once more, everything was back to normal, and even Karpukhin was smiling—except when he thought to ask himself the questions that no one had yet been able to answer.

I still clung to the falling-boulder theory, for want of a better. And I hoped that the Russians would accept it, so that we could stop this silly cloak-and-dagger business with Joe.

No such luck, I realized, when both Shapiro and Karpukhin came to see me with very long faces.

"Klaus," said Lev, "we want you to go down again."

"Well, it's your money," I replied. "What do you want me to do?"

"We've examined the damaged grid. There's a section of the thermoelement missing. Dimitri thinks that . . . someone . . . has deliberately broken it off and carried it away."

"Then they did a damned clumsy job," I answered. "I can promise you it wasn't one of *my* people."

Karpukhin never laughed, so I wasn't surprised that he didn't laugh now. But neither did Lev, and on reflection I realized I wasn't even amused myself. By this time I was beginning to think the suspicious Mr. Karpukhin might not be so far off the beam.

The sun was setting over the interior, in one of those typically lavish tropical sunsets, as I began my last dive of the day into Trinco Deep. Day's end has no meaning down there, of course; below about five hundred meters it is always dark. I fell more than seven hundred meters without lights, because I like to watch the luminous creatures of the sea as they flash and flicker in the darkness, sometimes exploding like rockets just outside the observation window. In these open waters there was no danger of collision, and in any case I had the panoramic sonar scan running, which gave far better warning than my eyes.

As I approached eight hundred meters I sensed that something was wrong. The bottom was coming into view on the vertical sounder—but it was approaching much too slowly, meaning that my rate of descent was far too slow. I could increase it easily enough by flooding another buoyancy tank, but I hesitated to do so. In my business, anything out of the ordinary needs an explanation; three times I have saved my life by waiting until I had one.

The thermometer gave me the answer. The temperature outside was five degrees higher than it should have been, and I am sorry to say that it took me several seconds to realize why. My only excuse was that I had had no occasion to visit the grid since it had become operational.

A couple of hundred meters below me the repaired grid was running at full power, pouring out megawatts of heat as it tried to equalize the temperature difference between Trinco Deep and the

Solar Pond up there on land. It wouldn't succeed, of course, but in the attempt it was generating electricity—and I was being swept upward in the geyser of warm water that was the incidental by-product.

When I finally did manage to reach the grid, it was quite difficult to keep the Lobster in position against the upwelling current, and I began to sweat uncomfortably as the heat penetrated the cabin. Being too hot at the bottom of the sea was a novel experience. So also was the mirage-like vision caused by the ascending water, which made my searchlights dance and tremble over the rock face I was exploring.

You must picture me, then, lights ablaze in that thousand-meter darkness, moving slowly down the slope of the canyon, which at this spot was about as steep as the roof of the house. The missing element—*if* it was still in the neighborhood—could not have fallen very far before coming to rest. I would find it in ten minutes or not at all.

After an hour's searching, I had turned up several broken light bulbs (it's astonishing how many get thrown overboard from ships—the sea beds of the world are covered with them), an empty beer bottle (same comment), and a brand-new boot. That was the last thing I found—

—before I discovered that I was no longer alone.

I never switch off the sonar scan. Even when I'm not moving and involved in something else I always glance at the screen at least once a minute to check the general situation. The situation now was that a large object—at least the size of the Lobster—was approaching from the north. When I spotted it, the range was about two hundred meters and closing slowly. I switched off my lights, cut the jets, which I had been running at low power to stabilize me in the turbulent water, and let the Lobster drift in the current.

Though I was tempted to call Lev Shapiro and report that I had company, I decided to wait for more information. There were only three administrative regions on the whole planet owning submersibles that could operate at this depth, and I was on excellent terms with all of them—in fact, I was on social terms with the majority of their rated crewmembers. It would never do to be too hasty and get myself involved in unnecessary political complications.

I did not wish to advertise my presence. Anyone working at this depth would have to use lights, and I ought to be able to see them coming long before they could see me. Therefore, though I felt blind without sonar, I reluctantly switched it off and relied on my eyes. Perhaps it was my imagination, but a curiously musical sound seemed to ring faintly against the hull of my vessel; I rechecked and assured myself that the sonar was in passive mode.

The quasi-musical sound grew louder. I waited in the hot, silent little cabin, straining my eyes into the darkness, tense and alert but not particularly worried.

First I saw a dim glow, at an indefinite distance. It grew bigger and brighter, yet refused to shape itself into any pattern that my mind could recognize. The diffuse glow concentrated into myriad spots, until it seemed that a constellation was sailing toward me. Thus might the rising star clouds of the Galaxy appear from some world close to the Milky Way.

That mental image momentarily brought to mind a correlate, an image of the great diamond-bright alien spacecraft then approaching our world, but nothing sustained the accidental connection.

It is not true that people are frightened of the unknown; we can be truly frightened only by the known, the already experienced. While I could not imagine what was approaching, I was sure that no creature of the sea could touch me inside ten centimeters of good Swiss armor plate.

The thing was almost upon me, glowing with the

light of its own creation, when it split into two separate clouds. Slowly they came into focus—not of my eyes, for I had always seen them clearly, but of my understanding—and I knew that beauty and terror were rising toward me out of the abyss.

The terror came first, when I saw that the approaching beasts were squids. All Joe's tales reverberated in my brain. Then, with a considerable sense of letdown, I realized that they were only about seven meters long—hardly longer than my Lobster, and a mere fraction of its mass! They could do me no harm.

Quite apart from that, their indescribable beauty robbed them of all menace.

This may sound ridiculous, but it is true: in my travels I have seen most of the animals of the undersea world, but none to match the luminous apparitions floating before me now. The colored lights that pulsed and danced along their bodies made them seem clothed in jewels—never the same for two seconds at a time. There were patches that glowed a brilliant blue like flickering mercury arcs, then changed almost instantly to burning neon red. Their tentacles, preceding them through the water, seemed like strings of luminous beads—or the lamps along an auto super-guideway, when you look down upon it from the air at night. Barely visible against this background glow were their enormous yellow eyes, uncannily human and intelligent despite their cat-like slit pupils, each surrounded by a diadem of shining pearls.

I am sorry, but that is the best I can do in words. Only a high-resolution viddiegram could do justice to these living kaleidoscopes. I do not even know how long I watched them, so entranced by their luminous beauty that I had almost forgotten my mission. Oh, and I must not fail to mention the music! The complex harmonics that filled the Lobster were nothing like the chittering of fish, or even the mournful groans and whistles of the great whales. . . .

It was quickly apparent that those delicate, whiplash tentacles could not possibly have broken the grid—that much was obvious. Yet the presence of these creatures here was, to say the least, very curious. Karpukhin would have called it highly *zuzpizhus*, or whatever the word is in Russian.

I was about to call the surface when I comprehended something incredible. It had been before my eyes all the time, but I had not realized it until now. . . . *The squids were talking to each other.*

Those glowing, evanescent patterns were not coming and going at random. They were as meaningful, I was suddenly sure, as the illuminated signs of New Broadway or Old Piccadilly. Every few seconds there was an image that almost seemed to make sense, but it vanished before *I* could make sense of it.

I knew, of course, that even the common octopus exhibits emotional changes with lightning-fast color changes. But this was something of a much brighter order, real communication. Here were two living electric signs, flashing messages to each other.

My doubts vanished. I am no scientist, but at that moment I shared the sort of feelings I imagine a Leibniz or an Einstein or an Aggasiz might have felt at the moment of some penetrating revelation. For then I saw an image of the Lobster, evanescent but unmistakable. *This* would make me famous. . . .

The images I imagined I saw (no, was certain I saw) moving over the rippling flesh of the squids now changed in a most curious manner. The Lobster reappeared, I thought, rather smaller. Beside it, much smaller still, were two peculiar objects—each consisting of a pair of bright dots surrounded by ten radiating lines.

As I said a little earlier, we Swiss are good at languages. But I flatter myself that it took a little extra intelligence to deduce that this was a formalized squid's-eye view of itself . . . and that what I had seen, before it vanished forever, was a crude sketch of the situation in which all of us found ourselves.

A nagging thought: why the absurdly small size of the squids, as they pictured themselves? *Were* they squids? Their light show had distracted me from certain other anatomical differences, which made them seem not much like familiar examples of their biological family. . . .

I had no time to puzzle this out. A third squid symbol had appeared on the living screens, and this one was enormous, completely dwarfing others. The message shone in the eternal night for a few seconds before one of the two creatures, retaining it, shot off at incredible speed, and my sonar reflected the rippling currents of its water jet. I was left alone with its companion.

The meaning of this act seemed all too obvious. "My God," I muttered to myself, "they think they can't handle me! That one's been sent to fetch Big Brother." Of Big Brother's capabilities I already had better evidence than Joe Watkins's anecdotes, for all his research and his clippings. So you won't be surprised to hear that at this point I decided not to linger in the vicinity.

But before I went, I thought I would try some talking myself.

After hanging there in darkness for so long, I had forgotten the power of my lights. They hurt *my* eyes—and they must have been agonizing to the unfortunate squid in front of me. Transfixed by that intolerable glare, with its own illumination utterly quenched, it lost all its beauty and became no more than a pallid bag of gray jelly with two big black buttons for its eyes. For a moment it seemed paralyzed by the shock; then it darted after its companion.

I soared upward through the black waters like a child's errant helium balloon through the sky, seeking the surface of a world that would never be the same again.

27

Klaus Muller's memoire continues:

There was consternation on the viddie nets; so I gathered within a minute or two of sticking my head out of the Lobster's hatch.

That an alien ship was within hours of Earth was old news now, several days old. Since it wasn't going to actually hit the Earth, who really cared anymore? No, the *new* news was, there was *another* alien ship in the skies, apparently identical to the first, which had suddenly appeared in the Mainbelt and was now accelerating on a converging course with the first—they were on a collision course *with each other!*

At Trinco Control they gave only a mild damn about all that—it was astronomers' business. Lev Shapiro and the rest were power engineers, and kept their attention focused resolutely oceanward.

"I've found your saboteur," I told Karpukhin, shortly after the crew had extracted me from the Lobster. "If you want to know all the facts about him, I suggest you get Joe Watkins in here."

Which was definitely *not* something Karpukhin wanted to hear—so I let him sweat a couple of seconds while I enjoyed the fascinating range of expressions rippling across his fat face. Then I gave my report—slightly edited.

I implied, without actually saying so, that the two big squids I'd met were powerful enough to have done all the damage to the grid. I said nothing about the conversation I'd, uh, overseen. That story could only cause incredulity, and besides, I wanted time to think matters over, to tidy up the loose ends. If I could.

This morning we have begun our countermeasures. I am going into the Trinco Deep, carrying the great lights that Lev Shapiro hopes will keep the squids at bay. But how long can this ruse work, if indeed intelligence is dawning in the deep?

I'd barely completed securing the Lobster for today's dive last night when I got word that yet *another* alien spacecraft had been sighted, a clone of the first two, accelerating inward from the Mainbelt. This was a garbled tale, which I thought due to wild rumors.

This morning there were more wild rumors. Alien ships coming from Venus, alien ships inbound from Neptune and Uranus! I couldn't afford to let myself think about all that. I tried to concentrate on the business at hand.

Last night I got Joe to meet me in the hotel bar. I'd intended to swear him to secrecy, but I soon realized I had a different problem: I despaired of ever getting him to stop ranting about world-sized spaceships, When Aliens Collide, etc. I needed desperately to get him back on the Trail of the Giant Squid.

Roughly half a liter of Scotch whisky did the trick. . . .

And Joe was indeed a great help, though he still knows no more of my discoveries than what I told the Russians. He filled me in on what wonderfully developed nervous systems squids possess, and he explained how some of them (the *little* ones) can change their appearance in a flash, through a sort of instantaneous three-color printing, thanks to the extraordinary network of ''chromophores'' covering their bodies. Presumably this capability evolved for camouflage, but naturally it has the potential for developing into a communications system—perhaps that's even inevitable, considering evolution's inventions.

One thing worried Joe.

"What were they *doing* around the grid?" he kept asking me plaintively. "They're cold-blooded invertebrates. You'd expect them to dislike heat as much as they object to light."

That puzzled Joe, but it doesn't puzzle me. I think it's the key to the whole mystery.

Those squids, I'm now certain, are in Trinco Deep for the same reason there are humans in the Mainbelt, or on Mercury—for the same reason Forster and his crew went to Amalthea. Pure scientific curiosity. The power grid has drawn the squids from their icy deep home, to investigate a veritable geyser of hot water suddenly welling from the sides of the canyon—a strange and inexplicable phenomenon, and possibly one that menaces their way of life.

And so they have summoned their giant cousin (their servant? their slave?) to bring them a sample for study.

I cannot believe that they have a hope of understanding the sample thus acquired. After all, as recently as a century ago no scientist on Earth would have known what to make of a piece of the thermoelectric grid. But the squids are trying, and that is what matters.

As I dictate this, I'm making the leisurely descent. My thoughts turn to last night's stroll beneath the ancient battlements of Fort Frederick, watching the moon come up over the Indian Ocean. I can't help but think of what our own race has been through, reaching for our nearby satellite hardly more than a century ago, after so many years of dreaming and wondering . . . then spilling out, onto and around the planets and moons and planetoids of the whole solar system. And then to encounter these strange events—awakening aliens from Jupiter!—all of it in such a little time, such a fleeting instant . . . cosmologically speaking.

So maybe after all I'll give in and let Joe use these meandering thoughts, this Joycean stream of consciousness—assuming everything goes well, of course!—in this book that he's taken into his head to badger me into writing. And if everything doesn't go well . . .

Hello, Joe, I'm talking to you now. Please edit this for publication any way you see fit, and my apologies to you and Lev for not giving you all the facts before. I'm sure that now you'll understand why.

Whatever happens, please remember this: they are beautiful creatures, wonderful creatures. Try to come to terms with them if you can.

On the day of Muller's last dive only one additional, partial sentence was spoken by him, as noted in this memo of that date from Lev Shapiro:

URGENT TRANSMISSION (with I.D. and time code. . . .)

TO: Ministry of Power and Energy Resources, North Continental Treaty Alliance, The Hague

FROM: L. Shapiro, Chief Engineer, Trincomalee Thermoelectric Power Project

Above is the complete transcript of the chip found in the ejection capsule of the Muller submersible, the "Lobster." Transcription completed this time and date. Remote search for the submersible was interrupted ten minutes ago by the unexplained rupture of the underwater videolink.

Interpretative remarks follow. We are indebted to Mr. Joe Watkins for assistance on several points. Herr Muller's last intelligible message was directed to Mr. Watkins and ran as follows: "Joe! You were right about Melville! This thing is absolutely gigan . . .''

28

>"One can hardly blame Muller for his confusion," says Forster, "After all, he'd done his best to concentrate on his underwater work, deliberately ignoring the events unfolding in the heavens. Certainly our surprise was as great as his. . . ."

Angus McNeil was the first of us to come awake and free himself from the medusa's life-support tendrils. He didn't know where he was, of course. He'd been asleep since the fall of Mars.

In proper time that was only a few years longer than I had been asleep, but in real time it was more than a billion years. No one was around to smooth his passage back to consciousness, and he was certainly puzzled to discover Klaus Muller's brightly painted titanium Lobster squatting there in the middle of the medusa's none-too-large, human-inhabitable space. Still, he managed to take the sight of the big machine in stride. Angus has come close to death more than once, I gather; in the process he seems to have learned to take a great many things in stride.

Angus peered into the Lobster's round viewport and found Muller peering back, rigid with terror. Muller surely wondered what sort of creature was confronting him; none of us looked much the better for the centuries we had spent under water. Angus spent the next couple of minutes, by his account, convincing the Swiss engineer that it was safe for him to come out.

By then the rest of us had begun to arise, creeping out of the watery drowning chamber into the medusa's central cell, pale and wet and wrinkled as prunes. For myself, this time I could find no energy, no spark of enthusiasm. I missed having Troy and Redfield there to ease the transition. The others looked as exhausted as I. Poor Marianne was the most pathetic of us all; her sorrows, technically a billion years or so in the past, were still fresh in her memory.

We were confronted by Muller, a blond-brushed, steel-bespectacled, rather plump Swiss burgher, sitting on the rim of his squat and ugly submersible's open hatch, plainly appalled at our appearance.

"What's the date?" I asked him, gasping and choking. He stammered out the year, but I interrupted. "No, no, what month? What day?" He told me.

It was the date I wanted to hear. It was the spring equinox. It was the day we had crossed Earth orbit in our own era.

"To the surface!" I cried—which frightened Muller enough for him to slide partway back into his machine. To the others I said, "If you feel as I do, you want to smell Earth's air and see the Earth's sky once more—if this should indeed be the last moment of our reality." Well, they couldn't have known what I meant, but they let me have my way. . . .

I went back into the water long enough to speak to our unseen Amalthean companions, who I had sensed controlling the medusa in their language of thumps and whistles.

We came up right at sunset, broke free of the water, and hovered over the bay in midair, offshore. The huge medusa's appearance caused a sensation—well described in numerous local news reports—but not until morning did the local defense forces organize a helicopter to come out and peer at us close-up. They'd had other things to do during the night, riots and near-panic, political and religious hysteria inspired by the multiple mirrors in the sky. . . .

Through the medusa's clear canopy we saw spread above us that fantastic sky. The lurid sun had not gone all the way down, and deep night had not yet settled, yet the sky gleamed with globes brighter than stars, trailing flame. And all of them were streaming toward the setting sun.

"*Goddess!*" I heard myself swear—it was a habit I must have picked up in the Bronze Age, and I was conscious of the odd looks I got from the others— "Where did they all come from?"

"What *are* they?" Jo Walsh demanded.

"World-ships," I said, for I had suddenly apprehended the appalling implications of what Thowintha had done.

I remember somebody pronouncing with great vehemence, "The uncertainty principle should hold true only in the microworld!"

And someone else objecting, "We went through the black hole—again and again. Because of that we've inflated microscopic uncertainty to the macroscopic scale. Uncertainty manifest and visible."

Then somebody else asked me (Jo, I think it was), "Were you expecting this, Forster?"

"I am expecting what Troy and Redfield called the state-vector reduction," I said. "They talked about world-ships—plural. Not thousands of them, millions of them. I think all the possible outcomes of the time loop must be up there."

"All? What about Nemo? He still has a chance?" That was from Bill Hawkins, who has a sixth sense for the really vexing questions.

"No matter, they're all on the way to destruction," said Angus. "They're all going to annihilate each other."

"Good for them. What about *us*?" Jo asked.

Nobody had an answer for her.

What followed that night was one of those half-informed, half-mathematical, half-physical, half-philosophical discussions. (On my part, now only half-remembered—how many halves is that?) At this remove I recall mostly my sloppy sentiment, my love for these people, whom accident had brought to our mutual fate.

Most vividly I remember the black waters below us and the blazing sky above us. I remember Klaus Muller, perched atop his stranded diving machine, his reticence visibly ebbing as he listened raptly to our surreal debate.

Thowintha had gambled and lost, I contended. Sh'he had kidnapped us and taken us back to Venus, meaning to rescue the Adaptationist faction before they could be destroyed by their rivals—an event sh'he must have witnessed in its primordial form. His'er own long memories indicated that we Designates had played a role in the salvation of him'er and his'er kind, but the details were hazy at best. Sh'he believed, or so I argued, that the Traditionalists would simply go on their way, leaving us to make the solar system in our own image.

Things didn't work out that way. First Nemo and the Traditionalists tried to destroy us—perhaps more than once. Eventually they realized that was impossible, inside the time loop. Then they knew they had to confront us at the *origin*. And at the same time they realized—or at least Nemo did— that they must exert their efforts to see that the origin was reproduced precisely, exactly.

Bill questioned me sternly. He said he understood well enough why Nemo and his aliens had failed to destroy us—because Thowintha had multiplied us, Xeroxed us, so to speak—but why was it necessary to reproduce the conditions of the origin so perfectly, in order to destroy us once and for all?

Jo came to my aid. "Think of a simple experiment. A photon is projected into a half-silvered mirror. Half the information about the photon's whereabouts goes through the mirror, half is deflected. Later this information is recombined. Which path did the photon actually take?''

''Both, of course,'' said Bill. ''*After* the fact we can say that. But you could have inserted a detector along one of the paths. If you got a photon, it had been taking that path. If you didn't, it took the other.''

''One could quibble, but close enough,'' said Jo. ''Now suppose that along these paths someone has inserted more half-silvered mirrors—so that information about the photon's wherabouts has been multiplied, that its potential paths have been multiplied.''

''All right, but that's why Nemo can't eliminate us,'' said Bill complacently.

''Suppose he *really needs* to squash that photon,'' Jo persisted. ''Where's he going to intervene?''

''After recombination,'' Bill shot back.

''Too late,'' I put in. ''He's got a stake in one path, one of the alternatives—it's his life, his only hope for survival. He needs to prevent the others from ever coming into being.''

''Why not *before* it hits the mirror?'' asked Angus.

Bill turned upon him scornfully. ''Fine for a photon. But in our case, any time before the origin would still be inside the time loop. Nemo tries that, there are all those other version of the path *before* we reach the mirror. . . .'' He paused, and we all saw the realization dawn on his face. He had talked himself into it. ''The moment of origin,'' he said. ''The moment when the photon hits the mirror. . . .''

Troy and Redfield—and Thowintha—knew as well as Nemo when the showdown must come. The outcome would be a statistical thing, without guarantees. But they supposed that we might survive. Which gave them a practical problem. Where were we to hide?

The deepest water on Earth is the Challenger

Deep in the Mariana Trench; its bottom is 10,915 meters below sea level, only about eleven kilometers down. The world-ship is thirty kilometers in diameter.

One version—the Ur-ship, or one of its later substitutes—was already in orbit around Jupiter. Ours went to hide in the Mainbelt instead, covering itself with a thick layer of worthless regolith. Still, its size was considerable; it was among the first asteroids discovered with a primitive telescope. In our era that asteroid has withstood two prospecting expeditions—and both times has managed to pass as worthless, for commercial purposes.

There Thowintha and his myriad companions settled to sleep once again. Here in the Indian Ocean—the Earth's emptiest quarter—we in the medusa settled into a similar sleep. We'd made sure to make our arrangements in a place and time Nemo was unlikely to interrupt us. We had about 2,000 years to wait, to see how it all came out. . . . Our Amalthean crew woke first.

As I have stressed, Amaltheans live and breathe *communication*—it may even be said that these magnificent intelligences become somewhat rattled in the absence of their companions. While we humans still slept in the peace of utter unconsciousness, the two crewmembers went exploring. They were soon attracted to the Trincomalee power project's heat-producing grid. And Klaus Muller's report gives some inkling of what happened next. . . .

A few days later, when our tentacled friends encountered Muller's submersible, they experienced an emotion akin to panic. Aboard the medusa we humans were still soundly sleeping, helpless. Would other humans bring a fleet of underwater vessels to seek out and attack us? The Amaltheans worried that they might have betrayed their trust, which was to preserve us until the moment of state-vector reduction.

Hastily they summoned the medusa to preempt Muller, and on his next dive they were waiting to seize him and his Lobster. From his last words on the commlink we know he mistook the thing that was attacking him (surely it was hideous in his eyes!) for a giant squid. Poor Muller only had time enough to eject an emergency communications capsule before his machine was captured. . . .

But at last our attempt to understand our predicament ground to a halt. Shining streaks of light smeared the star-spangled sky above us. Like comets, they all converged upon the sun, at last invisible below the palm-fringed western horizon.

Marianne spoke for the first time, a sad, quiet whisper in the night. "When will we know that we are dead?" she asked.

I turned to Klaus Muller, who had been peering at us from the top of his Lobster all the while as if we were the most extraordinary examples he'd yet seen of exotic undersea life. In that moment my heart went out to him—for although I am not noted for my psychological sophistication, I could recognize the effort he was making to hold onto his sanity.

"What time is it?" I demanded. He was the only one among us who would know. He looked at his chronometer and told me the time, to the second. "We are not dead," I said to Marianne. "The issue seems to have been decided in our favor."

"We'll live?" she asked.

"You mean *this* is the one reality?" Angus demanded.

"I mean we'll never know. We will all have died natural deaths by the time those multiple versions of reality reach Nemesis."

They all thought about that for several seconds. Only Angus and Jo were quick enough to catch me out, I think, for when Hawkins started to argue again—not from conviction, but from pure cussedness—Angus cut him off. "I suggest that we spruce up and find ourselves a drink."

* * *

In all the centuries in which I've lived—if only for a few days—I've rarely turned down a well-made product of fermentation or distillation. But this time I let Angus and Jo and Bill and Marianne go ashore without me; I was not yet ready to join them in their search for libations, or their encounters with customs officers. And apparently Klaus Muller shared my reticence.

"I've something to tell you, Professor," he said, when the others had gone.

"Call me Forster," I said.

"Forster?"

"Forster, yes. Think of it as my given name."

"If you wish." Muller was silent again, and I was afraid my impatience had scared him off.

"Well?" I said, trying to sound gentle and un-threatening.

"How do you think I came aboard this craft?" he asked.

"Didn't the Amaltheans bring you?" I asked tiredly, expecting no surprises.

"When this thing you call a medusa came at my Lobster, I thought it was one of Joe's giant squids, about to devour me. I wrote what amounted to a last will and testament."

"So you told us."

He looked at me through those thick round glasses of his, with a look that told me I was not nearly as smart as I thought I was. "Then I saw the woman," he said.

"The who?"

"The woman. The man joined her a bit later. And then the others."

I thought I understood his words, but I certainly did not understand his meaning. "Where did this happen?"

"At about eight hundred meters. She was very thin. Much of that will have been compression. At first I was uncertain how she could survive—well, to tell you the truth, I was sure I was hallucinating—but when I saw the dark slits along the sides of her chest, and the water intakes near her collar bone, I began to understand.''

''And the man?'' I asked.

''Like her. He had the intakes and the slits in his sides.''

''Gills.''

''You know these people?''

''We've been talking about them all night.'' I looked at him with a great feeling of pity. What he read on my face, I can't imagine. ''Troy and Redfield.''

''Ah.'' He was silent, wondering if he'd made a mistake by bringing up the subject. Who would confirm *this* story?

''What happened?'' I insisted.

''They signaled to me through the glass. They and the squids carried me toward the vessel. The humans stayed in front, making faces and gestures . . . trying to convince me they *were* human, I think. And then I was inside the vessel. That was the last I saw of them.''

''You said something about 'others','' I said.

He studied me, his blue eyes magnified by his round glasses. ''They kept well back. Only after I turned my lights on again could I see them, hanging back there in the darkness.''

''Can you tell me anything about them?''

''Only that they were exactly like the first two.''

''Exactly?''

''Exactly. Men and women who could have been their twins, happy as fish in the cold, dark deep. The pressure would crush an ordinary submarine. A week ago you could have described that sight to me, and I would have said it was my worst nightmare come true. But they smiled at me. They made funny faces at me, tried to make me laugh. It was almost as if they were dancing to entertain me. And—no doubt I was out of my mind—I took comfort from them.''

''That's what they wanted,'' I said. ''To save you. To save us all.''

"Where are they now? That's what I keep wondering. From what you've all said, I think I know where they came from. But where are they now?"

They had all vanished, I was on the verge of saying—either vanished or were about to. I pictured them wheeling in beams of watery light. Maybe they could see each other, but they knew they couldn't touch each other or exist in the same reality together. When the collapse of the wave function finally occurred, they would all (probably all—all but one couple, anyway) cease to exist. A thin apotheosis.

So, while I thought I knew the answer to Muller's question, I wasn't sure enough to defend my answer—or take the responsibility of making a myth of it. Instead I gave him a half-truth. "They've evolved into sea creatures," I said. "I don't think we'll see them on land again."

Or, I might have added, anywhere else.

29

"Those *others* . . ." A look of horror distorts Ari's face, and even Jozsef looks as if he has tasted something bitter.

"I have nothing more to say about them," Forster says firmly. "Nothing but this: Troy told me that, when she refused to murder Nemo, Thowintha said to her, 'Denial of sameness is a heavy burden.' "

"Which means?"

"Supply your own meaning. But consider that Thowintha was one with his'er world-ship. Perhaps we must learn to accept oneness with our world, which is also our ship. Perhaps Troy and Redfield, and even Nemo, in his way . . ."—and here Forster gives the commander a strange look, which goes unnoticed by the others—"have learned it already."

A hint of gray dawn pushes heavily at the tall library windows. The commander pokes at the last embers of the fire; the firewood is all gone, used up in the long night. "We will never know the details, then? They are all lost in the holocaust at the red limit?" Embers fall and shatter on the stone floor of the fireplace, and quick rhythms of transparent flame flutter over the brick red coals.

Forster has gotten the last of the smoky old Scotch whisky into his glass. He swirls it thoughtfully and sips. "If I have understood the formalism correctly, Penrose and the rest . . ."

"Penrose?"

"A twentieth-century mathematician and cosmologist. He suggested that information is lost in singularities—black holes. Whereas information is created everywhere at the quantum level, because at that level a single input has many potential outputs."

Jozsef is never more eager than when trying to understand the abstract. "You mean after the collapse of the wave function? At the same macro-level."

"Yes."

"So that all these matters will be determined when the objects that persist in our skies will have become extremely red-shifted objects . . ."

"Forgive me, Jozsef," Forster interrupts. "The issue will be decided much more quickly than that."

"But what happened to *you?*" Jozsef insists. "Those of you aboard the ship that became Amalthea? Those . . . others?"

Forster shrugs. "We live out our lives, I suppose. Somewhere on this rich Earth. Or an Earth like it." His smile creeps back, a soft, sad smile. "Back then, when the first world-ship went to ground . . . it was the Oligocene then. It must have been the *real* paradise."

"The first Designates were Linda and Blake, visiting Thowintha—the Amalthean Thowintha—in the distant past?" Ari wants to know.

"I think so."

"But Thowintha must have known to expect them," says Ari. "Gills and all." The concept of her daughter having suffered such a sea change was still repugnant to her.

"So then . . . different realities can communicate?" Jozsef asks, surprised. "Without annihilating one another?"

"Apparently this occurs routinely at the quantum level. I can give you the references—all the way back to Sidney Coleman, if you like."

"You spoke of a conspiracy between Nemo and Troy." The commander is silhouetted against the window; his features are lost in black shadow.

"At the risk of repeating myself . . . Nemo had

failed to prevent the evolution of the human race. He realized his only hope was to confront us at a place and time he knew we *must* appear. We realized this too. We got here first and hid—among the asteroids, and in the water."

"How did you good guys prevail?"

Forster smiles, but avoids the commander's gaze. "I'm new to the study of quantum mechanics."

"Forget that; put it in the notes," the commander growls. His voice is a rattle of stones.

"I can picture him living for thousands of years under the sea, spawning all sorts of myths. But there is only one reality, at the crucial junction, and Nemo finally realized that."

"Why are you so sure?" Jozsef asks.

"As a practical matter, Nemo's ship could have emerged from the black hole close to the last time we did, could have followed our ship as it went to Jupiter, could have destroyed it like a butterfly in the cocoon. Consider that Nemo and the Traditionalists certainly *did* find the world-ship orbiting Jupiter—Amalthea—and destroyed it. Many times."

"And . . . ?"

"Ignore Bell's inequality. Assume Nemo's attack succeeded at least fifty percent of the time—which *must* have happened. And by the same reasoning, in half the cases it *didn't* happen. Therefore the four of us are here now, around this fire."

"You mean half of Nemo's attacks failed?"

"In the sense that half the potential versions of him, half the potential world-ships he was riding, ceased instantly to exist, ceased to achieve reality—yes. *Only* half, though."

"Therefore you—and the rest of us—*had* to exist," says Jozsef.

"Evidently we do," Forster replies, and he can not prevent a self-satisfied grin. "Nemo came to understand that the only definitive intervention would come at the opening of the time loop. Which means that the decisive intervention must come as *all* the contending world-ships—every possible version of reality—simultaneously enter the sun. On their way to Nemesis.''

''He has lost his gamble?'' Jozsef asks.

Forster shrugs. ''We will know when the sun rises. Then every contending world-ship will collide.''

The commander presses him, her tone astringent. ''How did our heroes assure this great good outcome?''

''We haven't assured it,'' Forster replies. ''We only did what Nemo did—we did our best to insure that history was exactly as we knew it. Free Spirit, Salamander, everything. As for the rest . . . it *is* the outcome.''

The fire is low; the light in the library has faded. The big window at the end of the room is a framed picture of the universe, where dozens of mirrored world-ships still speed outward on columns of fire.

A few minutes pass, and Ari stands at the window, gazing at a morning sky spangled with blazing mirror-ships, a sky filled with strange angels.

One of those ships—one at least, more likely many—is carrying her daughter and her daughter's mate to the stars. Many more of her daughters are living under the sea. But as those ships vanish, so will the humans they have spawned.

''There they go,'' she whispers, too quietly for anyone but herself to hear. And she begins to cry.

There they go. Traveling at the speed of light.

Perhaps, if they survive the passage of the singularity, they will emerge into the Garden. And perhaps, if they have managed to marshal the resources of the aliens—the Amaltheans, the care-givers, the tenders of the Garden—they would undo what Ari had done . . . had done to her own daughter. And her daughter will then be able to conceive, and will conceive, and will give birth to a child, to children, and the children will truly be the children of a new age.

All of that is a day away, one day in the future. Then all the world-ships will meet within the fiery envelope of the sun; only one will emerge from that refiner's fire. That is the moment of origin. That is the moment when the photon meets the mirror.

All that is yet in the future, one day away . . . a potential future. Ari and her husband Jozsef and their friends, Forster and the commander among them, live on, on Earth. It is an Earth different from what it might have been, one different from what strict probability might have dictated.

This Earth witnesses the extraordinary flight of a giant medusa to join its mother ship, which it seeks out among a fleet of mirrored ships then crossing Earth's orbit.

It is an Earth upon which Bill and Marianne try again and have children. They have more than one, and they raise them more or less peacefully—at Oxford, where Bill has landed the sort of job for which he has always been best suited, in a universe of bicker and strut and mastery of the library catalogue. It is a world in which Marianne feels very much at home, knowledgeable and witty when she wants to be, diffident when she prefers.

This same Earth has many richer options to offer. It is, for example, a world in which Angus and Jo find themselves famous, the recipients of awards, publishing contracts, consulting stints, and other compensations which partially make up for the reality that they are no longer young enough to take to space.

And it is an Earth in which Klaus Muller, having repaired the Trincomalee Power Project, returns to his family in Switzerland. As the years unroll, his business takes him away from them from time to time; his boys do not not grow up without difficulty; his old own age and that of Gertrud, his wife, are full of human troubles. Nevertheless, Klaus and his wife do grow old, and his boys grow to be adults in a world whose skies get no fouler (and even began slowly to clear again), and whose land is tended with more care by those who live on it, and whose seas become cleaner.

Humanity, perhaps, has seen how close it has come.

For this, Ari can thank her daughter. Her daughter— all versions of her, she who knew herself as Sparta, all versions of her, diving boldly and with courage into the final holocaust—has in no predictable way, or imaginable way, nevertheless proved herself truly to be the Empress of the Last Days.

AN AFTERWORD BY ARTHUR C. CLARKE

And so, after six volumes, it's time to say farewell to the durable and resourceful Ms. Sparta, not to mention her wide spectrum of friends and enemies. I am extremely impressed by the way in which Paul Preuss has created a whole universe out of half-a-dozen short stories of mine, and I am delighted that the *Venus Prime* series has been so well received.

On re-reading the "Afterwords" to the previous volumes, I find that there is little that needs changing. The electromagnetic launcher which is the key element of *Maelstrom* (Vol. 2) now seems to be making an unexpected comeback, partly due to the Star Warriors, who have carried out some (so far ground-based) experiments with 'Railguns.' And, surprisingly, there is serious interest in such devices for launching payloads *from Earth*. For certain applications they would be much cheaper than rockets, and at least one company has been formed to exploit these possibilities. It is unlikely, however, that passengers will rush to buy tickets; accelerations will probably be in the kilogee bracket.

The hope I expressed for the Russian space-probe "Phobos 2" in the afterword of *Hide and Seek* (Volume 3) was, alas, unfulfilled. For reasons that are still uncertain, this failed to complete its mission—

though unlike its hapless precursor "Phobos 1," it did return much valuable information from Mars. But the fascinating inner moon remains untouched; there may still be a black monolith lurking there. . . .

I am more than happy to report that the much-delayed "Galileo" space-probe, mentioned in *The Medusa Encounter* (Volume 4) is at last on its way to Jupiter, via one Venus and *two* Earth flybys. All systems appear to be operating normally, and if it produces even a fraction of "Voyager" 's surprises when it starts reporting in 1995, I fear there may be no escape from a *Final Odyssey*. We may also learn the truth about the strange inner moon Amalthea, scene of much of the action in Volume 5.

The short story "The Shining Ones", which Paul Preuss has neatly embedded in this final volume, appeared originally in *Playboy* in August, 1964. It was reprinted in my collection *The Wind from the Sun* (1972), and with any luck, it may soon become a self-fulfilling prophecy.

The concept of Ocean Thermal Energy Conversion (OTEC) has been taken very seriously ever since the twin spectres of fuel shortage and the Greenhouse Effect started looming over the future. A number of experimental pilot plants have been built (notably off Hawaii, an obvious candidate), and there is little doubt that such a system can be made to work.

Whether it will be economically viable is another question: I still like the slogan I coined in the late 70s: "OTEC is the answer to OPEC." And if the sea level is indeed rising as a result of man-made global warming at the rate some scientists predict, we will need all the nonpolluting energy sources we can find. Thanks to the enormous thermal inertia of the sea, OTEC is the only solar-powered plant able to work twenty-four hours a day; it won't even notice when the sun goes down.

More than a decade ago, Dr. Cyril Ponnamperuma, the distinguished NASA and University of

Maryland biochemist (consultant on the Apollo and Viking Missions) and Science Advisor to the President of Sri Lanka* read "The Shining Ones" and declared: "We must make this happen!" Largely as a result of his enthusiasm, proposals have already been received from a number of engineering firms to build OTEC plants at the precise location I specified a quarter of a century ago—Trincomalee, on the northeast coast of Sri Lanka. Unfortunately, the mini-civil-war which until recently affected that area has prevented any further progress. As of early 1990, a fragile peace prevails in this region, and one can only hope that when reconstruction begins, priority will be given to tapping one of the ocean's most valuable—yet still unused—resources.

The giant squid which gives this story its name is one of my favourite animals, though I would prefer to make its acquaintance from a safe distance. By great good luck I was able to do the next best thing during the shooting of the Yorkshire TV series, *Arthur C. Clarke's Mysterious World*, which still makes frequent appearances on cable. We were able to film a specimen which had been washed ashore in Newfoundland, and even though it was only an immature female, a mere twenty feet long, it was an awesome sight. And the marine biologist who displayed it to us believes that adults may reach *one hundred and fifty feet* in length!

Some years after writing this story about deep-sea operations, I had the pleasure of snorkeling off Trincomalee with the man who has descended further in the ocean than anyone else—except his companion Jacques Piccard. When Commander Don Walsh, USN, took the *Trieste* down to 36,000 feet, he made one of the few records which will never be broken—at least until someone finds a deeper hole in the seabed than the Marianas

---

*Not to mention the first Director of the Arthur Clarke Centre for Modern Technologies, Moratuwa, Sri Lanka.

Trench. On our dive (maximum depth twenty-five feet) we met no giant squids; but I did encounter for the first time a creature which is a much more serious menace—the coral-reef-destroying Crown of Thorns starfish, *Acanthaster planci.*

Before winding up the *Venus Prime* series, I would like to answer a question I've been frequently asked: "Do you propose to do any further collaborations?" Well, it depends what you mean . . .

I've enjoyed working with Paul Preuss (though we've never met—even by modem), but I've now reached the (st)age when I wish to concentrate on projects which are exclusively my own. As Andrew Marvell almost said, "Ever at my back I hear, Time's jet-propelled chariot hurrying near."

There are still two volumes to go in the *Rama* trilogy *(The Garden of Rama* and *Rama Revealed)* which I'm writing with Gentry Lee, and Gregory Benford's 'sequel' to my very first (*c.* 1935-48!) novel, *Against the Fall of Night,* has just appeared. I should stress that *Beyond the Fall of Night* is entirely Greg's work—and I'm delighted that it's already received some very flattering reviews.

But Beyond Beyond? Well, at the moment I have exactly thirty-four (34) movie or TV options on my hands, and if even ten percent of them materialize that will put paid to any (ahem) serious writing for a few years. My energetic agent Scott Meredith *knows* this, but it won't stop him trying to get me involved in other collaborative projects. So in sheer self-defence, I've cried "No more—*unless* there's some element of great novelty and/or redeeming social value. . . .''

Well—the other day I came across this title (no, I haven't made it up, and I believe it's based on genuine historical research):

GEORGE WASHINGTON'S EXPENSE ACCOUNT
by
General George Washington and Marvin Kitman.

This has started me thinking of some interesting possibilities. I rather like the idea of

THE LAST MEN IN THE MOON
by
H.G. Wells and Arthur C. Clarke

How about it, Scott?